KEANE'S CHARGE

IAIN GALE

HERON
BOOKS

First published in Great Britain in 2015 by Heron Books
an imprint of

Quercus Publishing Ltd
Carmelite House
50 Victoria Embankment
London EC4Y 0DZ

An Hachette UK company

A CIP catalogue record for this book is available
from the British Library

HB ISBN 9781848664807
ExTPB ISBN 9781848664814
EBOOK ISBN 9781784293529

Printed an

KEANE'S
CHARGE

Also by Iain Gale

James Keane series

KEANE'S COMPANY
KEANE'S CHALLENGE

Jack Steel series

MAN OF HONOUR
RULES OF WAR
BROTHERS IN ARMS

Peter Lamb series

BLACK JACKALS
JACKALS' REVENGE

ALAMEIN

FOUR DAYS IN JUNE
A novel of Waterloo

For

Caroline Barty

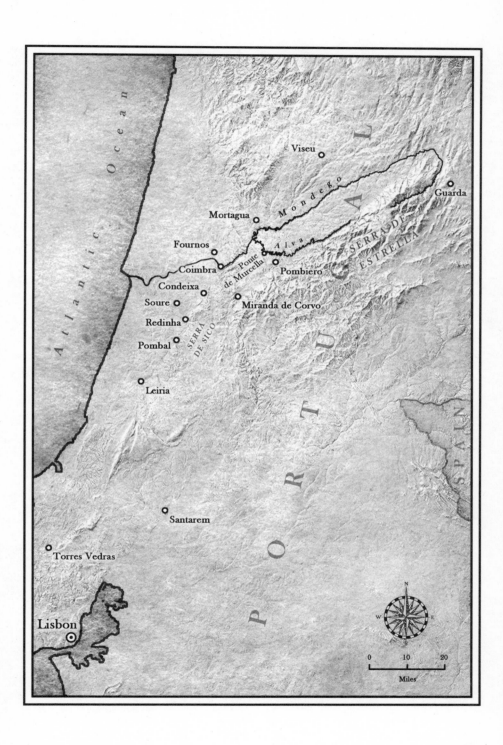

Atlantic Ocean

Viseu

Guarda

Mortagua

Mondego

Fournos

SERRA DE ESTRELLA

Coimbra

Ponte de Murcella

Alva

Pombiero

Condeixa

Miranda de Corvo

Soure

Redinha

SERRA DE SICO

Pombal

P O R T U G A L

Leiria

S P A I N

Santarem

Torres Vedras

Lisbon

N
W   E
S

0   10   20

Miles

1

The big man stopped and froze for a moment in the doorway, his square shoulders outlined in the half-light that came through the crack between door and frame. The men to his rear watched his every move and held their breath as, slowly, he extended his hand behind his back and then waved it at the ground three times in a signal to them to stop and stay quiet.

As one, they obeyed. There was no noise now. Old hands at secrecy, they had removed their sword belts earlier to avoid the clank and jingle and carried their weapons in their hands. Most of them were armed with a curved cavalry sabre, apart from one, younger than the others, who carried what looked like a shotgun and the leader, the big man, who held in his hand a larger, heavier sword.

The man waited and listened. From beyond the door came the sound of laughter and then someone was shouting. The tension inside the room was tangible. Seven hands gripped tighter on their weapons. Another laugh and then the sound of footsteps. Gradually fading.

The big man turned and shook his head and the men relaxed and smiled as he returned to them.

'Nothing. Just another lot of looters. They'll not find what they want in here. They won't trouble us.'

Captain James Keane sounded as if he knew what he was talking about and his men knew that he did.

For two years now they had followed Keane through this godforsaken country of Portugal and they would have done almost anything he asked of them and followed him anywhere. Keane knew it. Although sometimes he wondered why. And sometimes, too, so did they – at times such as this.

The sergeant, James Ross, a plain-speaking Glasgow man, a born fighter with a quick mind whom Keane had rescued from ignominy as a steward in the officers' mess, put their thoughts into words: 'Can I ask, sir, what is it that we're meant to be doing here?'

'As you are well aware, sarn't, we're here to do what we always do. We're observing the enemy. Those are our orders.'

'If you'll pardon me for saying so, sir, but we've not actually observed any of the enemy for the last day.'

There was a laugh from the others. It was true, thought Keane. His sergeant was, if anything, matter of fact. For the last two days they had been stuck in this dark room. Or to be more exact, in a damp tunnel, beneath the Portuguese city of Coimbra.

It was hard to believe that it had been just a week since they had beaten the French in battle, since he and his men and all of Black Bob's Light Division too had come charging down from the monastery on the ridge at Bussaco and into the French, driving them from the hill. A week since they had routed Massena's army. But, as he had often found to be the way, the fruits of victory had a bitter taste.

Wellington had been unable to follow up his victory and

could only hope that he had slowed Massena down. In fact, he had pulled back from the field of victory. Lack of manpower had exposed him and had the French but followed up, they might have inflicted wholesale slaughter. But both Wellington and Keane knew that Massena would not take that option. He would attempt to get past Bussaco, taking the northern road, and outflank the duke. But there would be no French pursuit. And Keane knew why.

Coimbra. As rich a prize as any soldier could hope for. Riches and women lay open for the taking. And that would be a temptation that Marshal André Massena, Prince of Essling and the most renowned plunderer in Napoleon's armies, could not resist. And so Wellington had got away, like a thief in the night.

But Coimbra had been left to the French and they still held it for the emperor. And Keane and his men were all that remained of the allied army. Left there to report to the duke that which he already knew.

They had been guided to the tunnel by a civilian. Doctor Thomas Roberts Sobral – half English, as were many of the well-to-do of this part of Portugal – was a kindly man in his advancing later years. He was also one of the staff at the university, a professor of chemistry. There was little Sobral did not know of the history of the institution and its ways. The tunnel had been carved out centuries ago, when the Jesuits still had control of the university. It linked two of the colleges with Jesuit churches and had been used many a time to hide fugitive Jesuit priests, hounded by the Church. Sobral had brought them here through a secret entrance, as the French army was at the gates. He had told Keane that it was the safest place for them and that, from here, they could emerge into the city to observe the enemy. The French would have no clue as to its existence and, in any case, as Keane knew too well, after a few days most of them would be too drunk to care.

Coimbra's nemesis had come two days ago in a single night of violence, the whole of which Keane and his men had spent in their refuge. Biding their time. Waiting for the right moment. Since then, they had made two sorties into the ruined city, watching as the French came and went through the great gate and listening in to the conversations on the street.

They had managed to ascertain the number of French and the identity of some of the regiments – exactly the information that Keane's superiors in Wellington's intelligence service had demanded.

And Ross was right. That day they had not left their lair, had not seen a single Frenchman. They had heard enough of them, though, as the enemy had drunk and stolen and raped its way through the ancient city.

Keane knew Coimbra of old. The city, standing high on a hill above the river Mondego, had been Wellington's headquarters twice before in the past year and it was here, in the Bishop's Palace, that he had first been commissioned by the duke as an exploring officer and given the task of raising the men he now commanded. He and his men had made their camp in a quiet olive grove just outside the walls. He wondered if now French tents were pitched in that place. For the Coimbra he had known was gone. On first acquaintance, he had thought it a vile place. A midden compared even to London or Cork. But later he had come to value the pleasant streets flanked with market stalls. But all that, the scent of lavender on the air, the music that caught the ear as you walked past a window and that curious contended atmosphere that had once reminded him of an English shire town, had now vanished. In its place was a scene of desolation. He had learnt to love this place, but now his greatest desire was to be gone from here.

Coimbra was a ghost town. The heart and soul of the nation had been deserted by its 40,000 inhabitants. Or most of them, for Keane knew there would be some diehards here. A few hundred or a few thousand who would not leave, for sentiment or money. And he knew, too, what their fate would be.

An army now teemed through the streets of the ancient city taking what they wanted like a pack of wolves falling on a flock of lambs.

He was sick of the thought. And sick, too, to the stomach. For, after two days, the air was becoming fetid in the tunnel and he wondered how much longer they might have to remain down here. He intended to make a final sortie that evening and, with help from one of his men, Sam Gilpin, a cat burglar by profession, had procured a couple of French uniforms with which to carry it out. Of course, he knew that, should they be caught, they would probably be shot as spies, being out of uniform. But that situation was nothing new to Keane. He gathered his men round him for a briefing.

'I intend to wait until nightfall. It shouldn't be long. Two of us will leave, take notes and return. Then we can all get away.'

'Won't be soon enough for me,' said a voice.

'Sorry, Silver? You said . . . ?'

'I said, sir, we can only go once we've seen enough.'

'Quite. So I can take it you're volunteering then?'

Horatio Silver smiled, knowing that his comment had caught out his commanding officer. He sighed. 'I suppose I am, sir.'

'I suppose you are too. Good, then – that's my party.'

The light through the door had all but gone now. Keane stood up.

'We might as well make a start. Come on, Silver.'

Keane threw one of the French uniforms at him. 'Yours. Into uniform. And try to think like a Frenchman, if you can. The rest of you, wait here. Sar'nt Ross, take command. If I'm not back within one and a half hours, take the men out, however best you can.' He gave Ross a slim leather pouch. 'My notes. Make sure they get to Colonel Grant.'

'Yes, sir. But I don't think there will be a need for that.'

'Nor I, but better to be safe, eh?'

Keane stripped off his uniform coat, a unique design in brown serge, worn by the Corps of Guides of which his unit was a part. It was based on a waist-length light cavalry dolman, but with black frogging. In its place he donned the hated blue-and-white tailed coat of a French infantry captain. He wore a white shirt, but it was grey and ragged after a year's campaigning and, through its thin cotton, the enemy uniform was itchy against his skin. He could feel, too, the coarse stitching where a patch disguised the bullet hole of the shot that had killed its original owner.

Both men placed the cumbersome, tall, black French infantry shakos on their heads in place of their light cavalry style helmets, but neither bothered to change his trousers and boots. Their grey cavalry overalls and the boots worn beneath them would not look so out of place in a French army in which most of the men now wore small clothes and leggings that were the most expedient and had often been captured or stolen from the dead.

Keane turned to Silver, who had clothed himself in the uniform of a dead French sergeant. 'Ah, the very image of a valiant *caporal chef*. Just take your sword, Silver. That's all we'll need.'

He was right. They were not going out to kill Frenchmen,

unless the opportunity arose, simply to observe them. To look and listen and take notes – that was their purpose – Keane's purpose, as one of Wellington's trusted intelligence officers. He and his men were the eyes and ears of the army.

There were nine of them, all told. Two of these, two of the finest, Leech and Archer, he had left behind at their base camp, hidden in the rocky olive groves beyond the city.

Though in the previous few weeks Keane had held command of a company, mainly Portuguese, he'd known it wouldn't last. And now he wondered if it ever would, whether, prized as he was by the duke in his present capacity, he might ever aspire to take a field command again, whether it might be as a captain or at a higher rank.

He looked at his command. All that was left now were his own men. He counted them off on a silent roll-call: Leech and Archer and those around him now – Ross and Silver; Sam Gilpin, the petty thief with a gift for mimicry; Jesus Heredia, a Portuguese trooper rescued from the gallows for a crime he didn't commit; Martin, the young man with the shotgun; and finally Garland, a bear of a man, handy with his fists and deadly in a fight.

There had, until recently, been one more of their number: Keane's old friend, Lieutenant Tom Morris. But Morris was dead and belonged, like so many of the people and things that haunted Keane's mind, to the past.

The two men moved towards the doorway and Keane listened and waited. Outside in the street he could hear two French voices. One, low and drunken, was shouting something about wine. The other, quieter and more sober, was arguing with him. It went on for what seemed an eternity and then, just as he thought they would descend into fighting, the voices became quieter, more distant. Keane pushed the door open a crack further. Peering through, he saw no one. He whispered to Silver, 'Now!' And together the two men emerged from the door, adopting an air of confidence. Just as the door swung shut behind them, several horsemen rounded the corner of the street. Dragoons – ten of them, with a junior officer at their head.

After the tunnel, the air was sublimely fresh and the sudden sunshine, even at this time of day, made Keane squint. He blinked, hoping no one would notice, and, taking the initiative, walked with Silver directly towards the horsemen. As they passed, he threw a cheery '*Bonsoir!*' at the officer who, having assured himself they were not worth arresting, responded with a nod and a grunt.

Silver spoke, surprised. 'They're provosts, sir. Out to take looters. Same as we do. That's not like the French, sir.'

'No, Silver, it isn't. And you're right. So we know there is some order, here. Someone's in charge of all this.'

This was not random looting. Keane had seen enough of that in fifteen years of soldiering to tell him that this was being sanctioned and regulated. The French army had been allowed its few days of excess, of doing what it did best, and now it was being reined in. And Keane thought he knew by whom.

Marshal Massena was behind this. He had done the same across Europe, emptying its treasure houses from the Vatican to Venice, and had made something of a name for himself. If Napoleon was the great thief of Europe, then Massena was his housebreaker.

Massena was as unpleasant a rogue as you would ever meet and looked the part with an eye patch. Keane had met him some two months back, in Almeida. He'd tricked him into providing information and, to top it off, had bedded the marshal's mistress into the bargain. He had an inkling that the man would know of that by now, that he had been duped, and he suspected, too, that he might have guessed he had also been cuckolded.

Keane knew one thing for certain. If he ever met Massena again, he would make sure that he was armed and, if he could help it, not outnumbered.

The street ahead of them was empty for only a few moments before a party of French infantry appeared from a side alley. They were laden with bags and objects. One of them carried a framed painting, a religious scene prized from an altar; another had strapped a gold chalice to his blanket roll. Their leader was an NCO with two red chevrons on his upper left arm signifying fifteen years in the service of the emperor. But there was no need for him to wear his experience on his sleeve. His face, scarred, tanned brown and prematurely aged, betrayed the secrets of a life spent in battle and its aftermath. The sergeant brandished a gold crosier, leading his men with it in a parody of religious devotion.

They were all obviously drunk and Keane wondered what might have happened had they appeared a few minutes earlier when the dragoons were still on hand. For, despite their drunkenness, most looked as if they might be capable of handling themselves in a fight.

The sergeant, seeing Keane and Silver, stopped and approached them, his crosier held out as if it were a sword. But it was not an aggressive move and Keane smiled at him. Again he thought, as the officer, it would look better to take the initiative.

'*Bonjour*, sergeant. Who are you?'

'Sergeant Bigoud, sir. Seventh line. These are my men, some

of them. And a few odds and sods we've picked up on our way. And you, sir?'

Keane thought fast.

'Captain Charles Mercier of the 45th, and this is my sergeant.'

Silver grunted. The sergeant looked at Keane.

'Lost your men, sir? I haven't seen many officers hereabouts, sir. They're mostly up the hill, where the British had their houses. Fine things to be had up there . . . sir.'

The word, repeated, took on a disrespectful note that, in the British army, would have earned the man fifty lashes, sergeant or not.

The French, though, were different. Keane laughed and clapped the sergeant on the back.

'Just as always, eh? Well, I'm happy down here. I'm from the ranks, me. Always will be, too. And, I'll tell you, this is the stuff of life to me.' Keane nodded to the sergeant's long-service stripes. 'You've been in a long time. Were you at Rome?'

The sergeant brightened and raised an eyebrow.

'Rome? That I was. Now, there was a victory. I went in a pauper, came out a rich man. Bought a farm in Normandy, I did. My brother runs it now. Lost his leg at Austerlitz. Those were the days, right enough. Were you there?'

'Yes. With Mortier. Still a ranker then, of course. Great days for a young man. And the women!'

The sergeant laughed. 'You stay down here with us, sir. You never know, maybe one day I'll get a commission, like you.'

Together now, they walked along the street, Silver following on, trying to mimic drunkenness in the hope that he wouldn't have to speak. His Portuguese was better than his French, and his Spanish was perfect, his mother having come from there.

There was a church on their left, a tall baroque building

with ornate towers and sculptures of the saints. The sergeant pointed. 'Let's try in here. I'm keen for some more gold before we get to the women.'

They entered the apse and, in the dim-lit coolness, Keane saw that they were not the first. The pews had been upturned and the tapestries ripped from the walls. A huge painted image of Christ crucified still hung at the far end above the altar and, at its foot, lay a body.

The sergeant shook his head. 'Shit. Beaten to it.' He turned to the others. 'Right, lads, anything worth taking, we take. Get a move on.' As they went about it with a precision born of habit, the sergeant walked the length of the aisle and Keane could see that the body was that of a priest, lying in a wide pool of his own blood. That of another man, also in vestments, lay off to the left.

'Saved us the trouble, whoever they were. Pity; can't abide men of God. Would have been a pleasure. Who believes now, eh? Apart from the bloody peasants we have to deal with.' He spat on the stones in contempt, leaving a gob of tobacco. 'They've no idea. They're fools. There is no God, is there? And do you know how I know that?' He didn't wait for a reply. 'I know because I've seen hell, and it's here on earth. What sort of God would let that happen?' He kicked at the body of the priest. 'Got no answer for that, have you, Your Holiness?'

He threw another kick at the head of the dead priest and Keane muttered an oath beneath his breath and tried to wrack his brain for the sort of thing that a Catholic might have said to bless the departed.

He was not a particularly pious man, and his family were Protestant Scots-Irish to a man, but he thought that he believed in something greater than the baseness of the world they lived in. In contrast to the sergeant, his own experiences as a soldier had taught him that there must be something else. He too had seen hell, and he knew there must, somewhere, be salvation. Even if we all needed a little help to get there. The sergeant's disrespect for a man of God cut down in a place of worship grated on his soul.

The sergeant, hearing Keane mutter, looked at him for a moment.

'Eh?'

'I said, "And good riddance to him and all of them."'

'Oh, yes. I'll second that. What have we got here?'

A soldier came up, clutching a pile of silver plate.

'That'll do nicely, Faron. And be sure to search the bodies for keys. I want this place stripped.'

It took ten minutes to remove from the church what it had taken five centuries to create. And, by the end of it, the building looked like a toothless cadaver, as cold and silent as the two dead priests.

The sergeant produced a bottle of red wine and offered it to Keane who, although loath to do so, took a swig. Silver, too, accepted the offer and it seemed to seal their place among the sergeant's comrades.

As they left the church, he laughed. 'Now what, sir? I'm feeling like a bit of fresh meat, if you know what I mean. All that robbing's got my gorge up. Let's see what we can find. How 'bout you, sir?'

Keane nodded. 'Ill take your advice, sergeant. I've not had a woman these past four weeks.'

'Then you'd better get one quick or you'll go half blind and yer pecker'll fall off.' He laughed and looked at Silver. 'You, too, cocky. Don't say much, does he?'

Keane shook his head. 'Lost part of his tongue in a fight with a peasant. Hurts to talk. He prefers to drink.'

They pressed on through the town and, every so often, the sergeant would stop at a doorway and summon two of his men to take a look inside. They came back shaking their heads. Then, at a large town house on a bend in the road that led to the upper town, they emerged grinning.

'There's a woman, sergeant. Classy piece. She's raving a bit, but she's got big tits and a nice arse.'

The sergeant laughed. 'Then she'll do, boys, won't she? Good enough for us, and sounds like she ain't got the pox.'

They entered the doorway and, even after fifteen years a soldier, Keane was shocked.

The house was that of a respectable bourgeois family. Merchants, perhaps, he thought, or something to do with the university. He thought for a moment he recognized it, but hoped he did not. For there on the tiled floor of the marbled entrance hall lay more bodies: a man and a woman in later middle age, well dressed, and, with them, a boy of ten. By the look of them, all had been bayoneted. From upstairs came the sound of hysterical shrieking.

'For Christ's sake! What's all that?'

The soldier spoke: 'It's the woman, sarge. Must be that kid's mother.' He pointed to the boy.

The sergeant climbed the stairs, taking them two at a time.

'Someone shut her up, before I do. I like a bit of spirit in a wench, but that's too much.'

Suddenly, from the landing, the woman appeared. She wore an ornate yellow silk dress, which had been to torn to expose one of her breasts. Her hair hung loose, as if torn from a fastening, and her face was a mask of terror and disbelief. She flew at the sergeant, her hands trying to tear at his face. He pushed her away but she came again, scratching his cheek. He shrieked and pushed her off, and then, with a massive effort, she came again and, managing to hold on to him, bit him on the ear. The sergeant yelled again and, picking her up by her shoulders, hurled her over the iron banister to the floor below, where she landed with a thud, cracking her head open on the marble.

He cursed, grabbed at his bleeding ear. 'Christ, I'm bleeding. The bloody bitch. I'll kill her.'

Keane looked down at her and her huge dead eyes stared back at him as the circle of dark blood pooled wider around her head. 'You already have.'

From the upper floors there was another scream now – high pitched and more terrible than the dead woman's.

A French soldier emerged, carrying over his shoulder a girl in her teens. Her hands had been tied behind her back and her hair showed the signs of struggle. This, thought Keane, must be the last of the family group, save the father.

'Look here, sarge! Look what I've got! A right lively one. Nearly had my eye out. Christ and Mary! What happened to you?'

The sergeant pointed with bloody finger at the dead woman.

'That. That's what happened to me. Look at this one! She's lovely. Aren't you, darling?'

The girl screamed louder now as the sergeant grabbed at her head with his bloody hand and jerked it up so that she stared into his eyes.

'I've dealt with your mother, see. And now you're going to give us what she can't. Give her to me, François.'

'What? But she's mine. I found her.'

'Give the bitch to me, I said. I'm the sergeant here.'

The man handed the girl to the sergeant. 'There you are. But it's not bloody fair. I found her.'

'Shut up. You'll have your turn. You all will.' He looked at Keane. 'You, too, sir.'

He pushed her up the stairs and Keane looked at the men with him, waiting their turn, joking with each other and half drunkenly boasting about what they would do with her. One of the men, a small corporal with a moustache and heavy stubble, left the queue and ambled to the front. He spoke a few words to the man at the front and produced something from his hand. The man dropped out to be replaced by the corporal, who had clearly bribed the man to get forward. Keane knew there was only one course of action. Leaving his place in the queue, he walked up to the corporal at the front.

'How much?'

'What?'

'I said, "How much?"'

'More than you could afford, sir.'

Again the word had no respect to it and Keane knew now that the French army had lost its way. Even here, he was taking notes for useful intelligence. He asked again. 'How much?'

The soldier looked at him with one eyebrow raised.

'You really want to know?'

'I asked you, didn't I? Name your price.'

'You'd never afford it.' The man thought for a moment, then smiled knowingly, anticipating the effect of his outrageous demand. 'Three hundred livres.'

Kane smiled and shook his head. It was a handsome sum – enough to buy as good a horse as you could want.

'A hundred.'

'Two fifty.'

'One fifty, no more.'

'Two hundred, no less.'

Keane waited for a moment. 'One eighty. It's my final offer.'

The corporal laughed and held out his hand. Whoever he was, clearly this officer was insane.

'Pay me.'

Keane reached into his pocket and drew out a purse. He delved inside and brought out another packet, which he handed to the Frenchman, having first taken out two large ten-livre coins.

'It's all there; count it.'

The man, unable to believe his good fortune, poured the contents of the packet on to the ground and, all pride gone, bent to count it. Then, satisfied, he gathered it all up.

'It's a deal. You can have her.'

Just in time, thought Keane.

The corporal laughed.

'You might have a wait, sir. The sarge likes to take his time with them. He always gets what he wants.'

'I'll wait upstairs, I think.'

Keane climbed the staircase under the gaze of the others, conscious that Silver was now quite far away from him, waiting his turn in line. He stood at the entrance to the bedroom. From inside, he could hear muffled screams.

Keane kept a careful watch on the men below and then, when they were momentarily distracted by a comment from one of them, he slipped inside the door. The bedroom was preceded by an antechamber and, as he entered, Keane reached into the top of his left boot and drew from the lining a slim-bladed knife that had been given to him by one of Don Sanchez's

Spanish guerrillas. Slowly, and taking care to tread carefully, he entered the bedroom.

The girl lay spreadeagled on the bed. Her hands had been tied to the bed posts and her legs were wide apart, with her ripped skirt and undergarments pulled up to her waist so that she was naked, save for a small band of clothing around her middle. The sergeant crouched over her, wearing his shirt, but naked, too, from the waist down. He did not hear Keane enter, nor did he see, for a moment, the change of expression in the girl's terrified eyes from one of terror to one of hope. And by the time he did it was too late. He felt Keane's blade at his throat and that was the last thing he felt.

Keane cut the man's throat with a swift, short movement and then quickly pushed his body off the bed as the blood began to spout. He used the same knife to cut the girl's ropes and then, pulling down her dress to cover her, he draped the dead man's coat around her shoulders and, with all his strength, picked her up and pushed her from the open window. She screamed as she fell and Keane looked after her. He had not checked, but had hoped her fall would be broken and, sure enough, she had landed on the straw roof of an outbuilding, crashing through to land in the mire beneath. He watched as she got up, and continued to watch just long enough to see her look back with gratitude as she rounded the street corner. Then he turned and rushed to the door.

'Help! Help! Murder!'

Keane ran out and rattled down the staircase as the men began to climb it. Thankfully, he saw that Silver was among them.

'She killed him. Cut his throat. He's dead. The sergeant's dead. I'll get her. I saw her go. I'll get her.'

He pointed past them and raced into the street. Having waited there for a sufficient time, Keane ran back into the house.

'No sign. She's gone.'

The corporal was looking at Keane now.

Silver noticed it and whispered to him. 'Sir, take care. I think he's guessed.'

Keane pretended to ignore the man's stare. At length, as the place erupted in panic and the drunken Frenchmen called for help, the corporal approached Keane.

'Sir, don't you think you should find help? Find the killer?'

He looked at Keane's sleeve and, glancing down, Keane saw that it was flecked with fresh blood. He wiped at it. 'Poor chap. Yes, we must find her. I was shocked. Didn't expect it.'

The corporal smiled at him. 'No. I suppose not . . . What's your unit, sir?'

Keane thought of one of the brass shako plates he had seen at Bussaco. 'The 105th. I need to find them.'

'You're a long way from home, sir. They were sent to garrison duty. At half strength, I heard. Got cut up bad at Bussaco.'

'Yes, that's right. Very bad. That's why I'm here. My whole company were casualties. What's left of them are here. In the hospital. Poor fellows.'

There was a party of dragoons in the street now, dismounted but carrying carbines, being led to the house by a group of the infantry. Hearing them, the corporal turned and, before he was able to say anything, Silver had clapped him on the back and pressed a knife to his side. 'One word, *mon ami*, and you're a dead man.'

The corporal froze.

Keane spoke quietly. 'Don't say a thing. Just come with us.'

2

Slowly, the three of them walked away from the house, Keane taking care to shield Silver from the gaze of the advancing dragoons. Silver, holding the knife to the Frenchman with his left hand and with his right arm around his shoulders, began to sway as he walked, shamming drunkenness, and Keane followed behind in a similarly shambling manner. With every step, they expected to hear a challenge from the dragoons, but none came and, as they reached an alley on the left of the street, Keane whispered, 'Duck down here.'

As they turned, the corporal jerked away from Silver and ran back into the street, waving his arms. He called to the dragoons, '*Au secours!*'

But Silver stuck close to him and no sooner had the words left his lips than the corporal felt Silver's slim blade slide hard into his side, level with his heart.

Keane cursed and, as the dying corporal slumped to the cobbles, he was already conscious of the shouts of the dragoons; he began to run down the alleyway, followed by Silver.

'Which way, sir?'

'To the tunnel? South, I think, back the way we came. We'll have to chance it.'

They turned left at the end of the street and ran on until Keane saw another lane leading back to the left again.

'Down here!'

The lane was narrow and dark, lined with filthy houses on either side. Both men gagged at the stench from the excrement which filled the open sewers to the left and right. The body of a Portuguese woman lay in one of them and further on a French soldier was vomiting against a wall.

After a hundred yards, they emerged at the far end of the street where they had started, at the spot where they had first seen the dragoons. Bizarrely, the street was now empty, save for two drunken Frenchmen outside the house where Keane had killed the sergeant, and he could only guess that all their pursuers must have run behind them. Thinking fast, he crossed the road and began to run in the direction of what he supposed must be south, down another small alleyway, followed by Silver.

They emerged in a small plaza filled with French soldiers. The men had dragged out wooden furniture – tables, seats and screens – from the church, which dominated one side of the plaza, and were burning it in the centre. The men stood, laughing, unaware of Keane's presence, while a group of Portuguese prisoners stood a little distance away, stoney faced. Keane scanned the place. Five streets led off the square. He chose the most likely and they sprinted for it. But, just as they reached the opening, he heard a commotion behind them and, turning, saw a dozen dragoons emerge from the other side of the square, followed by a mob of infantry. The officer pulled up his horse and signalled a halt, then scanned the square for a few seconds before his gaze alighted on Keane and Silver. The two men wasted no time.

Down the alley and cutting sharp left into another, Keane thought they might shake off their pursuers. But, as they paused for a moment to catch their breath, bent double, Keane heard French voices raised behind them and began to run.

He wondered if they should make for the tunnel door through which they had come into the town. It was in plain view and, if they were seen, it would be difficult to lose the dragoons. The secret internal entrance to the tunnel, though, through which they had been admitted, he knew from their guide, was in the cellars beneath the university.

This, he decided, would be a safer entrance, although they would have to alert the men at the other end before doubling back together to escape via the third way, which led directly from the tunnel system to an exit in the hillside below the city.

Silver spoke between breaths.

'How did they find us, sir? The place is like a warren.'

'They must have someone damned good with them.'

The dragoons were closing. A shot rang out and a carbine ball shot past Keane's head, smacking into a wall beyond. He looked for a second towards the noise and saw another dragoon loading and then, beside the dragoon, he saw a man in a different uniform: the blue and gold uniform of a French *général de brigade*. And the face above it, its sharp features under the fore-and-aft bicorne hat, sent a chill through him. He said the name aloud: 'Macnab.'

Silver followed his gaze.

'Christ. It is him, sir. It's the spy. Colonel Macnab.'

Yes, thought Keane, that's the colonel. Though he held no rank now in the army he had betrayed. For an instant, Keane was possessed with an overwhelming urge to run across the plaza and attack the man. This man whom he held responsible for so very many wrongs.

Silver sensed it and held him by the arm. 'No, sir, not now. His time will come. We know he's alive. And he's here. We'd best make ourselves scarce.'

They turned and ran and Keane could hear the drumming of the dragoons' high boots on the cobbled square behind them. It occurred to him that the man he had previously known as O'Connell, or Macnab, might equally well have recognized him, but he thought it unlikely. Nevertheless, he'd have had a good idea that a tall enemy soldier, who might be masquerading as a French officer, in the middle of occupied Coimbra had a fair chance of being James Keane. There were not that many of Wellington's exploring officers, and fewer still who would be brave, talented or foolish enough to attempt to pull off that sort of stunt under the very noses of the French. Keane was unique. As unique as the Irish spy in Massena's army who had, over the last few months, turned into his greatest adversary.

First, there had been the bomb in the house in Coimbra, then the messages intercepted, the cat-and-mouse games with parties of French who seemed to know his movements, not to mention those of Wellington's army. And then there had been the necessity for Morris's absence, which had led, in turn, to his friend's falling in love with Kitty Blackwood. And, finally, there had been Morris's death itself, at Macnab's hands, at the height of the battle of Bussaco.

All these things led to Macnab. And there was something else. Despite moments of doubt, and there had been and still were a few, Keane had grown over the past year to take pride in his job as an exploring officer, and determined to be the best.

The fact that there was now a man in French pay who seemed to be striving to outdo him filled him with fury and doubled his desire to win. Plus, there was the very fact that that man happened to be, as Keane was himself, an Irishman. The time would come, as Silver had told him. And, for Keane, it would not be soon enough. But now they had to run.

Their flight took them through more of the city's narrow backstreets. Keane cursed the place. Every vennel looked like the next, every thin, piss-poor lane with its collection of rubbish and fetid debris and its washing – days, weeks old – strung out on a line between between its buildings. He stumbled over something – a body, lying in the running sewer that was the gutter – and, managing somehow to regain his balance, ran on. Behind him he could hear the men coming, their breathing getting louder as they went. And there was another noise – one that caused him concern. He had heard it before and he knew it for what it was. It was the sound of pursuit.

He turned left, then right, then, following his instinct, turned left and instantly wished that he hadn't.

They had blundered into a huge plaza, exposed on all sides to anyone who might be watching. On three sides, the tall marble buildings of the university rose to the sky and, on the fourth, the way lay open to a view of the mountains.

Opposite them, close to the open side of the square, two men sat at a table. As Keane and Silver entered the square, the men looked up. Keane fixed them in his gaze, saw a flash of uniform – gold epaulettes – then detected a movement. Then, as the men rose to their feet, he managed a feeble smile.

He looked around for others and saw no one but a dog and a woman carrying oranges in a wicker basket on her head. Seeing them, she turned and ran.

Keane yelled, 'Silver, how the hell did we end up here?'

'No idea, sir, but I reckon we're 'bout as far from home as we could be.'

Keane looked around and, realizing that they had taken a wrong turning, headed off towards an alleyway. 'On me. Stay close.'

Once again, they found themselves in the warren of filthy streets. And now Keane sensed that the men he had seen in the square were behind them – along with whoever else had been in pursuit before. The dragoons. Macnab.

They found themselves in another street and, this time, heading fast downhill. Low, wide steps of shiny stone rang out with their footsteps as they clattered down, twisting round in a spiral. These streets were where the students had lived and spent their days. But now the cafés were boarded up, or splayed open by the invader, and the students were long gone.

At last, they emerged from the university quarter and found themselves among the decorated buildings in what had been the Jesuit area – the old colleges that had been proscribed by the Inquisition. Here it was, Keane knew, that their own salvation lay, for it was close to here that they had originally gained access to the tunnel, in those final few moments before the French had first arrived in Coimbra.

Keane turned to Silver. 'This is it. We're close now. Close to the tunnel. Remember?'

Silver nodded and then, quite suddenly, stopped and held up his hand, warning his officer to be silent. Keane knew better than to disagree. Both men listened and, above the general row of the place, heard nothing for a moment, and then, sickeningly, the repeated thud of hard leather boots on cobbles.

Keane whispered, 'Good God. How did they manage that? How the hell did they find us?'

'Macnab, sir?'

Keane shook his head. 'Come on. I've been in these filthy clothes for too long. Let's get out of here.'

He stood for a moment, looking at the streets, and then, recognizing one of the corners, pointed it out to Silver.

'Look, there. That's the way. Come on, quickly.'

The two men ran down the street and, gaining the shelter of a porticoed entrance to what had once been a Jesuit church, pushed at the huge oak doors. They opened and Keane knew that his instinct had been right.

They moved slowly into the nave and, turning to the left in the dim light, tried to find the door they knew to be there. The place smelt of a stable yard – horse shit and leather – and, looking underfoot, Keane realized why. The French had made it into a barracks for their horses and the place was ankle deep in manure.

Ten paces further on, and just before the grilled entrance to a side chapel, he found what he had been searching for: an oak door, only about five feet in height. The forgotten side entrance of the old college.

Without another word, the two of them entered and found themselves, as they had some days ago, in a vaulted atrium. To their left lay the main entrance doors, long disused, and, high above them, a brass ring hung on a chain from the roof, missing the ornate chandelier which had been there for two centuries. Light filtered through a window above the doors and, through the dust, they began to make out the lighter patches on the stone walls, which marked the sites of vanished paintings – looted, not, for once, by the French, but by the Inquisition when it had proscribed the Jesuits.

Keane led the way to their right and down a narrow corridor, which had once provided access to the college kitchens. But, counting the paces as he went, he stopped before he reached them and stood over a hatch in the floor. He lifted the heavy iron ring at its top and the hatch swung upwards easily and revealed the first of a set of stone steps leading down. Taking care, Keane placed one booted foot on the top step and made his way down, followed by Silver, who pulled down the hatch after them, shutting out the light.

The dark was all enveloping, the only light coming from a few gaps in the wood of the hatch.

Doing their best not to slip on the algae-covered stone, they reached the bottom of the steps, where they emerged in a low-vaulted room, its ancient stone walls dripping with moisture. There was no door and, at first, it appeared to be no more than a cellar or a dungeon, but, having been here before, Keane was not panicked. Moving as swiftly as he could in the darkness towards the end wall, he looked at it but saw nothing. He began feeling his way carefully and trying to remember what the old man had told him – to count the stones, from the top left corner and then downwards and then right again. He recalled the coordinates: ten, three. Ten stones in, he stopped and then moved down – three stones, about level with his waist. Slowly, he moved his hand around the stone and then, to his relief, found the place where there was no mortar. Keane inserted his finger and pushed. There was a faint click, like a lock turning, and he pushed, moving the stone so that half the wall swung open on a massive pivot. The two men slipped through the gap and then, careful to close the false door behind them, went on. It was dark here and smelt of the damp of ages.

There was no noise from behind them. They paused for a

moment, regaining their breath. Keane drew out a pistol from his belt and, reaching for a bullet, pushed it into the muzzle before ramming it home. He primed the pan and tucked the pistol back into his belt. It was always best to be ready, even though they felt secure in the knowledge that the dragoons would never find them here. He was just about to say as much to Silver when, from beyond the door, he heard the sound of scraping – or, more distinctly, the sound of trailing scabbards grating on stone. And with it came the noise of raised and anxious voices.

'Christ, they've found the stairs.'

Turning down the tunnel, the two of them ran as fast as the darkness allowed. Keane's mind was befuddled by the impossible. How, he asked himself, had the dragoons found them so fast? Macnab was with them. He was the only answer. Somehow he had found out about the door.

They came to a junction where three corridors met each other. Keane recalled the right way from before and together they entered. Sure enough, after a hundred yards, they began to see light and hear voices. Keane stopped and listened, and then, recognizing one of them as that of Ross, went on. The men were waiting where he had left them, but turned as one on his approaching, their swords drawn.

Keane motioned to them. 'It's me. We must be quick. The dragoons are hard on our heels.' He turned to Ross. 'Macnab's with them. Or O'Connell. Or whatever he calls himself.'

The sergeant swore. 'That black bastard? Did he know you, sir?'

'No, I don't think so. But who can say? God alone knows how he found the trapdoor. Come on.'

They turned to go back and find the way leading to the

hillside, which their guide had told them about. With any luck, he thought, the French would not have discovered the secret entrance. But, there again, they had Macnab with them and he seemed to have ways of finding everything.

They had reached the crossroads now and Keane pointed them all towards the left-hand way. But, just as he did so, a flood of light was let in from the left, quickly followed by the familiar thud of cavalry boots on stone.

'That's them! Save yourselves! Get out! Ross, you're in command.'

He pushed Garland and Martin down the tunnel, and then Ross. But it was clear that the sergeant wasn't going to move.

'I'm not leaving you, sir.'

'It's an order.'

'Don't care, sir. I'm not going.'

'Nor me, sir.' Silver was beside them.

'Very touching, both of you, but we can't all stay and fight here. There isn't room. Sarn't Ross, you're in charge. Now get them all out. See you on the hill.'

Ross turned and ran down the tunnel after the others. But Silver stayed and smiled at Keane.

'Can't get rid of me, sir.'

'We'll see about that.'

'Perhaps we'll get out before they find us.'

But Silver's wish was not to be granted. They made ready to follow Ross but, just as they did so, two French dragoons emerged opposite. Keane knew that they would not fire in here for fear of their carbine bullets ricocheting off the stone, but he saw the dim light glinting on their swords. He shouted after his men. 'Run!' Then, turning, he faced the dragoons.

The two men came at them and Silver met the first with a

deft parry. There was barely space for all of them to fight in the tunnel but Keane thrust his sword towards the other dragoon, feeling it hit home and sink in. The man fell and Keane, withdrawing the blade instantly, parried that of the following dragoon, who clambered over his comrade's body. Behind him, he could hear the men making their escape and, to his front, the sound of the tunnel filling with the French. As he fought with the man, Keane used his left hand to reach into his belt to draw out the loaded pistol. Two more cuts – one to the body, parried, and a riposte to the chest. Keane held the dragoon's blade with his own and lunged to the man's heart. The blades clanged, steel on steel, and the dragoon made another thrust. Keane's blade ran round that of the Frenchman and skewered him beneath the chin, pushing home, running up and into his brain.

The next dragoon was on them almost instantly and before Keane had time to withdraw his blade from the first. Still holding it, with the blade embedded in the dragoon, he presented the pistol and, in an instant, had cocked it before gently squeezing the trigger. The gun spat flame and the ball hit the dragoon in the chest at point-blank range, exploding from his back in a welter of blood.

Keane pulled his sword from the dead dragoon and, cleaning it on the man's tunic, returned it to the en-garde position. Silver was alongside him now, his sinewy body squeezed into the tunnel next to Keane's taller frame. Both men stood at the ready, and both responded with simple, clear parries when the dragoons attacked. Keane's was the more elegant style, with quick, deft strokes of the blade, learnt in the *salle* in Paris when he had lodged with his aunt. Silver's cuts were more of the barrack yard – hard and strong, with no room for error.

Keane drew first blood just as the other Frenchman hit home on Silver's forearm. The Englishman recoiled but didn't drop his guard and, as Keane went in again with another attack, Silver did the same. This time, both men hit together. Silver's was lethal, a great hammer blow that cut the dragoon through the collarbone and into the chest, sending him sprawling on the floor. Keane's pierced his opponent in the chest and the man sprang away. But Keane was on him again and placed his sword into precisely the same place. And this time he made no mistake. The blade pierced the Frenchman to the heart.

Keane looked at Silver and saw that the man was grinning, delighted as a child to be here with his officer. Ahead of them, the corridor was empty. Silver whispered, 'Think there are any more to come, sir?'

'As much as I would love to stay here, slaughtering Frenchmen, Silver, we have other business to attend. Come on.'

Now it was their turn to run. The tunnel behind them was blocked by the six bodies and that might just allow enough time to gain several hundred yards advantage. Perhaps enough to get out. Pushing himself to the limit, Keane ran the length of the tunnel and saw figures ahead of him and, beyond them, a sudden shaft of light. The others had found the hidden door in the hillside and were free. And it was then that he realized they were coming towards him.

Martin reached him first. Keane exploded, 'What the hell are you doing? I told you to get out.'

'Not without you, sir. Or Silver.'

'You're a bloody fool. And damned insubordinate.'

'Wouldn't leave you, sir. Are we going to fight them?'

'No, Martin. We're going to bloody run. Come on.'

Pushing the boy back down the tunnel, Keane yelled towards the others. 'Get back! We're coming out! Get into the hills!'

Then he ran for his life, followed by Silver. And by the French.

They thundered along the length of the tunnel and, within a few minutes, had made the entrance. Keane pushed Martin through the narrow opening into the air and the boy stood, regaining his breath. But the French were closing on them. Keane grabbed him. 'Come on – up there.' Together, the three of them ran from the tunnel and into the long grass. It was only a few minutes before they heard shouts to their rear. There was the crack of a shot and a carbine bullet zinged past Martin's head and thudded into a tree.

They increased their pace. The others were well ahead of them now, as Keane paused and cast a glance back at the pursuing French. He had thought that the dragoons might have given up by now. But they still came on, enraged by the deaths of their comrades and encouraged by the shouts of their officers.

Martin had turned, too, and, without a word of command, knew what to do.

He raised his gun, the musket that had been Keane's old game gun, a peerless weapon in the hands of the right man. And Keane knew that Martin was that man. He tucked it into his shoulder and took aim. He lined the bead of the barrel up on one of the green-coated men and gently squeezed the trigger.

The gun cracked as the hammer hit home and spat the ball from the barrel. As the smoke cleared, Martin looked to check what he already knew. The dragoon officer lay dead, shot through the heart. The green-coated men stopped, thrown by their officer's death. Their shock did not last long, but it gave Keane all the time he needed.

With Martin and Silver, he turned and scrambled up the hill-side, grabbing on to any roots and bushes he could to help him.

At length, one by one, they reached the horses in a clearing hidden behind a natural wall of stones. They were just as Keane had left them, guarded by Archer and Leech. And with them stood a woman, the tenth and last member of the troop. Gabriella Ramos was Silver's common-law wife. He had rescued her from a life of prostitution in the backstreets of Lisbon. While, at first, Keane had been as sceptical as the others about taking a woman into danger and combat, over the past year she had become as good a member of the team as any of the men, and he was grateful to have her. Besides, Keane had seen lesser women fight like devils for the guerrillas and he knew that, whenever the time came, Gabriella could acquit herself as the equal of any man. It helped, too, that she was pleasing on the eye. For, even though she was Silver's woman, and Keane's sense of honour would have kept him from trifling with her, there was something about having a woman in the camp that calmed him, something he missed and yearned for, no matter how much he might feel at home in the company of men.

He smiled at her and nodded towards Silver, who was just behind him, up the hill. Just to let her know that he had returned him to her, as he had promised. As he always did.

The French had recovered and, once again, were swarming up the hillside now, but encumbered by their heavy boots and slipping on the grass.

Keane yelled at the men, 'Come on! Mount up!'

Martin looked at him. 'Permission to try for one more, sir?'

Ordinarily, Keane would have ordered him to horse, but now, here, after all the killing and misery he had witnessed in the city across the valley, he nodded his head. The young man knelt at the stone wall and took careful aim. Again the gun sang out and Martin's exultant shout and smiling face told Keane that the emperor had lost another of his dragoons.

With Martin in the saddle at last, they turned their horses and rode away from the city. And, as they did so and Keane turned his horse towards the British lines, his thoughts went to the teenage girl he'd thrown from the window earlier and whether, like them, she had managed to escape the French. He thought it unlikely. Most probably she had been taken and ended up, once more, at the end of a long line of men. Robbed of decency, robbed of respect, robbed of her soul. A symbol of her country's destruction. He pitied her and her countrymen and hoped that, against his intuition, she had managed to get away and hide herself somewhere in the city. He would never know. But, without knowing it, she had given him more than enough to fill his report to Wellington. The French army was out of control. Low in morale and high on indiscipline, Massena's men were not the stuff of a conquering army. They were a rabble. And a rabble that could be defeated.

3

Arthur Wellesley, Duke of Wellington, stood with his back to Keane in the cool, lofty interior of the house he had taken for his headquarters in the little town of Leiria and breathed a sigh as the door closed behind the red-coated, red-faced officer who had just left their company.

Saying nothing to the other staff officer who stood with him, in the shadows, close to the fireplace, Wellington turned to Keane. 'Now then, Captain Keane, to business.'

Keane, who had witnessed the duke's exchange with the departing officer, said nothing.

'Lost for words, Keane? That's unlike you.'

'I was merely thinking, Your Grace, that I had never before seen Major Cavanagh in such spleen.'

Wellington smiled and nodded, his pleasure evident. 'Yes, Keane. You're right. That was a rare sight. Perhaps I did press my point rather. But, you see, the man has been undone. He had thought to have gained the upper hand and he has finished with nothing on the table.'

Keane looked puzzled.

'Major Cavanagh, as you know, Keane, voices the opinion of

St James's, here in Portugal. In many ways, he is the sounding box of the Prince Regent himself.

'As you have just witnessed, Major Cavanagh had thought that Marshal Massena might have retired on Almeida and cancelled his invasion, so badly mauled was he at Bussaco. He thought that I should follow up and had reported as much to his masters at St James's. But I am afraid that that was never my intention. And so Major Cavanagh has been made to look a fool and, for such a man, that is the worst fate. To pretend to be the eyes and ears of the army, to have the knowledge of the general's mind was his essence and now that is gone.

'Unlike you, Keane. You, in truth, are the eyes and the ears of my army. Now, tell me, man, what news have you?'

'Firstly, Your Grace, the news that, from all we hear, Marshal Massena has no idea of the existence of the lines. His officers believe that the whole country lies wide open, beyond Santarém, to all arms.'

Wellington smiled. 'Good, that is indeed good news. He has no idea at all?'

'None at all, Your Grace. You have quite outwitted him.'

Wellington nodded. 'Continue.'

Keane and his men had ridden hard from Coimbra to find the duke. But such was the pace of the retreat that it had taken them two days to reach headquarters, here at Leiria.

'It appears that, just as they arrived at Coimbra, the customary French supply of fourteen days' bread, taken from their last bakeries, was exhausted and they began to rely upon the land. They have no provisions, save what they can find.'

Wellington smiled again. This was exactly what he had hoped for: the marshal, duped into believing the country was open and not realizing that the Portuguese people had at last embraced the British policy.

His face grew solemn, though, as Keane related all that they had seen in Coimbra: the wanton destruction of the ancient buildings and artefacts; the random slaughter of priests and civilians, men, women and children; the looting, authorized by Massena on behalf of Bonaparte, and the rape of the girl; the killing of the sergeant and their skirmish with the dragoons. All the while, the duke stood in silence. At the mention of Macnab, however, he looked alarmed.

'That man is there?'

'Most certainly, sir. And, had I but had the time and opportunity, you can be sure that he would not now be alive.'

'Yes, I am aware of your . . . vendetta. But that man is more than just an object of your hate. He was a spy in our midst, Keane, and he is still a spy for Bonaparte. Such a man will now have the ear of the marshal, if not the emperor himself. And you can be sure that, wherever he is, there will be something more to it than common, everyday soldiering. I am deeply sorry to hear about Coimbra. But I had guessed as much would happen. But we did what we could, Keane. All that we could.'

The citizens of Coimbra had welcomed the duke and his men, garlanded them with flowers and sung *fados* in praise of their victory. But when it became clear that what they intended was to abandon the city, their joy had turned to despair. For Wellington had ordered his army to retire to Lisbon.

Conscious, perhaps, of the past, Wellington had ridden to Coimbra and personally supervised its evacuation. Only a year before, he had abandoned the citizens of a Spanish town to the mercies of the French invaders, and he regretted it. The decision not to relieve Ciudad Rodrigo had not been one of the duke's more glorious enterprises.

Keane, too, bore it on his heart. He suspected that Wellington's strategy, and his apparently planned decision not to follow Massena, was in part at least inspired by the fact that he had to justify his scorched-earth policy, by which he had instructed the people of Portugal to burn their own farms to save them falling into the hands of the French. The lines of Torres Vedras, the ornate system of forts stretching across Portugal, which would prevent the French from gaining entry, had cost a king's ransom and more. What would England say, were Wellington now not to use them? There was politics afoot here, politics with London, and, as always, thought Keane, as with all politics, at the end of the day, the decisions taken by men such as Wellington and those in the government at home had real impact on the ground with men such as himself.

The duke coughed and Keane realized that he had been daydreaming.

'As I was telling you, Keane, we are hard pressed. A retreating army does not love its general and the men cannot understand how, if they won a battle, they are falling back. We have had trouble, Keane. Why, just this morning I had four men hanged on the spot for drunkenness and looting. Now order is restored, but the sooner we reach the lines the better.'

'Yes, sir. We'll all be happier then.'

'We will, Keane.' He hesitated. 'But not you, I'm afraid.'

'Sir?'

'You are to return to the hills about Coimbra and await further orders.'

Keane groaned inwardly and hoped that it had not been too evident. 'Orders from whom, Your Grace?'

'Why, Colonel Grant, as always. He is out in the field.'

Keane had been surprised that his immediate superior and mentor, Colquhoun Grant, Wellington's chief intelligence officer, had not been at their meeting and that, in his stead, had been the other staff office. Throughout their interview the man had remained in the shadows behind Wellington but now he stepped forward slightly. In the light, Keane was able now to make out his face, which, with its high forehead and aquiline nose, was familiar to him.

'Colonel Grant is in the field, sir?'

'He is; his choice. You know Grant, Keane. He is better employed with the guerrilla than with a retreating army. There will be little for him – or indeed a man such as you, Keane – to do once we have reached the lines. He has work for you. Important work. Isn't that so, Sir George?'

Wellington at last turned to the staff officer, whom Keane had recognized as the Quartermaster General, Colonel Sir George Murray.

'Quite so, sir.' Murray smiled at him with the indulgence of a superior who clearly knew what his fate was to be. 'A pleasure to have you on board, Captain Keane. Word of your endeavours has travelled fast. The Prince Regent himself is among your admirers.'

'I am honoured, sir.'

Wellington continued, 'With Colonel Grant taking on a more active role, Sir George will now become your immediate commanding officer.'

'Sir.'

This was all he needed, thought Keane – some pudding-headed pen-pusher from St James's as his commanding officer, someone who knew more about orders and establishments than the reality of life at the front line.

Murray smiled again. 'I'm sure that I shall find you as able
an intelligence officer as Colonel Grant has. He has great faith
in you, Keane. We shall need every scrap of information we can
gather if we are to rid this country of Bonaparte's scourge.' He
held out a packet, handing it to Keane. 'Your orders. Colonel
Grant will provide the detail.'

Wellington nodded. 'Goodbye, Keane, and good luck.
Remember me to Colonel Grant. And if, as you say, Macnab is
in Coimbra, I'm sure that he was right to ask for you.'

Walking back to his horse, Keane pondered the meeting and
the presence of Murray. He realized that there must have been
a reason why he had been allowed to witness Wellington's
rebuke of the odious Major Cavanagh. The duke was telling
Keane something, impressing upon him the importance of his
strategy, enabling him to better understand it. And, he thought,
perhaps he was also attempting to strengthen the resentment
Cavanagh already bore to Keane, whom he considered had
betrayed his cause to Wellington some months before. Keane
hated such politicking. But he knew that, in his role, he was
bound to be caught up in it. And he knew, too, that, given such
a role, to excel in it was the only way in which he would be
able to gain advancement in the army and any chance of the
wealth he so desired.

He was still not sure, though, that he was wholly Wellington's
man. Not yet. There was a freedom of spirit in Keane that would
not ever allow him to be anyone's man. And perhaps that was
the reason he was so good at what he did. Murray, he would
reserve judgment on. But written orders? It was the first time
he had been given the like since joining the exploring officers.
He pulled the packet from his coat and tore it open. It was
written in a slim, spidery hand – Murray's own, he presumed.

Reaching his horse, Keane mounted up and, followed by
Silver and Heredia, who had accompanied him as an escort
from their bivouac on the outskirts, rode through the town,
on to the road.

Back at their camp, his news was not best welcome.

'We're going where, sir? Back to Coimbra?'

'That's it.'

Garland spoke: 'Can I ask why, sir? The place is full of
Frenchies. They've killed all the Portos what was left. Why
aren't we going with the rest of the army, sir? Back into
Portugal, behind the lines?'

'Because we're not like the rest of the army, Garland. You
know that. Is that why I dragged you lot out of the prisons of
Lisbon and gave you back your lives?'

It was not strictly the case. In truth, only four of Keane's men
had been rescued from prison and, of them, only Garland and
Heredia from the death sentence. But there was a truth to it.
Keane's men were, all of them, unique.

Ross took him to one side. 'Sir, would I be right in thinking
that one of the reasons why we're going back to Coimbra
might be that you have a score to settle with a certain Irish
gentleman?'

Keane shook his head. 'No, you're wrong there, sarn't. That
doesn't enter into it. It's on the duke's orders. And we are to
meet Colonel Grant there.'

'You wouldn't, then, have persuaded the duke to send us
back?'

Keane smiled. 'Coimbra is the last place I want to be, Ross,
believe me.'

It took a matter of minutes to pack the camp. Gabriella

strapped the big cooking pot to the side of her horse and they set off quickly, as Keane had taught them.

The road was crammed with people. Some of them troops, others stragglers – Portuguese, mostly – all of them desperate to catch the tail of the retreating army. Most of them, though, were civilians.

Keane's report had included much on what he had seen of the French shortage of supplies and the fact that, even with their looted booty, they were struggling and suffering. But, he thought, if the French suffered, the suffering of the people of Portugal was twentyfold worse.

The people on the road were terrified by the stories they had heard of the French. Men, women and children milled together, walking blindly behind one another like so many sheep.

It seemed to Keane that the entire population of central Portugal had abandoned their homes. Tens of thousands of them. The strong and healthy had taken to arms and were either serving under General Beresford in the reformed Portuguese army, had volunteered for the militia and the *ordenanza*, or had gone with the guerrillas.

The old and the decrepit, with mothers, girls and young children, were left to walk on foot with the army. The lucky few travelled on donkeys or mules. Luckier still were those with carts. Most, though, simply carried in their arms all that they could of what was left of their wealth. The rest had been destroyed or buried or left for the French.

Keane wondered at their bravery, their sheer determination not to be conquered. He wondered, too, if the people of his own dear country would have behaved in the same way. Would they have accepted the orders of some foreign general to leave their homes, abandon their farms and everything they had and destroy their country? He very much doubted it. But he knew that, if such a situation were to remain a fantasy, it was up to him and his men and the rest of Wellington's army to defeat Bonaparte here, in the peninsula, before he could again contemplate an invasion of England or Ireland.

Such was the impact of the destitute refugees upon Keane's party that there was little to say as they made their way back along the route they had so recently taken. Going now against the flow of fugitives, they made poor time and Keane was thankful that at least the weather was fine and the road dry.

The flow of civilians stopped as they grew closer to Coimbra and Keane knew that, from now on, they might meet a French patrol at any turn. So, for that reason, leaving the road at Pombal, they took to the hills, climbing their horses carefully up over the rocks and scrub. Keane sent Martin out to scout for the enemy and, slowly, they crested the *serra*. A competent cartographer, like all his fellow intelligence officers, Keane had taken care to map the area on two previous occasions and, with local knowledge, too, had managed to draw up a reasonably accurate chart, certainly better than anything the army might have had. Using this, they navigated the ancient donkey tracks and, with better speed, found themselves close to Coimbra when Martin returned, riding hard. He reined in next to Keane.

'The French, sir. Massena.'

'Speak slower, boy. Catch your breath. Where are they? On your tail?'

Martin, breathless, shook his head. 'No, sir. They didn't see me. Massena's whole force – a great blue serpent, snaking along the road – on the move. They're moving on Condeixa, heading for the road to Leiria. In a single column.'

'He's abandoned Coimbra?'

'One of the guerrillas told me. Left a garrison there. And all his wounded.'

Keane smiled. A garrison. But how many? And in what state would they be? he wondered. Still, he was sure that Massena would not leave fewer than three battalions to defend the city. And a few batteries. It was what Wellington had predicted. Nevertheless, he knew that he should confirm this knowledge to the commander. He drew out a sheet of parchment from his valise and scribbled on it in pencil before turning in the saddle to find the man he wanted.

'Heredia, take word to the duke. Ride like the devil – hard as you can. You'll find us in the old camp clearing, above Coimbra.'

Heredia, the Portuguese soldier whom Keane had rescued from the rope and who had been key to uncovering the presence of the spy, Macnab, in the British staff, turned his horse and, tucking the note inside his coat, rode off to find Wellington.

So, thought Keane, Massena had marched and it seemed that now Keane and his men were, once again, well and truly behind enemy lines.

They found the clearing with little difficulty and it was just as they had left it. Keane had suspected that returning here so soon would not be good for morale and he was right. The mood of the men was sullen. Gabriella's, worse still. She had said nothing since encountering the refugees on the road and now, as she stirred the pot for their supper, she kept her thoughts to herself. Silver sat close to her, but even he could not draw a word from her lips.

Archer was the first to speak: 'Why do they do it, sir?'

'Do it?'

'Why must they destroy everything of beauty? Carry away

what has taken centuries to amass? Look at Coimbra: its buildings ruined, its art looted, its books destroyed.'

Keane had been in Coimbra many times, but he had never
really considered the place. Its streets, to him, had always
been a meandering maze of alleyways, filled with ordure and
vermin. But, especially with Archer's take on the place, Keane
could see that its buildings must be important, of some age,
and that the art he had seen carried on the backs of French
soldiers was the sort that was valued by dilettanti.

'I'm not an educated man, Archer. Would never pretend to
be. Not like you. I can see beauty in things, but you know their
value – their real worth.'

'Coimbra's a sort of Portuguese Oxford, sir. It's the oldest
university in continental Europe – dates back to the thirteenth
century. Think of all that learning. Hundreds of thousands of
books alone. God knows what the French can want with all that.'

Garland nodded. 'Boney's orders, ain't it? Wants it all for
himself.'

Gilpin, the thief, spoke up: 'Nah, it's more than that. It's
the law, isn't it? The French killed their king and then Boney
took over and now it's a free-for-all. They just take what they
want – gold, treasure, women – everything.'

Gabriella looked up at them. 'Women last?' She sneered at
Gilpin.

'Eh?'

At last she spoke, and there was venom in her voice. 'You
said women after gold and treasure. We are less important.
It's the same for you as for the French. We are nothing. Pieces
of meat.'

Gilpin stood up. 'Hold on, that's not what I meant and you
know it.'

Silver bristled. 'Let her be. She's on edge, Sam. She knows what you meant.'

Keane watched them, careful to gauge whether their argument might boil over into something else, as it had in the past. He was thankful he'd had the wisdom to send Silver's old rival, Heredia, away with the despatch.

Gabriella went on, 'Look at my people. Look at them with nothing and still the French take from them. Perhaps they would be better to stay and fight and die in their homes.'

Keane decided it was time to become involved. He shook his head. 'It's vital that they leave nothing to the French. It's the only way.'

'Why? Why must you destroy a country to save it?'

'There is no other way. The French need supplies and live off the land. Deny them those supplies and they cannot live. The army will go hungry and then the army will be forced to retreat. Wellington knows that. I'm sorry if it's hard for your people. But it's what we must do.'

Gabriella said nothing, but Keane could see the anger in her brown eyes.

Silver placed his hand on her arm, but she shook it off. He spoke now: 'I know it's the generals' orders, sir, but did you see those people? Women. Babies. Christ, it's hard to watch that.'

'Better to watch that than see what the French would do to them.'

Knowing that his commander was right, Silver fell silent.

Martin spoke: 'And if we don't fight them, who will? Someone's got to send Boney back to France.'

'And we won't stop there, will we? We'll drive him from this glorious country and through Spain and then we'll march into Paris and throw him off the throne. Won't we, Captain Keane?'

Keane leapt to his feet and turned towards the sound of the voice and, as he did so, a figure emerged from the shadows, accompanied by the simultaneous click of five carbines being cocked and made ready to fire.

But Keane was smiling, knowing the voice of old. 'Colonel Grant?'

The figure emerged from the shadows and the men eased the hammers back down on their guns.

Colquhoun Grant was in his late thirties with a shock of tousled dark brown hair, the ruddy complexion of a son of the soil and a similarly craggy countenance to the commander in chief.

He wore a dark blue cape and white buckskin breeches over hussar boots and, beneath the cape, a hint of scarlet betrayed the fact that he was in uniform – the uniform of a colonel on the British staff. Grant would never have dreamt of going in disguise. Not for him, playing the spy. Above all else, in his own mind, Colquhoun Grant was a gentleman.

'James, damnably good to see you. I'm sorry I missed you in Leiria. But you met Sir George?'

'Yes, sir.'

'Don't be confused by first impressions, Keane. He's no fop. He's a good man, James. A very good man. And a damned fine officer.'

'Really, sir?'

'Really, James, and don't you ever forget it.'

There was something in Grant's tone that made Keane take notice. The usual, almost fatherly advice was gone, replaced by a snap, which told him that the colonel was in deadly earnest. Perhaps he had been wrong about Murray being no more than a St James's desk Johnny. It was true, he was sure, and well meant, but Keane could sense in Grant's voice a tone of regret and something that was not quite envy. He did not think that Grant could be envious of anyone.

'Yes, sir.'

Grant walked into the firelight and the men stood to attention. 'At ease, all of you. Good to see you all. In fact, good to be out in the field myself again. Too long cooped up at headquarters. It's not good for a man, eh, Captain Keane?'

Keane laughed and the men shared his laughter, grateful for Grant's arrival to diffuse the tension in the camp.

He walked across to Keane and the two sat together. 'You have a new mission, James.'

'Yes, sir, although, as yet, I'm not entirely sure what it might be.'

'You are aware that Macnab's on Massena's staff. Or O'Connell, if that's the name he goes by.'

'He'll always be Macnab to me, sir.' He paused.

'So you know he's with Massena?'

'Yes. I saw him. He found our route into the city and chased us out. Where is he now, sir? With Massena or still in Coimbra with the garrison?'

'I don't know. That's for you to find out.'

'Is that my task? To find Macnab? That will be a real pleasure.'

Grant shook his head. 'I'm afraid not, James. There's more to it than that, although I'm sure that Colonel Macnab will prove to be a very evident part of it.'

Keane nodded. 'Before you tell me more, sir, what I really want to know is how the devil Macnab found the tunnel.'

'You don't know?'

Keane shook his head.

'Sobral told him.'

'The doctor? Doctor Sobral would never tell them.'

'Of course not – not willingly. But the French have their methods.'

'He was tortured?'

Grant nodded. 'But we don't think he's dead. They seem to want him alive. I suspect it's Macnab's doing. The man knows more about Coimbra than the French have yet found out and he might be of use to them again. So another of your tasks is to get our friend Doctor Thomas Roberts Sobral out of Coimbra – whatever's left of it and him.'

'I saw some of the damage.'

'There's more now, done just before Massena left. I have it from spies that, quite apart from all the loot they've carried off, the town hall was burnt down and the causeway. We've no idea of civilian losses yet. But I'm sure we won't need to look hard. The French are not the tidiest of murderers.'

Keane shook his head. 'I can give you a few for certain. There's a family – a mother, father and son – and two priests.' He thought, too, of the girl he had saved and wondered again if she had managed to hide from the French. 'And another woman. I doubt there will be many survived.'

'The main thing is you got out, and it's damned good to see you in one piece.'

'Those poor people.'

'Yes, but there was nothing to be done, Keane. We managed to get most of them away. Those others just wouldn't be told. How much did Sir George tell you?'

'I think I got most of it, sir. He's replaced you?'

'Not exactly. I've kept my rank. But Sir George is now in overall command of all of the intelligence officers, along with Sir Charles Stuart.'

'The political envoy? But he's a civilian.'

Keane had never met Charles Stuart, but everyone had heard of him. He was the son of the old prime minister, Lord Bute, and had made quite a name for himself in court circles. The previous year, he had been appointed envoy extraordinary to Portugal.

'Precisely. But you know he's been working undercover here for years, with the juntas, establishing contacts – and that the French had no idea.'

'May I ask why?'

'Why?'

'Why have Sir George and Sir Charles been put in command of intelligence?'

'You know more than most, Keane, that the duke has been spending thousands on intelligence gathering. All that silver for Sanchez and his guerrillas is just a tiny part of it. And it's not going to get any less expensive and St James's wants to know why and if it's worth it. So they've made everything more formal. It's politics, Keane; steer clear of all that, if you want my advice. Only, this time, you can't and nor, I think, can I. Anyway, it suits me to be here – away from all that blessed intrigue. And, of course, with me back in the field and Sir George at the helm, it looks to St James's as if the expense might be justified.

'Anyway, that's enough of that. Now down to business. We need to find Macnab and we need Sobral. But, more than that, we need you to go into the city and find a piece of treasure.'

Keane sighed. Here then was the crux of the matter – the essence of his new errand. 'Treasure, sir?' He smiled. 'But that would be looting, sir, wouldn't it? Isn't that what Boney's men do for him?'

Grant shook his head. 'Don't try to be funny with me, Keane. This isn't any piece of treasure. And we're not in the habit of looting, James. This is something quite unique. It's a book.'

Keane stared at him, incredulity spreading across his face.

'A book, sir?'

'A book. But not just a book.'

Keane held up his hand and laughed.

'I'm sorry, Colonel Grant, but a book is a book, if you ask me. If you don't mind my saying so, sir, it looks as if you're asking me to take my men back into Coimbra, under the noses of the French, to find a bloody book!'

Grant ignored the insubordination. This was Keane, after all. 'Yes, a bloody book. But think, James. Think back, if you can, to your schooldays, to the college, to Armagh. Do you recall anything about the ancients?'

Keane wracked his brain for the lessons at the Royal School in Armagh. The old schoolroom in Abbey Street and lessons with Doctor Fellowes about heroes of Greece and Rome and British history. Troy and Rome and Homer and Virgil and Thucydides.

'We learnt about the Greeks, sir. That I can remember. And something of the Romans. And Socrates and Plato. The philosophers.'

'Well, this book is a repository of just such knowledge – ancient knowledge.'

'A school book? Philosophy? Can I ask what use that is to us here, sir?'

'Well you might and, in the field, of course, it's of no use at all. But it has other value, James.'

'Where is this book, sir?'

'We have to presume that it may still be in Coimbra. It is one of only two known copies in existence. The other disappeared some years ago from the Vatican library. This version was kept here, in the library of the university.'

'But why do you need me to get it, sir?'

'Because, if you don't, then Massena most certainly will. In fact, he might have it already.'

Keane smiled. 'He really wants it so badly, does he? This book? I had no idea the marshal took such an active interest in philosophy.'

'You're quite right, James. He doesn't. But he does want the book. Very badly.'

'Just because it's full of ancient writings?'

'More than ancient writings. Hieroglyphs, Keane. You've heard that word before, haven't you? Know what they are?'

Keane's face brightened as he began to understand. 'We found some of those in Egypt, sir – when I was at Alexandria. In fact, I recall the Frenchies being pretty keen on getting them, back then. I even heard that Boney had established a regiment of scholars.'

'You're quite right. He did just that. Sent a crack team of experts, in uniform, out with a special troop of infantry to take the things back.'

'So what are these Egyptian things doing here?'

'That's just it. No one knows and no one knows quite how old the book is or what secrets it contains.'

'Secrets, eh?' Keane sat up at the word.

'It contains certain secrets. At least, according to Sir George it does. Otherwise, why would Bonaparte want it?'

'So it's Boney that wants it – not just Massena.'

'Good God, man, have you been listening at all?'

'But you said that Marshal Massena wanted it.'

'Marshal Massena wants it so that he can give it to Bonaparte. And why does he want to give it to Bonaparte? Because, as we speak, the good marshal is in danger of being recalled to Paris, away from his army. He is in high disfavour, Keane. He not only lost at Bussaco, but he has imperilled the emperor's army and taken his men deeper into Portugal. Boney won't like that. Plus the fact that Massena had his mistress out here with him.' He smiled at Keane. 'As I believe you are only too well aware, James.'

Keane grinned and was transported in his mind back to a languid afternoon, some months before, at Massena's old headquarters, in the town of Almeida, on the Spanish border, to an hour spent in the company of possibly the most beautiful, most enticing woman he had ever encountered. Henriette Lebreton: mistress to Marshal Massena and wife to an officer of the French dragoons. He had promised to take her away from Massena, to come back for her. But he had not. He had let her down and he wondered where she might be now.

'I see, sir. That paints a rather different picture. Clearly, the book is of great importance.'

'Ah, at last, Keane, you begin to see. Now, perhaps we can begin.'

'Can I ask the name of the book, sir?'

'You can, though I doubt it'll help you. It is called the *Très Sainte Trinosophie*.'

'Christ, that's a title, sure enough.'

'Certainly, and, as you will have guessed, it's in French, too, unfortunately. It was annotated and edited, apparently by a man named Cagliostro, a French count in the late eighteenth century. He was a Mason and got into serious trouble with the Pope over it.'

Keane smiled. 'That sounds more interesting.'

Grant continued. 'Cagliostro died during the Revolution. But he always carried his copy of the book with him. How it might have got here, I don't know.'

'You know a lot about it, sir.'

'That's dear Doctor Sobral again. He's our oracle in all these matters. It's a short book – only ninety-six pages long – but it's handwritten and divided into twelve sections, representing the twelve signs of the zodiac.'

'So it's a lot of rot.'

'Yes, if you like. I suppose, if you're a Mason, it isn't. According to Sobral, it's full of stuff about rites and Masonic mysteries. The pictures and tables are the most interesting part.'

'And it's all in French?'

'Yes, and in hieroglyphs.'

'Egyptian drawings.'

'If you like.'

Keane whistled. 'Some book, sir. You're sure we need it?'

'James, this comes directly from the peer, Sir Charles and Sir George. They want it. More precisely, they don't want Bonaparte to have it.'

'Isn't the peer himself a Mason? I had that from an officer in the 33rd.'

'I have no idea. How the devil should I know that? Anyway, Keane, that is not our concern.'

'How on earth will I recognize it, this book?'

'Oh, you'll know it if you see it. It's shaped like a triangle, bound in red morocco leather and the text is embellished with hundreds of figures, well drawn and brilliantly coloured. And there are small symbols at the beginning and end of each of the sections. All the way through, there are scattered letters,

words and phrases in ancient languages. And there are magical symbols – figures resembling Egyptian hieroglyphics. It's
these that most interest Bonaparte. My men in Paris have
been alert for some time to the fact that he has an interest in
the occult.'

'Sir?'

'Black magic, Keane. The mystical. Call it what you will.
Superstition.'

'That mumbo jumbo? I had no idea.'

'It's a weakness of his, Keane. Every man has a weakness and
some day it will prove his undoing. This is one of Bonaparte's
and it's up to us to see if we can use it against him and to our
advantage. These hieroglyphs he believes to be the essence of
an ancient religion. He even thinks they can bestow magical
powers on those who understand them.'

Keane laughed. 'Magical powers? Christ! Boney? That's rich.
He might think that, but we can't possibly, sir, can we?'

'Of course we don't. We're living in a modern world, Keane,
not the Middle Ages. But the point is that, at the end of the
manuscript, there are a number of leaves written in strange
ciphers, possibly the code used by St Germain's secret society.
But that's not important. They are ciphers so hard to decipher
that all the Pope's own scholars could not do so.'

'By "ciphers", I take it you mean what we might call "codes",
sir?'

Grant nodded. 'Yes, precisely. That is one of the key reasons
why we must find it. If the French get their hands on this book,
quite apart from whatever it might mean to Bonaparte with
his liking for Egyptian mystic nonsense, it also could have a
real value.'

'In the codes?'

'Yes. We know that, for some time now, the French have been trying to establish a code for their messages. A *grand chiffre*. It's the only way they will ever be sure of maintaining secrecy. Every dispatch rider they send out has the truth tortured out of him by the guerrillas. But, with an impenetrable code such as this, no amount of torture would be able to extract information. With their vast armies, if the French can gain the upper hand and prevent us from understanding their intentions, then our advantage is lost.'

Keane nodded. 'When you put it like that, sir, I see quite clearly. What you're saying is that Boney can use this old book to create a code we can't even hope to break – not even Archer.'

'Not even Archer, your great code breaker. Yes, I remember him with the telegraphs. He invented the new codes for them.'

'He's quite brilliant, sir. I'll bet he could break these ones.'

'But there is every possibility that he couldn't and that's the reason we've got to get our hands on the book. Massena might have it already, but we have to find out.'

'So, back to Coimbra it is, then, sir.'

'I'm sorry, James. But there's really no other way. If the book is still not with the French, then it's somewhere in the city.'

'When do we go?'

'As soon as you can. Tomorrow, if possible.'

'All of us?'

'That's up to you. But I wouldn't take the girl.'

'Very well. Is that all, sir?'

'No, not quite. There is one more thing, James.'

He reached inside his waistcoat and drew out a piece of paper.

'I have a letter for you, James. From Sir George. Some additional instructions to the ones he's already given you.'

Keane took it and began to unfold the letter.

Grant shook his head. 'You don't have to bother, if you wish. I've read it already, of course.'

Keane smiled. He should have guessed. 'Of course you have, sir. And?'

'It is to do with Trant. You do know of Nicholas Trant? Or Sir Nicholas Trant, as he likes to style himself. He is a brigadier general in the Portuguese army.'

Keane nodded. Of course he knew of Nicholas Trant. Knew the name, at least. The irregular commanding officer of a brigade of Portuguese militia had been a thorn in Napoleon's side for these last few months, conducting covert operations behind enemy lines. Keane was surprised that their paths had not yet crossed and had supposed that they would, at some point. Perhaps sooner than he had thought.

'Yes, sir, of course. The militia commander. What of him?'

'He's operating hereabouts. It's highly likely that you will encounter him very soon. Indeed, you're charged by Sir George, in that letter, to help him in any way you can.'

Keane nodded. 'I'll do everything I can, sir. You know me.'

'Yes, James, I do. But there's one thing: he's his own person, if you understand me. Trant is an individual, James. The duke calls him a brilliant officer, but says, too, that he's also as drunken a dog as ever lived. Trust him, if you will, but be on your guard, too. But the main thing is that we see Trant, maverick that he is, as a vital element in the strategy.'

Keane scanned the letter. It was written in a spidery, almost womanly hand.

You are to assist Colonel Trant in every manner possible and with every means at your disposal. His work is vital if we are to harass the enemy in the rear and divert his energies from our greater purpose.

'So I'm to help Colonel Trant, sir? Is that it?'

'Yes, James. Read Sir George's letter. Help him however you can.'

'However I can, sir? Really?' He smiled.

Keane knew from the past that such orders were often impossible to obey and he could tell from Grant's countenance that this was precisely the case with these.

'So tell me, sir, am I to be directly under his command?'

Now Grant smiled. 'No, Keane. Not directly. But shall we say that, should Colonel Trant suggest a course of action, you may want to follow it.'

'With respect, that's not a very clear order, sir.'

Grant smiled and shook his head. 'Oh, my dear James, I think it is. You know the drill. Discretion. That's why we employ you in this way. You and your flock of jailbirds.'

Keane thought for a moment, stirring the embers of the fire with a stick before speaking. 'And what is the more important, sir? Colonel Trant's orders or the book?'

'Both, Keane. Both are important to us – to Wellington – but in different ways. Only you can decide which will take precedence.'

'That hardly seems fair, sir. Should I make the wrong decision, then the fate of the war might go against us.'

'That's quite true.' He smiled. 'And that's why I recommended you to Sir George for this mission. In fact, I can't think of a better man for the job.'

4

As dawn turned to morning and the sierra began to awaken, the party advanced through the long grass, down the hill towards the exit tunnel. It had been just a week since this had been their means of escape from the French.

Keane was loath to re-enter the city by this route, but, given that the French still held Coimbra, there was no alternative. He presumed that Macnab, whether or not he was still in the city, would have either blocked the entrance or at least posted a guard at one or both of the doors. But with these he would have to take his chance. They were almost there when Keane looked back momentarily at Ross, behind him, and then looked up to the left, startled by a noise. Gunfire – from the west.

Keane looked again at Ross.

'Guns, sir.'

'Yes, but whose guns, sarn't? And where from?'

Archer spoke. 'Off to the west, sir. Towards Fornos, I'd say.'

Fornos, thought Keane. If Massena had left a garrison in Coimbra then it was more than likely that he had also maintained a presence in Fornos. 'Have we men there still? Guerrillas, d'you think?'

'Probably, sir. The rearguard's long gone. Could be militia.'

Another burst of fire. Keane shook his head. 'We'll push on. It's not our concern and we're pressed for time.'

His tasks preyed upon his mind, as they had through the night. Firstly, he knew that he must find Doctor Sobral and get him out. He wondered what condition the poor man would be in. The French had a particular way with torture. Keane had seen it too often. Then there was the book. That bloody book. Perhaps, if he still had a tongue left in his head, Sobral could tell them where they might find it. The library, Grant had said, contained three hundred thousand books. If Sobral couldn't help them, perhaps Archer might have a chance, thought Keane. But even he would be hard-pressed without a proper clue as to its whereabouts. And God knew what state the French had left the library in. Or even if there still was a library. Three hundred thousand books would have made a big bonfire on a cold peninsular night.

Slithering down the last few yards of the hillside on the dewy morning grass, they reached the entrance to the tunnel and, to Keane's surprise and relief, found that the French had posted no guards there. Nor had the entrance been sealed. One by one, they slid into the tunnel and, stooping in the low space, began to make their way through the blackness. They had not yet been joined by Heredia, returning from his mission to Wellington, but had left Gabriella with Leech at the clearing, with orders to send him into the city on his arrival.

Foot by foot, they made their way along the tunnel and then, in the blackness, Keane tripped, stubbing his toe on a solid object. Kneeling down he touched it and felt something cold and soft. In seconds, he realized that he was touching the face of a dead French dragoon, left in the tunnel after the combat the previous week. He sprang back and, peering into the gloom, saw in the half-light three frozen faces, ashen white in the mask of death.

'Dead French. Let's hope that's all there is down here.'

They continued and, after a while, saw a crack of light ahead of them. A few minutes more and they gathered behind the door into the street. Again, there were no guards. It was strange, thought Keane, and he wondered why Macnab or any French officer would not have stationed a man here. He whispered to the others, 'I'm going to take a look outside. Wait here.'

Then, easing the door open, conscious of every exaggerated creak, he peered cautiously into the street.

The place was alive with French soldiery. Infantrymen in blue coats, some hatless, some without their weapons, were running hell for leather on the cobbles, and, from what Keane could tell, all were consumed by terror.

For less than an instant, he wondered why. Then he looked to his left and found the answer. Horsemen, a party of twelve of them, rounded the corner, bearing down upon the Frenchmen, their sabres whistling in the air. From their blue uniforms and British stovepipe shakos, they looked like Portuguese, but it was clear that these men were not of the regular army. Their clothing was more that of infantry than cavalry. This, he thought, must be related to the gunfire they had heard from the hill.

The cavalry careered into the French, packed as they were in the narrow street. A few of the infantry still had their muskets and attempted to thrust bayonets at the horsemen. But they were ponderously slow and the torpor of days of looting and drink had taken its toll. Now it was the Frenchmen's turn to pay. The cavalry sabres sang in the air and fell among the screaming French. Those without weapons raised their arms in surrender or to shield their heads. But the sabres fell with the force of vengeance. As Keane looked on, he saw a French soldier extend an arm in entreaty, only to have it lopped from his body. Another horseman drove his blade hard into the skull of a sergeant, splitting it in two.

Keane watched the massacre unfold and, after all that he had witnessed in the city previously, wondered if revenge was the answer. The Portuguese, though, had a score to settle and he knew well enough that there would be no point begging them for mercy.

Within seconds, the street was filled with the bodies of dead and dying men and the cavalry were cleaning their sabres on French tunics.

Keane stood, his own sword in his hand, ready to defend himself lest the Portuguese should take him for a Frenchman and continue their killing. But their commander, his rank evident from the gold epaulette on his shoulder, spotted Keane, his brown uniform and light cavalry helmet quite distinct from the French, and rode across, followed by two troopers.

The officer spoke in Portuguese. 'You are Portuguese?'

Keane answered in the same tongue. 'English. Captain James Keane of the Corps of Guides.'

The officer, who was in his early twenties, smiled at hearing his native language and saluted. 'Capitan Ernesto Loyola, *Legión Académico de la Universidade de Coimbra.*'

Keane nodded and translated in is head: the Coimbra University Legion. What the devil, he wondered, was that? It was no unit he had ever heard of, certainly. Still, he thought, surveying the carnage before him, they seemed far from amateur. He looked at the man and saw a boy, his face bristled and swarthy with the weathering of campaigning, his forehead lined with worries beyond his age – but still a boy.

'You've taken the city, captain?'

The student smiled and looked about him. 'So it would seem.'

'The French have left?'

'They have. They left only a few men here. You have seen how we deal with them.'

Keane nodded. 'Yes. I was here before. I saw what they did.'

'Then you will know why we do what we do. There is no place for mercy in this war.'

'How many of you are there?'

'Fifteen hundred. Horse and foot. Of my own regiment, just two hundred.'

'And the others?'

'We are all Portuguese. They are mostly militia. Our commander is Colonel Trant.'

Keane smiled. The boy might be as brave as any soldier he had met and not a bad swordsman, but his youth and naivety showed in his response. No veteran soldier would have given their numbers so readily. Keane also noted the pride in the young man's voice as he spoke their commander's name.

'You know of him?' Captain Loyola asked.

Keane nodded. 'Yes, of course. Colonel Trant's fame precedes him. In fact, I have orders to make contact with him.'

'You are alone, captain?'

'No. My men are with me.'

'Then you would do well to come with me. This place is not safe. There are too many men here with death in their minds. I will take you to Colonel Trant.'

*

Keane sent Silver to collect the men and, together, led by the captain and his troopers, they made their way through the streets. Everywhere lay signs of the rape of the city and its ancient houses. Doors lay smashed and furniture and personal possessions were strewn across the cobbles, sad reminders of the vanished inhabitants. Keane wondered if they would ever return here and how many had been slaughtered by the French. Dead Frenchmen lay in every street. But how many had been killed by the Portuguese liberators and how many were victims of their own comrades' earlier drunken violence, it was impossible to know.

And there were other corpses, too. Most of the Portuguese civilians murdered by the French had been left where they had fallen. The place reeked of death and, as they passed several of the houses, Keane glimpsed shapes of what might have been either rats or dogs in the shadows, presumably making the most of the unexpected source of food.

Silver, who was walking alongside him, spoke quietly: 'This is bad, sir. Worse than I thought it could be. Worse than Oporto.'

Keane nodded. Oporto, the site of their first action as a unit, had been a grim sight. Marshal Soult had taken the city in one of the first actions of the new campaign and its inhabitants had suffered the same fate as those of Coimbra. The French had pillaged the city without mercy and, by the time Keane and his men had taken the town with the army, most of the slaughtered inhabitants' bodies had been thrown into the river. This was different. There was no convenient equivalent of the Douro in which to dump the evidence, and burial was out of the question. They might, he thought, have burnt them. But it was the obvious indifference of the French to their victims that struck him most – that and the sure knowledge that such

scenes were bound to be repeated across the country as long
as the war raged on. Atrocity had become the hallmark of the
war in the peninsula as it had not been in any other of the
campaigns in which he had served.

'It's a mess, Silver – a tragedy that should never have been
allowed to happen. It pains me to say it, but I'm wondering
if the duke learnt anything from what happened at Ciudad.
You can't just leave a city undefended and allow the French to
walk in. If he keeps on doing this, then this is what's going to
happen again and again.'

'It's what he thinks will win us the war, sir. But I can't see it.
I'm a soldier, sir, like you. He's a fine general, sir. The best there
is. But he don't understand people – how they think, how they
won't leave their homes. Thank God my Gabby can't see this.'

They rounded the corner and Keane almost retched. There,
in the gutter, lay the dead body of a young girl, half of her
head eaten away.

Silver exclaimed, 'Christ almighty!'

The girl could have been no more than twelve. She wore a
white dress with red bows at the shoulders and she had fallen
in the spasm of death so that her legs splayed out in an unreal
position, like some marionette. Her disfigured face looked up
at them with an expression not of pain, but curiosity. She must
have known nothing about what had happened to her. In his
twenty years in the field, it was one of the most awful things
Keane had seen. He looked away.

Their Portuguese companions rode on, apparently unaf-
fected, though Keane knew that could not be the case. They
had simply seen this too many times. And he wondered how
such a sight being commonplace might affect them. This was
the catalyst for their vengeance.

Silver swore again. 'We should give her a decent burial, sir. Why don't they stop?'

'Too many of them. There are just too many. They don't have the time, Horatio. And they probably have orders not to stop.'

Orders from Trant, Keane thought, and wondered what sort of man would give such orders.

He tried to remember what Grant had told him as they had sat over the campfire. Nicholas Trant was no ordinary soldier, he had said.

'He's an Irishman. Protestant. Commissioned into the 84th and fought in the low countries. He was given an Irish regiment. Led them at Minorca in '98, when we took the island from the Spanish. Trant was the agent general for the prizes –' Grant had raised his eyebrows – 'the man in charge of distribution of booty. He was skilled at dealing with the economics of war. Some said, a bit too skilled.'

There had been no scandal. Trant had kept his rank. The way Grant had smiled as he spoke made Keane wonder if Trant might be the sort of man it was worthwhile becoming better acquainted with.

By '99, Trant had been a major in the Minorca regiment. 'You might have come across him in Egypt,' Grant had said. 'They were at Alexandria, in support of the 42nd.'

Keane had not encountered him. He was quite certain that he would remember such a man. He wondered, though, whether Sergeant Ross might recall him, having himself been in the 42nd, the Black Watch at Alexandria.

Grant had said that, with the peace, when the regiment was disbanded in '03, Trant had left the army. But he came back – as an ensign. Keane had been intrigued.

'Yes, in the Royal Staff Corps, no less. He's been here in

Portugal as a military agent since '08. And he served in the Lusitanian Legion.'

Keane had heard of the unit. Who hadn't? he wondered. Raised in the summer of 1808 from Portuguese refugees in London, it had been officered by the British under no less than Sir Robert Wilson. Keane had served under Wilson in Holland in '97 and had huge respect for the man who was renowned for his dash – and for saving the Austrian emperor from capture by the French. After the Egyptian campaign, Wilson had endeared himself to every private by calling for the abolition of corporal punishment in the army.

Grant had told Keane that Wilson had also acted as a secret agent for the government in Prussia, in 1807. It was from this position that he had been given command of the Lusitanian Legion. Based in Oporto – and, latterly, in Coimbra – they had fought as light infantry, riding behind the lines. They had defended Almeida in December 1808 and, with Trant as a leading officer, had raided into Spain. Grant had added that Trant had been a lieutenant colonel by now, in the Portuguese service.

Grant had added that there was perhaps something else, too, that Keane should know. Trant had lost his wife after his son was born, and it had changed him. Hardened him. Grant's parting words had been said in earnest: 'Just make sure you look out for yourself, James . . . and your men.'

Keane came back to the present with a word from the young officer: 'We're almost there, captain. Look, there he is now. There is Colonel Trant.' There was a note of pride in his voice and, as he pointed, Keane followed his gaze.

Nicholas Trant stood in the shade of an olive tree, high on the citadel of Coimbra, beside the old cathedral. Tall, quite the equal of Keane in stature, he had a chiselled face, sparkling blue eyes and a shock of dark brown curly hair. He wore his coat close buttoned to the neck with an inch of his cream silk stock protruding. He wore the blue uniform of the Portuguese army, heavy with gold trimmings, and Keane noticed that his chest was adorned with medals.

He smiled at Keane and nodded. Then he spoke and Keane saw at once why Trant's name had become so well known. His presence was huge and it was matched by the voice – a deep, booming voice that filled the courtyard with its warm, mellifluous tones, imbued with a subtle, charming Irish accent that betrayed his roots.

'I was told we had an English officer in the city. Of course, I thought it unlikely, but here you are. Captain . . . ?'

'Keane, sir. James Keane.' Keane wondered how Trant had known of his presence so quickly.

Looking at him, he thought of Wellington's description of Trant: 'As drunk a man as ever was.' The drunk seemed remarkably sober at present. Placid, even, given the scenes he had witnessed in the city and the revenge Trant's men appeared to have exacted.

'Captain Keane, welcome to Coimbra. We have liberated the city.'

'Yes, what's left of it. Your men seem intent on butchering their prisoners.'

Trant smiled. 'You should know, captain, that I have issued orders for the killing to stop. British or Portuguese, we must be careful to show mercy and to save face. Besides, there has been enough killing. Don't you agree?'

'Of course, colonel. If we kill the French in this way, we do no more than lower ourselves to their own level.'

'My own thoughts entirely, captain.'

'Do we have any idea how many French Massena left as a garrison?'

'There was only a small garrison, if you can call it that. Barely five hundred men. Mind you, there must be over four thousand Frenchmen in the hospital – both the wounded from Bussaco and those ill from disease and sickness. I have forbidden my men to enter the place. I do not want to be accused of massacring helpless wounded. In the streets, it was anyone's guess how many there were left behind. But you can be sure that there are a few less now than when we entered.' He laughed. 'Besides, who knows what diseases there are there in that hospital? Typhoid fever, I'm willing to wager.'

'Do they have medical staff?'

'Yes, the French are well provided. That's one thing they can do properly. We could learn some lessons there. Did you see the state of our surgeons after Bussaco? Regular butchers' shop.'

He shook his head and Keane realized that perhaps Trant was not quite so placid, after all, that beneath that calm face there lurked a spirit, a passion and a ruthlessness. He thought of what Grant had told him – of the man's past. He had Danish roots, Grant had said, and, looking at him now, Keane fancied he could see the Norseman in him. But there was no mistaking his Irishness, and not just in his accent.

Trant was some years Keane's senior, having been born, he remembered Grant telling him, in the same year as both Wellington and Napoleon. Like Bonaparte, he had been educated at a military school in France.

Trant was thinking. 'Keane? You're Irish, are you? From the north?'

'From County Down, sir.'

'Then we are countrymen, Captain Keane. Along with the duke and not a few of the common soldiery. Speaking of which –' Trant noticed Keane's unit, gathered behind him – 'these are your men?' He looked them over with what Keane knew to be a seasoned eye, then paused and seemed to count them. 'These are all your men? Really?'

'All save two, sir.'

He looked at them again, taking in their diversity. 'They look like an interesting bunch. Damned curious faces, some of them.' He paused and smiled again, and Keane knew what was coming. 'It's not much of a command, surely, for a man of ambition, such as yourself. You do have ambition, I take it?'

It was an unusually direct question from any officer. From Trant, it was loaded with possible meaning. Keane knew what it was he wanted to know and thought that, for once, he would oblige.

'I do, sir. I have need of advancement.'

'Then we are again alike, Keane.'

It was another blunt reply and seemed to expect an answer. But he gave none.

Trant showed his annoyance with the next question: 'How do you come to command so few, Keane? For a captain?'

'I am an exploring officer, sir, and a guide. My men, too, are guides. We scout for the army.'

'You spy, Keane. That is what you do.'

'It's not a word or a description that I tend to favour.'

'But that is, in truth, what you are. You play the spy for Wellington. And very useful a job you do, too. We all do, do we not? You, I, Colonel Grant?'

Keane was taken aback. Again he had not expected such a

direct response from a British officer – even one such as Trant, a maverick in the Portuguese service.

'Oh, don't mind me. I speak my mind. You'll get used to it. We have need of spies, Keane, or whatever it is you choose to call yourselves. The duke will not win this war without good knowledge and good intelligence. Better intelligence, at least, than the French. That and the support of the people. I can strive for the one and dabble with the other. You, I believe, have something of a talent for the cloak and dagger.'

'You flatter me, colonel. But you are right about the war. I believe we are his best advantage. Intelligence is everything. How else can he win against so many of the enemy?'

As he paused, Keane realized that, for some time, his words had not had to contend with the firing, which all the while had filled the streets. 'They've stopped fighting.'

'Yes. I told you that I had ordered an end to the killing. We have the city. We must be merciful now. And, what's more to the point, we must find you quarters.'

'You intend to stay here? With your militia?'

'Of course. I have taken back an ancient city and created a running sore on Massena's backside. Why would I leave? I can defend this place with my men. To some of them, indeed, it's home. To others, the place of their education. And you, too, Keane. You are here with your little band. And I hardly think Marshal Massena will be returning here very soon. He is too busy chasing the peer.

'I have taken the Bishop's Palace as my headquarters. You are welcome to take a room there tonight. We can find you your own residence in the morning. My aide, here, will help you.'

He called to a young man, standing a few paces off, wearing the full dress uniform of a Portuguese staff officer. 'Luis, this is Captain Keane. Find him a room in my quarters and have someone see about his men.'

Keane shook his head. 'Thank you, colonel, but there is really no need. I prefer to be with my men.'

'Nonsense. That may be so, but – this once – I insist. You will billet with me. I can see that we have much to talk about. And now, captain, I will leave you. I need to question the commander of the garrison. Until, shall we say, six o'clock? In my quarters. My man tells me there is something of the remains of a cellar – some bottles the French didn't find.'

'Yes, sir. But I think that perhaps I should also speak to the commander. It is, after all, one of my duties.'

'Yes, of course. You're right. But allow me to go alone first, if you will.'

Keane nodded. 'Yes, sir. Of course.'

Trant spoke again to the aide: 'Lieutenant Romero, escort Captain Keane to my quarters. See that he finds a bed.'

As Trant walked away, Keane cursed beneath his breath. He wondered why the colonel should want so badly to speak with the French commander. He knew from experience that it was better to be the first to interrogate a captive – whatever your methods and whatever your purpose. What, he asked himself, could Trant hope to glean from the man? He knew the extent of the garrison, surely, by now, and the man's orders were plain: to hold the city. A task in which he had clearly failed. What else was there for Trant to know?

Keane watched him go, followed by three of his officers, in the direction of the hospital, then motioned to the aide to wait for him, that he would follow after speaking to his men.

'Sarn't Ross, all of you, they're finding us all billets for the night. Colonel Trant intends to stay here and so shall we, until we find what Colonel Grant needs. Be careful of the Frenchies; they're bound to be in a murderous mood. They thought they were the victors and now they find they're the prisoners and not the jailers. And you'd better be sure to mind Colonel Trant's men, too. They're Portuguese, but they're militia. And they're not the same sort of militia that we've met before. I don't know what he's up to, but I'd swear there's something going on here beyond the colonel's orders and I intend to discover what it is.'

It was around an hour later that, having installed himself in a room of the Bishop's Palace, Keane found himself approaching the hospital. It was curious, he thought, that his billet should be the very building in which, only a year earlier, he had met with Wellington when it had been used as allied headquarters. Stranger still that, up until two days ago, it had been head-quarters to the French garrison and, before that, to Massena himself. Keane seemed to dog the man's footsteps.

Thinking of Massena brought his mind to thoughts of Henriette and, remembering her as she had been in the mar-shal's quarters at Almeida, he wondered whether they would ever meet again.

He crossed the central plaza of the university, the Pátio das Escolas, and paused beside the entrance to the library. Three hundred thousand books! Good God. What chance did he have? Curious to see what three hundred thousand books might look like, Keane pushed one of the doors open.

He was not used to libraries. He had never been a scholar. School, to him, had been a necessary thing. It had given him all that he needed – a grounding in the classics and the ability to read and write and manage rudimentary mathematics, which he had put to use both in the field and at the card table. Above all, it had taught him how to bluff. It had, in effect, made a good liar of him. When asked by a master a question to which he did not know the answer, he would manage to reply in such a way that suggested he did. It was a skill, and one, once learnt, never forgotten.

He had only once visited a library – a *bibliothèque*, in fact – once, in those long vanished days when he had lived in Paris with his aunt, his mother's sister, who had married a Frenchman. But, even among the books, his mind had not been on matters of learning. He had been fourteen. Those had been the days when, deceiving his aunt, he had spent his hours in the Marais, the Palais Royale and the Place Dauphine. Women had been his study then. But it had been closer to home that his chance had come – with his beautiful cousin, Sophie, four years his elder, at eighteen. They had gone together to the library in the old Palais Royale and there, hidden from view among the learned texts, she had taught him things that no book ever could.

A year later, Keane's uncle was dead, murdered by the Revolution, and, when the Royal family were arrested, he had returned to Ireland. He had not seen Sophie again and he had often wondered, with some real sadness, whether the Revolution had claimed her, too, as Madame Guillotine had his aunt.

The great library doors creaked as he pushed at them and at once he knew that he had entered another world. The very air was different in here to that of the street. Yet even here were signs of recent events. Just inside the doors, a dark pool of dried blood marked where someone had fallen, French or Portuguese, and the doors themselves and the walls around them had been cratered by musket balls. The place smelt of

age and, he supposed, of centuries of scholarship, and it drew
him back at once to that blissful moment in Paris.

There was an atrium and, beyond it, another door. He walked
in further, his sight adjusting to the gloom. And there all resem-
blance to his previous experience of libraries ended.

Beyond the second doors lay the books – shelves of them,
reaching thirty feet to the ceiling – and, above them, painted
woodwork and coats of arms in richly enamelled and gilded bla-
zons. Around the walls and the shelves ran a galleried walkway,
also elaborately carved and gilded, reached by staircases, some
of which had been smashed down by the intruders. The place
seemed to be deserted, now, but Keane saw around him further
evidence of the French occupation. Books lay about him on
the floor, their pages torn and ruined, their leather bindings
trampled, ripped and detached. He bent to pick one up and
looked at the cover.

Keane would have been the first to admit that he was no
scholar, but he'd had a respect for learning instilled in him by
his mother and his aunt that bordered on reverence.

He surveyed the room in awe, as much at the richness of
the decoration as the sheer volume of learning. Three hundred
thousand books! Again, Keane asked himself what he was doing
here. He was a soldier and, not for the first time, he wondered
if he was truly the right man to be an intelligence officer,
whether he might not be better at the front line, leading a
company of men, as he had done. His men were loyal, but
he missed the everyday challenge of leading a company – the
smell of the powder smoke, the rush of excitement as you
closed with the enemy. Even the crack of the bullets around
his head. It came back to him from time to time. Not always in
battle. It could happen at the quietest of moments. A sudden

noise would make him start and he would find himself momentarily frozen. And he was there again, back in the line, yelling the familiar commands, seeing his men achieve the impossible. Five rounds in a minute. Watching the blue column, its eagle-crowned tricolours waving above, as it halted and fell apart and then broke and ran.

Curiously, he felt more threatened now, here in this place of dusty learning, than he'd felt on any battlefield. He felt enclosed, restrained, imprisoned almost. As if all the knowledge around him were trying to suffocate him. He felt his heart pounding and realized that the noise he could hear was his own breathing. Remaining calm, Keane replaced the book carefully on a shelf.

A library was no place for him. Yes, he would do his best to accomplish his task. He would find the book, and Sobral, too, if he could. But someone else would do the searching – for the former, at least. Archer was the answer. Walking briskly through the library, he made for the front door and, once out in the cool of the evening, felt somehow easier. His breathing relaxed. His heart stopped pounding in his chest. He would find Doctor Sobral. He would fetch Archer. Just as soon as he had spoken to the French commander.

The hospital was a large, two-storey house on the edge of the university area of the old town. Whitewashed and pantiled, from the outside it looked as if it might have been a granary or even an arsenal. Keane entered and found himself in a pleasant cloister around a central garden. He walked down a long colonnade and through two doors that led to steps. At the top of these, he was met by two French infantrymen, who, to his surprise, did not appear to have been disarmed. They did not wear the white and blue uniform of the ordinary rank and file. These men wore dark blue coats and overalls with orange, red and black facings. Keane tried to place them. They too looked at his curious, hybrid uniform with some suspicion before saluting and admitting him.

Inside, Keane was overwhelmed by the stench of putrefaction. Here were the French infantry, hundreds of them, packed into a space barely large enough to contain them. They looked up at Keane with faraway staring eyes. He knew battle fatigue at once. These were the men from Bussaco – the men he had helped to beat, barely a month ago.

Keane was about to enquire of one of them the whereabouts of the commander of the garrison when a man appeared from the rear of the ward.

He wore a similar uniform to the two soldiers on the door and, at last, Keane recognized it. The commander of the French garrison was a captain of the marines of the Imperial Guard. At first sight, he looked quite the part, with his dark blue hussar cut, frogged tunic and the classic Imperial Guard trimmings of that colour Keane had seen nowhere else. *Aurore*, the French called it – a shade of brilliant orange. They said that Bonaparte himself had a hand in designing the uniforms of his men, at least of the guard. And, if that was the case, thought Keane, then the little Corsican ogre, when he was eventually deposed, might enjoy a promising second career as an artist.

The man broke his reverie abruptly, speaking in French. 'Sir? What is your business here?'

Keane replied in English, deliberately. 'I am a British officer. Captain James Keane. I am looking for your commanding officer.'

'You have found him, Captain Keane. Capitain Jean-Michel Lievremont.'

Keane began to notice details about the officer that suggested he was not all he had at first appeared. The man looked back at him through a veneer of command, with tired eyes that seemed to yearn for the rest he might find as a privileged officer prisoner in the warden's lodgings of an English jail before being exchanged back to France in return for some British officer.

Keane tried to imagine what was in his mind. He had been left by Marshal Massena with just a short-strength battalion of his men to keep watch over this plundered city whose rape he had been powerless to stop. He must have been astonished to observe Trant's militia approaching. Massena's generals would have assured him that all the enemy troops were with Wellington, on the run back to Lisbon. He had nothing to fear, they would have said.

The captain must have looked at the column of militia and the horsemen and wondered how best he could possibly defend a city with less than a battalion and no artillery.

Keane smiled at him and spoke again, but now in French. 'You were left behind?'

The man seemed surprise to hear his mother tongue. 'You speak French.'

Keane smiled. 'Of course, but not very well, I'm afraid. Why you, captain? Why only you?'

The young captain smiled. 'We are the emperor's guard. There are not too many of us left in Spain. The emperor took most of us back to France with him when he went. My friends went to fight the Austrians and the Russians. But I was left in this godforsaken country.'

'You're marines, aren't you? Sailors.'

'Yes.' The man laughed. 'And so I know that you will ask, what are we doing here, in the middle of the countryside?'

'No, not really. You're soldiers and you just go where you're ordered. Just like the rest of us.' It was a clumsy attempt to establish a rapport and Keane was relieved that it appeared to have the desired effect. The two were joined, as brothers in arms.

'Yes. You're right, there. We go where we're ordered. Though why the devil we are here, God only knows.'

'This is a valuable place. It commands the roads, dominates the land for miles around. It is of vital strategic importance.'

'Then why leave it? Why go in pursuit of Wellington?'

'Your marshal has a plan and, to accomplish it, he has to defeat us before the winter. He sees Wellington retreating, despite the fact that he has just won a victory. Massena is close to being disgraced and here is an opportunity he cannot allow to go: the chance to push Wellington and his troops into the sea. What would you do?'

'I wouldn't have left this place filled with the sick and wounded. Look at these poor bastards.' He gesticulated to the room and, again, Keane took in the desolate scene.

'Yes, you have a point. It would perhaps have been more charitable to move them. They haven't much chance here, have they?'

The captain looked grave. 'Better than the poor sods cut to pieces in the streets out there. I heard the screams.'

'The Portuguese had good cause, didn't they? You know what your countrymen did? Did you try to resist?'

The man nodded. 'Of course. Who wouldn't? Any soldier would. And we are the guard. We barricaded the hospital and fired down from there. I couldn't help the poor buggers in the streets. Those horsemen cut them to pieces.'

'Who were they?'

'They were students.'

'Students? Of what?'

'The classics, arts, sciences. They attended the university here.'

'No wonder they bore a grudge. Who commands them?'

Lievremont smiled, 'You've met him. Just now.'

'Colonel Trant.'

Lievremont nodded again. 'He's quite a character.'

It was Keane's turn to nod. 'He certainly is. What did he say to you?'

'He said that we were to cooperate fully or he would pass us over to his men, the students. He said that he, Trant, and a few English soldiers, yourselves, were all that stood between us and death. That the Portuguese militia would like to tear us limb from limb.'

'And I dare say he may be right. What did you say?'

'That we would do what we could to cooperate, but that we had a duty as soldiers to confound the enemy in any way we might.'

'You're a brave man, captain.'

'I am merely a soldier, doing my job. That is all. All that I know.' He paused for a moment and stared into Keane's eyes and Keane could see the fear, the loss of hope. 'We were told that the Portuguese had no fight in them. That they were cowards and would run before our bayonets.'

'They lied to you.'

'The emperor would never lie.'

'Your generals lied. The Portuguese are a brave people. Their soldiers fight well, when properly led. Your generals knew that.'

'They would never have admitted it. To Massena, all the people here are scum.'

'You don't agree with the marshal?'

He shook his head. 'He's a liar – of that I am certain, now – and a thief, too. He gave orders to sack this place. Orders. I know that the emperor has taken treasure from all over Europe. From Rome and Venice. But to sack this place? This is a place of learning. Now the world believes that the French are worse than barbarians. The Huns and the Goths of the ancient world are nothing compared to us.'

'You know your history, captain. Did you read the classics?'

'Captain, my father was an educated man. A doctor. A *philosophe*. There was no need for me to attend a university. I learnt everything at home – from him. He would be appalled at what we are doing here, what we have done throughout Europe.' He stared vacantly at the wall.

Keane thought that perhaps now, when the man was at a low ebb, as disaffected as he was likely to become, this was the time to start questioning him.

'Do you suppose that your marshal is planning to return? He must have heard about Colonel Trant's having captured the place by now.'

Lievremont shrugged. 'Not as far as I know. He vowed that he was going to chase Wellington into the sea.'

So, thought Keane, there was the proof that the French did not have an inkling about the existence of the lines at Torres Vedras.

'Surely, though, he must have intended to leave supply bases on his route.'

'It is not our way and you must know that. We live off the land.'

'Don't you realize that Wellington has issued orders to destroy the land? The Portuguese are burning their own crops and killing the livestock as they go. Where did you think the people of Coimbra had gone? How many were left here for your men to kill? Your army will have nothing. No provisions. No supplies.'

'We carry a modicum of basics.'

'But how long will they last? A week? Two? How many men did the marshal have with him? The entire army? Or did he split it? That way, he might have more of a chance. And what of the horses?'

'He was going to split the army, to leave garrisons as he went. He'll keep the best with him, to fight Wellington and defeat him. His cavalry, too – they can move faster. They will find their own supplies, operate outside the army on the march.'

It was everything that Keane had hoped to learn from the officer and, when he had a chance to get word of it to Wellington, would provide valuable intelligence. It had been given readily and perhaps unwittingly. He was not sure if Lievremont realized how much he had said or, if he did, whether he really cared. He had spoken of his duty as a soldier but, in reality, thought Keane, the fight had gone out of him.

'It won't work, captain. Look at the Portuguese. What do you see? A people, resolute in their defiance. They have been doing this for months. They have become used to it.'

Lievremont nodded. 'Yes. I know what has been happening, we all do, but still Massena does not believe it. He refuses to believe that a people will go to such extremes. He tells us that these are no more than isolated incidents intended to frighten us. That we will find food when we go after Wellington.'

Keane shook his head and laughed in a way that chilled the Frenchman.

'But he's wrong, captain. There will be no food. No crops

to make your bread, no livestock, no wine. Nothing. And so your army will starve. Face the truth, captain. If Wellington's plan works, very soon you and your men may well be the only survivors of Massena's army.'

5

Keane sat with Trant in the shade of the vine-hung colonnade of the Bishop's Palace and watched the sunshine play on the stones. The scent of lemons came on the air and, with that arcane skill known only to soldier-servants, Trant's Portuguese orderly had not only found a table, but had draped it with an altar cloth from a looted church and, on this, the man had placed a cold bottle of rosé wine.

Keane's men had gone with Trant's in search of quarters for the night, and the two officers sat at the table on their own as the shadows grew longer on the wall and the sun began to lower on the distant mountains. It was a bizarre interlude, thought Keane, to be sitting here in such tranquillity when around them the world lay in chaos. But he had learnt to value such things and, besides, he was intrigued. Trant had given him a cheroot, one of the small cigars favoured by the Spanish and Portuguese. Keane eyed it uncertainly, but eventually followed Trant's suit and, lighting the end, breathed in. The sensation was pleasant – until he began to cough.

Trant stopped talking and smiled at him as he recovered from the fit. He had been waxing lyrical about Ireland and his family;

he seemed hugely proud of his history. Now, having allowed Keane to clear his lungs, he continued in the same vein.

'My grandfather, Sir Dominick Trant of Dingle in county Kerry, wrote a tract. It was quite famous, in its day. Infamous, you might say. "Considerations on the present Disturbance in Munster", it was entitled. He wrote it in 1787 and it went to three editions. Three editions!' He stared at Keane, as if awaiting some exclamation of approval. None came. 'You know it?' He raised an eyebrow.

Keane shook his head. 'No, I am afraid I have to admit that I don't, colonel.' He coughed again and looked at the cheroot in his hand. 'By God, these things are devilish. What d'you call them?'

'Cheroots. Picked up the habit when I was here before – back in '98. Minorca. That's a tale worth telling, right enough.'

He drew on his own cheroot and blew a slow ring of smoke, which hung in the air before them, slowly disappearing. 'I remember the first one I had. Worse than you, just now. Spewed up my guts. But I persevered, you see. Got to persevere. Otherwise I'd have lost face with the locals. And that wouldn't do. Not at all. Won't do now, neither. But you'd know all about that, wouldn't you, captain? Now, where was I?'

'You were just telling me of your grandfather and his infamous tract.'

'So I was, and you hadn't heard of it. It's of no matter. It concerns the problem of the insurgents – those who would imperil Ireland. You will recall the troubles we had some years ago. He defended the tithes against them and called for measures, if you know what I mean. Measures.'

'To punish them?'

'Precisely. Well, some took against him. Sir John Colthurst

called him out in a duel, thinking it a personal slight and, sad to say, my grandfather killed him. Shot him between the eyes. We've always been good shots, the Trants. My father was in the army and my uncle the East India Company.

'Of course, my family was not always so partisan as Sir Dominick. We were Catholics, originally –' he laughed – 'followed James II to France and were attainted. But by my grandfather's time we'd seen the light. My grandfather was a barrister. Great taste in art. He would have loved this place. He practised in Dunkettle. As you might guess, most of his clients were of the smuggling fraternity.'

Keane nodded sagely. But, having not set foot in Ireland since leaving there, aged seventeen, to take up his commission, he would not have guessed. And he wondered, quite frankly, why Trant should be giving him such a tiresome torrent of information. Could it be he was eager to impress? Keane presumed so and, if he was correct, it might betray an apparent insecurity in the man, which was not, at first, evident.

Trant continued, 'Where's home to you, Captain Keane? Or should I say, where do you long to be, if not here?'

'Ireland, of course, colonel, like yourself. But you knew that.'

Trant nodded. 'Of course, but where exactly is home? You and I both know that blessed island can be a very small place.'

'County Down. We had a farm. Nothing great to speak of. But enough.'

'But you left to be a soldier. Is that it? The sound of the guns in your ears? The siren call of fife and drum?'

'I was purchased a commission.'

'By your father, was it?'

More questions. 'By a family friend. My father's dead. Long dead.'

Trant's face fell and he paused, seeming genuinely affected. 'I'm sorry. Was he a soldier, your father?'

'Yes. He died in America, fighting the rebels.'

'Now that was a war, if you like. Taught us everything we know, if you ask me – the real way to fight. Good tactics, Keane, sound tactics.'

He took a long draught of rosé and wiped his mouth on his sleeve. 'When were you commissioned?'

'Ninety-five. I was seventeen. Into the Inniskillings.'

'Ah, the 27th. Old friends of mine. A fine regiment, with a fine past. Then we are almost contemporaries. 1794: date of my commission. October. Bought into the 84th. I'd been at school in France. Of course, the Revolution put paid to all that.'

Keane smiled and found himself speaking. 'In France? So was I. In Paris.' He stopped, thinking that now, perhaps, he had given away too much. It was not in his nature to be so revealing and he wondered why he was doing it. There was something in the manner and character of Colonel Sir Nicholas Trant that had made him open up, giving away too much of his past to a man he did not know, Irishman or not. Trant had a way that made you feel relaxed in his company, ready to talk. But Keane had not yet the measure of him. Not enough to trust him. He resolved to be more guarded.

Trant went on: 'I went home, back to Ireland, and you must have, too. Where was school? At home?'

Again, thought Keane, he has me trapped. 'The Royal School, Armagh.'

'That's a fine establishment. And wasn't Lord Castlereagh himself there and, if I'm not mistaken, the duke, for a short while?'

'I believe so. But long before my time.'

Trant smiled, warming to his subject. 'The duke and I are exact contemporaries. Did you know that? No, how could you. Exact with Boney, too. All three of us, born in '69.'

He paused and took first a drink and then a long puff at the cigar before continuing.

'I have been here before, you know.'

'So you said, colonel.'

'With Sir Charles Stuart. We took Minorca. My baptism of fire, that was, at Flushing, and then it was south to the Cape of Good Hope. A thankless place. November '98. Twelve years ago, almost to the month. And I don't mind telling you it was a fine posting for a young man.'

He paused, as if remembering. 'Prize money, Keane. More than you ever saw. More, certainly, than we shall find in this war. Different then, of course. They appointed me agent-general for prizes. And I was seconded to the Minorca regiment. Did you hear of them?'

Keane nodded. 'As a matter of fact, I did.'

'The Queen's own Germans. Queen's own scoundrels, more like. The times we had! But it opened my eyes to soldiering. Showed me what could be.'

Keane knew what he meant. If there was one thing soldiering could bring, it was the opportunity for sudden fortune. Keane knew about that as much, he suspected, as Nicholas Trant. Hadn't he found Soult's baggage train with its cargo of silver coin? Of course, most of it had gone to Wellington to pay the guerrillas and the army. But Keane and his men had taken their share, just as any man would.

It occurred to Keane that he and Trant had something in common, apart from their Irish heritage. Both of them were anxious to acquire wealth. 'Weren't the Minorca in Egypt?'

'Quite right. We fought with the 42nd. Your mob were there, were they not?'

'Yes. Alexandria. If you fought with the Black Watch, you might know my sergeant. James Ross?'

Even if he did, Trant showed no sign of recognition. 'No, can't say I do. The peace with France in '01 did for my ambition. How did you fare?'

'I stayed in.'

'You were more fortunate than I. My regiment was done away with. Just gone. So I went too. What else could I do? Resigned my damned commission, sold it and left the army. Went back to Ireland. Biggest mistake of my life.'

He was suddenly silent and Keane wondered what he might mean.

Both men took another drink and, having finished the bottle, Trant called for another, which the orderly somehow managed to conjure up. Immediately, the colonel poured himself a glass, which he managed to down in one. Grant's report of Wellington's comment had been disarmingly accurate. The man was as big a drunk as you could find.

Trant suddenly began to speak again. 'Of course, I rejoined – at the bottom. An ensign.' He shrugged. 'An ensign in the Staff Corps. Took me three years to make lieutenant colonel.' He smiled and took another drink.

'Three years?' Keane was genuinely impressed.

'Three years.'

'How did you manage it?'

'That's the thing. Same as the Minorca regiment. That's what I'd learnt. Go for foreign service. Lieutenant colonel in the Portuguese service. Local rank.'

'So you were still just a lieutenant in the British army?'

'Precisely. And by now I might be no more than plain Captain Trant to the redcoats, but in this blue coat I'm Colonel Trant of the Portuguese. I hold a colonel's commission, I have a colonel's command and I draw a colonel's pay.'

It occurred to Keane that, while he might also be a colonel of militia in the Portuguese army, Trant was still a captain in the Royal Staff Corps. That made him curiously close to Keane's own command. Part of the Staff Corps' duty was gathering intelligence and Keane wondered how much Trant might still be involved in this. Had Grant been entirely truthful with him? Might Trant not also be engaged in covert operations? Certainly it would explain his endless questioning. But then why not tell him? It must have been clear to Trant that Keane and his men were behind enemy lines with the purpose of intelligence gathering. Trant, it seemed, was here to harass the enemy with his militia. But might there be more to him than that? Keane had had his differences with Wellington for some time now and had not put his faith in the commander's every word. His callousness at Ciudad had been a turning point, compounded by what had happened here at Coimbra.

But now, for the first time, he began to doubt Grant's veracity and wondered if his replacement by Sir George Murray at headquarters and his greater presence in the field might not also have had some other motive, of which he was unaware. He felt exposed, insecure and excluded. Quickly, though, he told himself that such suspicions were groundless. They were mere suppositions based on nothing more than his presumptions about Trant. But it unsettled him. He took another drink and listened again to the colonel.

'I had five years in the Staff Corps before I found myself here again. Imagine my surprise, Keane, to be sent to Portugal as a military agent. Me – a humble lieutenant. Imagine my amazement to find that I was now lieutenant colonel! It was the duke's doing – Sir Arthur, as he was then. I was summoned to fight for him at Roliça. I took my men. Good men. A Portuguese corps – fifteen hundred foot and more than two hundred horse.'

'You fought at Roliça?'

'Aye, and Vimiero. We turned the French left at Vimiero and held the reserve there with Black Bob.'

Keane spoke: 'I heard that you were with the Lusitanian Legion.'

Trant looked interested. 'Yes, that is so. What do you know of them?'

'I have the greatest respect for Sir Robert Wilson, sir.'

'And I, too. They were good days. We certainly shook up the French. Ever heard of a man called Sanchez?'

Keane pricked up at the name. Don Julian Sanchez had been one of the first guerrilla leaders he had dealt with in his new command. 'Yes; in fact, I know him quite well.'

'Do you now? I knew him too. Damn good soldier.'

Keane moved back to the subject of Trant's real purpose. 'I'm intrigued. What exactly is the role of a military agent, colonel?'

'You are quite aware of that, I'm sure, captain.'

'No, really – do tell me.'

'I had similar duties to your own, captain – liaison with the locals. But the main thing is that I was a fighting soldier. I was not a spy and I wore uniform – the uniform of the Portuguese. We made the Frenchies run about. By God, we did.' He laughed. 'Should have seen them. One night, we managed to creep up on their pickets as they sat at their fires in the advance posts. That showed them. Kept behind the walls after that. We never gave them a moment's rest. That was our watchword. We did well, Keane. Damned well. Pushed them out of Alcántara. Do you know, I believe that it was my actions in those battles that persuaded the duke that the Portuguese can fight. Of course, I was there when poor John Moore was killed.'

'You saw him die?'

'That I did. Where else would I be? I left with the rest from Corunna.'

'But you came back?'

'Of course. These people are mine, now, and I theirs. I'm a big man here, Keane. How could I ever give that up? Yes, I came back. But what's more, I was sent back here.'

'By the duke again?'

Trant shook his head. 'No. Most certainly not. Not the second time. I'm sure he was looking out for me. I was always convinced of that. But it wasn't the duke who sent me back. How could it be? He has never believed that we should cut and run and leave the country to its people. But those who sent me back here did. That's exactly what they wanted to do. Wanted me to arrange plans for the evacuation of all the British population from the country. Not just the army, Keane, mark you, but the entire population. All those Warres and Cockburns and suchlike. The whole damned parcel of our connections.'

Keane whistled under this breath. 'The Blackwoods?'

'Aye, them too – him and his precious wife and daughter and all their nephews and hangers on – the whole lot. That was to be my role.'

Keane thought for a moment. This was news indeed. The Blackwoods he knew – only too well. Indeed, their daughter, Kitty, had been, until recently, the object of his affections. Until, that is, his late friend, Morris, had taken her. Again, the awful voices rose within him. And his feelings were torn apart between mourning for his dead friend and jealousy for the girl. A pointless jealousy that now could never be fulfilled and, in any case, was irrelevant. There was another face in Keane's head now, another name in his heart. And he wondered if their paths would cross again.

'What were your plans?'

'Oh, much the same as the Royal family. They, of course, went to Brazil, where, as you know, they still are. We were hoping to go there, some of us, the others, back to England. It was a headache to organize, I can tell you. But it was never to be. Thank God. That's why the duke is the saviour of this country.'

'Even though he burns her fields and allows such massacres as this and that at Ciudad?'

'Yes, captain, even so. I know these people and, believe me, I sympathize with them. But I now believe that his plan is the only way, if these people want to be free. That is why I raised the corps.'

'The students of Coimbra?'

'They existed already, of course. But they were not a proper fighting unit. You know the sort of thing. They liked parades and uniforms, but as to fighting . . . We – '

'You changed that.' Keane cut him short.

'I like to give myself credit for having created as good a force as any in the Portuguese army. You saw how we took this place. It was done slowly. I had only five hundred, at first, then more and more came to me. After Oporto, it was easy.'

'With the reports of the massacre.'

'Exactly, and we – how shall I put it? – made sure that those reports were widely broadcast.'

'And in some detail.'

'Soon, I was in command of three thousand men.'

'And then they had to make you a colonel.'

'Better than that; by the time Wellesley got to the Douro and took back the city, I was governor-general of Oporto. I owe so much to the peer – my career, for one thing. I have the problem, Keane, of being too many things to too many people. I am ubiquitous. I was promoted captain in the Staff Corps in June 1809, but the good office at St James's afterwards informed me that I would be removed from it unless I resigned his Portuguese employment. That, of course, I would not do. By God, I was brigadier to the Portuguese. It was the peer who saved me, yet again. He wrote to St James's and, do you know what he told them, Keane? He said that there was no officer the loss of whose services in Portugal would be more felt.'

It was the final straw. Keane had at last had enough of Trant's self-promotion. The man was certainly fascinating and they did seem to have much in common. But Trant was something that Keane was determined he would never be: he was self-important. He stood up.

'If you'll excuse me, colonel, I really must go back to the hospital.'

Trant poured himself another glass of wine. 'Really? Must you? Just when we were getting on so well. I really wouldn't bother, if I were you. It's full of pestilence. You should be careful you don't catch something, captain. Why d'you need to go?'

'I need to speak with the commandant. Lieutenant Lievremont.'

Trant laughed. 'That boy? He's out of his depth, the poor bugger. Massena was mad to leave him in command. What was he thinking of?'

'I think he may have more to tell us yet.'

'Do you, now?' He paused, smiling. 'How will you get it out of him?'

'I have my ways.'

'You're a canny man, Keane. I would never have taken you for a spy.'

Keane bristled. 'I prefer not to use the word, myself.'

'Oh, I see; still a little conscious of it? Well, I know only too well the effect it has upon our fellow officers. I've never enjoyed great favour in the mess myself.'

'I don't find it a problem.'

'Oh, come on, old chap. We both know what the others think of us. "Conduct unbecoming a gentleman" and all that. It's the secrecy. They can't abide it. Going behind the back of the enemy – and behind their own, for all they know. Fact is, they trust no one.'

'With good reason, colonel. You do know that, until recently, we had a French spy in our own staff?'

'Yes, Colonel Grant acquainted me with the fact. And he is still at large?'

Again Keane stiffened, only too aware that Macnab, as he had come to think of the man in his own mind, had evaded him. 'Yes. But I will find him.'

'You say that with feeling, Captain Keane. Something personal?'

'He killed my closest friend.'

'Really? I had heard that you and Lieutenant Morris had grown somewhat apart.'

Keane stared at Trant. How on earth could the man know anything about Tom Morris? Least of all the nature of their friendship after Morris had become engaged to the object of Keane's affection. 'What do you know of that?'

'I told you, captain, I know many things about many people. I make it my business. It's just as you do, yourself. We are in the same trade. Are we not?'

It was too much. 'No one knows about that business, save for a few close friends. How could you?'

'I have my ways. Don't feel uncomfortable, captain. I'm sure you must know a few things about me that you have perhaps not yet divulged. You mustn't feel guilty for Morris's death. That was Macnab's doing and, besides, isn't it grand to have a vendetta to pursue? Believe me, it makes the chase so much more exciting.'

6

He found the men in the abandoned tavern that had become their billet. Garland had found two bottles of wine that had somehow been missed by the French and he and Silver were making their way through the second while Martin cleaned his gun and Archer tried to rescue some pages of a manuscript that the looters had thrown on the fire. Ross stood in the shadow, watching.

'Right, on your feet! We've got work to do.'

Silver looked at him. 'Work, sir? What work could we do here, in this godforsaken place? All the work needed here's been done, looks like to me.'

Keane walked across to him and, with a single deft movement, snatched the bottle from his grasp. In an instant, Silver rose, staring with drunken eyes at his commanding officer, who stood quite still, holding the bottle. There was a barely perceptible half move from Silver – just a hint of something that might happen – and then Ross was on him. The sergeant's fist smashed into Silver's jaw, knocking him to the ground. Silver sat up, shook his head and pushed himself to his feet. But the sergeant was standing over him.

'Want another?'

Silver managed to stand and, swaying, looked first at Ross and then at Keane, who spoke.

'Let's forget that happened, shall we? Or, rather, it didn't happen. Did it, sergeant?'

'No, sir. Nothing happened at all. Did it, lads?'

They murmured a 'No'. Keane looked at Silver, who was rubbing his bruised jaw.

'Right. Sober up fast and get your kit together. You too, Garland.' He looked around, but the others were already up.

'I need to talk to Lieutenant Lievremont again. He knows more than he's telling us.'

With Keane and Ross leading the way, they left the tavern and walked through the streets of the old town in the direction of the hospital, and again Keane noticed the destruction wrought by the French. It was the senselessness of it that appalled him most and the evidence of wanton brutality. The dark stains that spattered so many of the whitewashed walls bore testimony to the number who had been put to the sword here.

They were a short distance from the hospital building when they heard a commotion up ahead. Keane stopped and the others halted with him. He listened and heard the sound of raised voices – and cheering.

Ross turned to him. 'Sounds like someone's rabble-rousing, sir. I'd know that noise anywhere. Barrack-room politics, that's what that is.'

Ahead of them, a company of Trant's blue-coated Portuguese militia was standing in the street. Keane noticed that these were not the Coimbra university unit, but other regular militia, and, he presumed, less educated. Among them, their leader, a young sergeant, was speaking. Keane hoped they might not be seen. He waved a silent command to the men and they split to either side of the street, melting into the shadows.

His Portuguese, good enough to pass spoken, was better still in listening, but he wished that he had Heredia with him to grasp the nuances of the sergeant's argument.

The sergeant was passionate. 'What are we going to do about it? I ask you that, comrades. Shall we just stand here and let the French pigs get away with it?'

Cries of 'No!' filled the street now, rising to a frenzy.

The sergeant responded in echo. 'No. They should pay! All of them! You've all seen what they did here. They've defiled our cities, just as they have our women. They kill our children and our elders, slaughter babes on the end of their sabres. Why should they live? I say we take the hospital and that every man of them should be put to the sword.'

There was another cheer, louder. 'Kill the French!' The men were keen to move now and Keane had to think fast. There was clearly no way that he, with his tiny force, would be able to take on even an under-strength company of militia. But he had to do something to prevent another atrocity of the worst kind.

He found Ross. 'You heard that?'

'Yes, sir. My Portuguese isn't very good, but I can see they're out to get the French – the wounded.'

'They intend to kill them all – everyone in the hospital – the marines and the wounded. All of them.'

'What can we do?'

'The only thing is to join them. Make them think we're out for blood, too. Then, when we reach the hospital, stick to me and break away. We must warn the marines.'

The mob had moved now, following the sergeant along the street towards the hospital. Keane signalled to the others and together they joined the rear of the ragged column. Some of the Portuguese looked round, but seeing evidently English faces and the distinctive Tarleton helmets unique to the British cavalry, took them to be friends. Besides, they appeared to have joined the party.

Gathering momentum, they moved along the crowded streets, collecting further militiamen as they went. At length, they reached the hospital. To Keane's horror, however, where there should have been a guard posted at the door, there was none, and the door itself stood open.

Seeing his chance, the Portuguese sergeant ran towards the building, followed by a number of the men. Keane was up beside him too, his long legs taking him faster than the others. He pushed forward towards the building ahead of the rest of them, anxious to be at the front when the attack began, desperate to warn the marines, but pretending all the time to be part of their lynch mob.

He called to the sergeant in Portuguese. 'Let me in first! I claim the first of those bastards.'

They reached the opening together and, as they did, the sergeant turned to him and stopped. 'And who the hell might you be?'

'I'm a British officer and, if anyone's going to be the first to kill those bastards, it's me. I saw everything that happened here. Everything.'

The man stared at him and, for a moment, Keane thought that he might have to kill him. 'What are you? You're not one of us. I don't know you, do I?'

'Your colonel does. Colonel Trant. I'm a British officer. My name's Keane.' He paused. 'But it's "sir" to you, sergeant. And now, get out of my way. This is my fight.'

The sergeant weighed up Keane's height and build, then stood back, uncertain as to what he should do. The officer had mentioned the colonel, Colonel Trant, and that name was enough to make the man hesitate.

Keane saw his chance and looked to find the others. But they were with him already.

'Sarn't Ross, all of you, in here. With me.'

Keane pushed past the sergeant and, as he did, thought it best to make sure and, turning, gave the man a powerful shove in the chest so that he toppled back on to two of his own men. Keane pushed through the door and, in an instant, Ross, Silver, Martin, Archer and Garland had followed him. The sergeant was yelling at them now, furious. Calling them back. Screaming oaths.

Keane carried on. With the others, he ran through the entrance and into the covered colonnade of the hospital, in the cool shade of which some of the French wounded had been laid to look out at the cloistered garden with its tall cypresses and lemon trees.

He shouted at them in their own tongue: 'Get up – all of you! Anyone who can, get up. Save yourselves! Look – there.' He pointed to the doorway where the sergeant was leading the militia into the cloister. Some of the French tried to stand; few managed it. The others did not seem to hear him. Keane carried on along the corridor, followed by his men. Garland stooped to help a French infantryman to his feet and propelled him along the cobbles before him. Martin did the same and, within minutes, a half dozen of the French were running, or hobbling, with them.

Keane could hear the Portuguese behind him now, running after them, yelling death to the French, their boots hammering echoes on the cobbles of the colonnade. He wondered how many of them had noticed his men helping the wounded and supposed that it did not matter now. And, as the thought came to him, so did the screaming. It was the sound of the wounded being bayoneted and sabred. Men were begging for their lives, calling for their mothers.

Silver was up beside him, breathing hard as he ran. 'Christ, sir, they're killing all the wounded.'

Still running, with his arm wrapped around the waist of a Frenchman, helping him to safety, Keane gasped, 'Nothing to be done. We've done what we can. We have to save the others.'

Martin was looking back and he saw the bayonets and sabres rise and fall, slicing and stabbing into the defenceless French.

Keane saw him and stopped. 'Martin, to me – now. Leave them.' The boy turned and Keane saw the look in his eyes: pleading, desperate. Keane yelled at him again with more urgency as the Portuguese closed on them. 'To me, now, Will! At the double! Now, boy!'

Hearing his Christian name, Martin snapped back to reality and, pulling himself away from the scene, rejoined the others as they continued to run towards the end of the colonnade.

He rounded on Keane, forcing him to stop. The wounded Frenchman pulled himself free and carried on as the boy spoke. 'Sir, look at them.'

Keane fixed him with a stare. 'Enough. They brought it on themselves. We've done our best.' Then, with no more words, Keane grabbed him by the arm and pulled him away from the militia. There was nothing to do now but get further into the hospital, find Captain Lievremont and his marines and defend the building as best they could. And, if possible, get word to Trant. It was the only way in which to prevent a greater massacre.

There was another door ahead of them and Keane seemed to recall that it led into the administrative offices of the hospital, surely where they would find Lievremont and his men.

Beyond the door there was a wooden-banistered staircase and Keane ran up on to the first step. There were shouts from above.

Keane yelled back in French. 'Friends! We're friends. Captain Lievremont, is that you?'

Boots clattered on the stairs and there was a commotion.

To their rear, Keane saw the Portuguese in the doorway and yelled at Garland, 'Shut that door! All of you!'

Garland put his broad shoulders to the door and pushed it against the Portuguese; then Silver was with him, and Ross. The wooden door slammed shut and, in an instant, they had dropped the iron bar behind it. At that moment, Lievremont appeared above them on the staircase, his sabre in his hand.

'What the devil?' He saw Keane. 'Captain Keane? What is going on?'

'Quick, man – back up the stairs and barricade the door.' He motioned his own men to go up and Lievremont, seeing their uniforms, let them pass.

'Captain Keane, what is happening?'

Keane pointed back down the stairs, towards the door. Outside, the Portuguese were pounding at it with their musket butts. Soon they would find something with which to break it open.

'I was coming to find you, but it looks as if we got here just in time. We need to get word to Trant. We must get him to stop them, take command, or we're all dead.'

Lievremont stared at him and then down the stairs, his face blank. Keane was not surprised. He had no idea what action the young man had seen, although, to be in the guard, he must have proven himself somewhere. But he had thought that he might behave like this under pressure. Perhaps his nerve had gone. Keane had seen it before in men under his command. An incident would happen in the field, something of untold horror that made an indelible impression on the mind, and then, when circumstances called for it, the nerve, which before had been so strong, would fail. In fact, Keane himself had not been immune and he had noticed recently that, when under pressure, he would play with the tips of his fingers as if there was something on them.

He looked at Lievremont and, seeing him tense, as men do when under fire, grabbed him by the arm. 'Those men out there intend to kill you, captain. Can I suggest that I follow you back up the stairs?'

Without waiting for a response, he pushed Lievremont up the staircase and, at the top, found another double door leading to the offices. As he remembered, beyond the offices lay the main wards of the hospital. From below came the sound of splintering timber as the militia broke down the lower door. Keane ushered the last of the French wounded through the doors and, together with Garland and Ross, followed them into the administration offices. Then, turning, he pushed the doors shut and locked them. Lievremont was standing frozen to the spot.

'What have we got? What furniture?'

'Furniture?'

'Furniture – something heavy.' Looking around the room, Keane focused on a huge oak armoire. 'That. That'll do.' He shook Lievremont by the shoulder. 'Help me, man! For God's sake.'

The marine stared at him and then, suddenly understanding, ran to the armoire and began trying to shift it across the floor.

Keane turned to his men to ensure they would be ready for a fight; they were loading their carbines and tearing off cartridges from the strips in their leather ammunition pouches. He pointed to the armoire. 'Sarn't Ross, put that big bugger there across the door.'

Ross and Garland began to move the armoire and, helped by the others – not least, Lievremont – managed to manoeuvre it across the room and push it against the door.

Keane could hear the Portuguese at the top of the stairs now, as they reached the other side of the door. He could make out the sergeant's voice, shouting commands.

Turning to his other men, Keane said, 'Once this door's secure, check the rest of the wards. We need to barricade all the entrances.'

'Who are they?' Lievremont asked him.

'Portuguese militia. The same unit that took the city. But they've been drinking. They want vengeance for what happened here, what your countrymen did. To be honest, I can't blame them.'

'I told you before, captain, I am not proud of that.'

'I did not presume you would be. Still, it was your army.'

'There are many different sorts in my army. Every army has a bad element.'

'Of course, even my own. But it seems to me that Marshal Massena's army has more of a "bad element" than others.'

Lievremont said nothing. He smiled and shrugged. 'And what now?'

'Now we wait. How many men do you have?'

'An under-strength battalion, as I told you. Perhaps four hundred men. We have some wounded who can walk, but not enough guns for them.'

'They'll try to break in. And, eventually, they'll manage it. We have to be ready for them.' He looked around, counting. There were perhaps eighty marines among the patients.

'Where are the rest of your men?'

'In two other rooms like this, above us, and in their own quarters.'

'Where's that?'

'Up another staircase, across the courtyard. Look, you can see from the window.'

The two men walked through the office to one of the ward rooms and over to the window in the interior wall. Looking out, Lievremont pointed to a red, pantiled roof. 'They're over there; that's the barracks.'

Keane scanned the building. A stone staircase led up to a balustrade on which the two sets of doors on to the cloister were shut and there seemed to be no sign of life. But, even as he looked, with a splintering of glass, one of the windowpanes exploded outwards and first the butt and then the barrel of a musket poked through the hole.

'Thank God they're there,' said Lievremont.

'They're in there, all right. Best thing for them. Better if we don't try to reach them. Wouldn't do any good. Let's hope your men upstairs do the same as us. We have to get word to Trant.'

Keane found Sam Gilpin, arguably the most agile of his men. 'Gilpin, take yourself off and find Colonel Trant. He'll be at the Bishop's Palace. Can you find it?'

'Yes, sir. I know where it is from when we were here before.'

'Right. Go and inform Colonel Trant what's happening here. Tell him we need him to come at once and order his men to stop. Tell him that, if he doesn't do that, we'll all be slaughtered. Tell him they've already killed the wounded.'

Gilpin walked to one of the windows and, opening it, pushed himself out and on to the roof. Then, employing all his agility as a cat burglar and the skills learnt in the slums of St Giles, he clambered silently over the rooftops and, dropping down on to the ground, ran for his life.

The ward was filled with wounded men in various states of dress and injury. They lay on the few bloodstained beds and sprawled on the floor on filthy mattresses or, in some cases, just on a greatcoat or a pile of straw. The place stank of excrement and putrid flesh – sweet and sickly, filling the nose and mouth. Blood lay slick and congealed on the wooden floors.

At the other end of the ward, a door opened and, hearing it, Keane spun round, thinking it might be more of the Portuguese. But what met his eyes was more shocking than any foe. A woman stood framed against the doorway – a woman he knew at once.

Henriette Lebreton had recognized him too and, for a moment, both of them stood transfixed as, all around them, the marines and Keane's men went about the business of barricading the room. He shouted at one of the marines, 'The door! Close it and turn the lock!' Then, slowly, he began to walk towards her.

Lievremont had seen her, too, and went fast, past Keane. 'Henriette, you should not be here.'

'I heard gunfire. What's happening, Jean?' She looked again at Keane. 'Captain Keane.'

'Miss Lebreton.'

Lievremont looked puzzled. 'You know her? Henriette, you know Captain Keane?'

'Yes, I know her and Miss Lebreton knows me.' He paused and gazed at her. 'I didn't know if I would see you again.'

'Nor I, you.'

'But how on earth do you know each other? Miss Lebreton came here with the marshal. Marshal Massena. She was with the army.'

Keane nodded. 'Yes, I know; we're old friends.'

Lievremont let it go. 'Well, I'm afraid that now is not the time to chat. If you recall, captain, we are under attack.'

Keane cast a glance at the marine and saw instantly from his manner that he and Henriette were, or had been, something more than comrades in arms.

Lievremont smiled at her. 'Henriette, my dear, you must go to the upper floors. You can see we're being attacked.'

Keane shook his head. 'No. She's better staying with us, here. Let her stay.'

'No, she must go to a higher level. It will be safer up there. We have to think of her safety first, captain. Can't you see that? We're the first point of any attack.'

Henriette looked at Keane. 'James?' There was a quiver in her voice.

Without waiting, Lievremont took her by the arm and started to lead her towards the door. Keane waited for a moment and then began to follow them, not entirely sure as to what he would do, but certain of one thing, that he did not want to let Henriette go from his sight.

He shouted towards them, 'Leave the door. Don't open it.'

Then, just as Lievremont and Henriette reached the other end of the ward, there was a shot from the corridor beyond and one of the doors flew open, its lock blasted in a mess of wooden splinters. As the smoke cleared, six Portuguese militiamen pushed into the open doorway.

Keane called out, 'Sarn't Ross, to me! They've got round to the rear.' He began to run down the ward, towards Henriette, and, as he watched, one of the militia, a big man welding a cavalry sword, took a swipe at Lievremont, but missed. The marine's own sabre, quickly drawn, swung forward and took the man in the stomach, skewering him against the wall.

Another of the Portuguese swung at the marine and was met by Lievremont's fist. A third man grabbed Henriette by the arm. She screamed and scratched at her attacker, gouging a scarlet furrow down his cheek. But he kept his grip. Two other militiamen were on Lievremont now, one with a bayonet on his musket that caught the marine on the upper part of his right arm.

As Lievremont pushed against the two men, Henriette lost her footing and, falling, was dragged from the room by two of the militia. Keane closed on them just as a Portuguese infantryman took aim at the marine captain. But the shot that rang out was that from Martin's gun, its bullet making a neat black ring in the Portuguese soldier's forehead. As the man fell, Lievremont saw his chance and grabbed Henriette by the waist. Another of the Portuguese pulled her away, tearing her dress.

And then Keane struck. He raised his sabre and brought it down hard on the man's head, slicing through his shako and into his skull. The man fell, poleaxed, to the floor, a piece of the dress still clutched in his hand, and, as he did so, Lievremont managed to pull the girl free. Keane moved fast and, with Ross and Garland, heaved at the doors, pushing them shut. Within instants, there were more men behind them, holding the doors against the Portuguese. Lievremont slumped to the ground and Henriette, breathing heavily, knelt to tend him.

Keane called behind in French. 'Quick! I need more men.'

Lievremont managed a cry. 'Hurry! Help him'. At his word, six of his marines ran to the door and, with Keane's men, pushed their weight against it. Keane found a huge iron bar. With Ross, he managed to lift it and together they slotted it into the iron slots behind the doors. As it dropped, the men holding the doors, marines and guides alike, began to move back. Some stood, doubled up, others rested their heads against the walls.

Keane turned back to the room. 'Thank God.'

He looked down at Lievremont, whose arm, covered in blood, was being bound up by Henriette, using strips of fabric torn from what was left of her dress.

He bent down. 'Captain Lievremont, I must thank you. If you had not acted so swiftly, I can't think what might have happened to this young lady.'

The Frenchman smiled up at him. 'It was only what any man would have done, captain, to save any woman.'

But she was not any woman, at least not to Captain Keane. And, as he looked at Lievremont, he guessed that Henriette was not just any woman to the French captain, either. Knowing that it would be unwise to betray anything of his feelings for Henriette, either to Lievremont or to his own men, Keane straightened up and tried to avoid her gaze. But, as he did so, their eyes met for an instant and that was enough to persuade him that what they had had together still existed.

He watched as she bound Lievremont's wounded arm and something about the captain's manner and the way in which he had come out so quickly with his last comment made him

uneasy. Unless he was very much mistaken, there was something between the two of them.

He turned away, unsure how to play the situation. He was
adept at subterfuge, a skilled spy, as Trant had reminded him.
He could talk himself out of a corner and deceive a French marshal. But here he was lost. Of course, he had loved women, many
of them. And for every one he had felt something. But always
he had cut and run. That had changed with Kitty Blackwood.
He had not felt the urge to run. Nor had he been given the
opportunity to advance the situation. And then it had been too
late. But now, surprisingly, he felt the same for Henriette. He
sensed that he had changed; he now sought something more
than the easy, undemanding and unambiguous relationships
he had known in the past. But, at the same time, he realized
that, here, he was totally at sea. Complex matters of the heart
were not his forte and luck had never been kind to him in such
things, only seeing fit to smile on him at the card table and
on the battlefield. Suddenly thinking that Henriette might be
more attached to Lievremont, he felt a curious anguish.

Blanking out the problem, he turned to Ross. 'Sarn't Ross,
make sure the doors are properly closed and block them with
whatever you can.'

Henriette, had just finished tending Lievremont and was with
another of the Frenchmen, when from the garden, a ragged
volley of shots hit the windows, sending shards of glass flying
into the room. Henriette started and gave a short scream, and
the wounded men lying in the beds directly under the windows
tried to take cover as the jagged glass rained down on them.

There were more shots. Keane screamed an order: 'Get them
out of the beds and into the room. All of you, stay back from
the windows.'

Lievremont yelled a command and a score of marines began to help the wounded from their beds. One of them, however, ignoring him, aimed into the garden and cracked off a shot in retaliation. 'Don't fire back! Hold your fire!'

Keane looked at Ross. 'Christ, we'll be killing the Portuguese ourselves in a minute. Where the devil's bloody Trant?'

Two more marines were over at the windows, now, joining their comrade to fire down at the militia. Keane turned to Lievremont. 'Captain, will you kindly tell your men not to shoot unless they are attacked?'

Lievremont shouted, repeating the command, and the marines ceased firing, but not before they had done their damage.

Outside, they could hear the militia again – an angry buzz of hate – and Keane guessed that one of the marines' shots might have struck home. But he knew that the noise was just that. There was little the Portuguese could do, aside from burning them out. He wondered if that was a possibility and began to worry, praying that Gilpin would find Trant in time.

He stood at a little distance from his men, watching Henriette. Looking at the way she tended the wounded, he wondered what was happening in her mind and whether her feelings might mirror his own.

Ross reported, 'That's it, sir, they won't get through the doors in a hurry.'

Hardly had the words left his mouth when there was another shattering of glass and two missiles came flying through the windows, trailing smoke and shrouded in flame.

Instinctively, the men sought cover and Keane ran to the missiles, which had come to rest close to one of the wooden barricades. He stamped on them and saw that they were pitch-soaked torches, with, thankfully, no explosive charge. As he did so, three more of the torches came through the windows.

'Put them out! Use water – anything. Piss on them.'

It was what he had dreaded and, as another barrage flew in, one of them striking a wounded grenadier, he heard battering at the door closest to the entrance stairs. Although they managed to put out the flames, the damp cloth on to which the pitch had been poured caused the torches to smoke with incredible ferocity and an acrid pall of the stuff soon filled the room.

Keane shouted to the coughing, retching defenders, 'In the centre! On me. Form square.'

Lievremont, too, was shouting commands now.

As they fell back into the centre of the ward, several more of the torches flew through the windows, but these were quickly extinguished. Keane stood in the centre of the hollow square, coughing on the smoke from the torches, while outside the battering continued against the door. 'Make ready. Be ready for them.'

But Ross had been right: there was no moving the doors and, within fifteen minutes, the Portuguese had given up.

And so they waited. The smoke cleared, leaving a smell of burnt wood, and the floor was awash with water, blood and urine. Under Lievremont's orders, the eighty marines had formed up with Keane's few men into a loose square formation, away from the windows, in the centre of the room. The wounded, almost two hundred of them, were huddled together in the middle, Henriette among them.

She had not said a word to Keane since she arrived, not least because of the attack. But now, in the calm, their eyes met again and this time there was a questioning look to her expression.

The doors had remained closed and, although from time to time they shook as the frustrated Portuguese made an effort to break them down, they held.

Gilpin had been gone an hour when Keane became aware of a change in the noise from outside. Voices were raised in anger and, among them, he heard another, more familiar. He ran to the door and pushed closer. The booming Irish tones were unmistakable.

Keane shouted to Ross, 'It's Colonel Trant. Pull down the barricades.' Faster than they had gone up, the tables, beds and other objects were taken down and, within minutes, the doors were opened.

Trant stood before them at the head of his men and Keane knew that Lievremont's marines were still behind him, at the ready, prepared, should the militia ignore their colonel and rush to the slaughter. But there was no rush.

Trant smiled at him. 'A misunderstanding, Captain Keane. That's all. Nothing more.'

'A misunderstanding that very nearly had us all killed.'

'Come on, now, Captain Keane. It was only a few of my men and they have been disciplined.'

'They have?'

'The ringleader has been dealt with. He should not have agitated in such a way. It destroys morale and establishes a mob mentality. I won't tolerate it.'

'You've had him shot?'

'Of course. What else do you suggest? This army, like the British army, works on example. I won't flog them, if I can help it. But I will hang and shoot, if I need to. Now, are you recovered?' He looked around the filthy, reeking ward with disgust. 'I told you this place was not good for the health.'

Keane smiled. 'We need to clean it up, colonel. Make it into a hospital. Perhaps your men could lend a hand.'

'Of course. After all, they had a part in making the mess.'

He noticed Henriette, standing close behind Keane, between him and Lievremont. 'I see you have met the charming Madame Lebreton. Her husband is one of our enemies, but I am sure a gallant one. Perhaps you would like to join us for dinner, madame? We will make a pleasant party now that our numbers have increased. Look, Captain Keane, I have brought you a visitor.'

He stepped aside and, for the first time, Keane noticed another figure standing behind Trant: a man in civilian dress. Small, dapper and with a beak-like nose topped with a pince-nez. He knew him before the man stepped forward to introduce himself.

'Doctor Thomas Roberts Sobral, at your service.'

7

The following day, Keane's men were reunited. He sent for Gabriella, Leech and the horses and with them had come Heredia, returned from delivering his report on Coimbra's situation to Wellington. Massena's army, as ragged as it might be, was now between them and the British lines. They were, in effect, cut off. It was nothing new to Keane and the others, and Trant, too, seemed unperturbed by the situation. Trant had assured them that his men would not attack the French again and Keane chose to believe him.

While Doctor Sobral was clearly the focus of his mission and, by right, should have been occupying his time, it was Henriette that Keane found most in his thoughts.

And so it was that, although he had told Ross and the others that he had a meeting with Doctor Sobral – which was, in fact, perfectly true – he had omitted to mention that he had contrived en route to see Henriette, at the hospital.

Walking alone as he made his way through the filthy streets towards where she nursed the enemy wounded, Keane was haunted by a sense of guilt. He had promised Henriette that he would come back to Almeida, would take her away from Marshal Massena. But, for once, Keane had not kept his word. It had dogged him ever since. He had to have the chance to explain it to her. He hoped she might forgive him and even, perhaps, take him back. He could not help but wonder how on earth it would conclude, this mad flight of fancy and lust that had begun in Almeida all those months ago.

Drawing closer to the hospital building, he told himself, as he had done throughout the long night, that it was pointless. Even if she were to forgive, quite apart from being the mistress of a French marshal, she was also married to a captain of dragoons in the enemy army. And now there was also the question of Captain Lievremont. They had not had the chance to speak privately in the mayhem of the action and he still could not tell the extent of her attachment to the captain.

But, just as loudly, another voice in his head reminded him now, as it had done when every hour had struck on the church clock through the long night, that such things had never stopped him before.

Henriette was his – his by right – by right of the fact that he loved her. She was his to take and no one – no propriety, no wealth, no rank and no captain of the Imperial Guard – would stand in his way.

He rounded the corner of the street and entered the hospital.

The approach to the hospital and the corridors had been cleared of bodies, but there were still signs of the struggle that had taken place there: patches of dark blood on the walls and discoloured, dried marks on the tiled floors.

Keane walked quickly and, passing up the stairs, soon reached the ward where he knew she must be. They had not arranged to meet, but he hoped that she might have thought he would return.

She saw him from the other end of the ward and smiled as he approached.

'I had to come and see you,' Keane said. 'I have a meeting with Doctor Sobral. We don't have much time. I just wanted to talk.'

Henriette handed a pile of bandages to one of the French orderlies and promised she would return within minutes, then she walked with Keane into the corridor. She spoke: 'I'm glad you came. I was hoping you would. I wanted to talk.'

'I owe you an apology.'

'I was wondering when you would mention that. I waited, James. A long time.'

Keane said nothing for a moment. 'I'm sorry. There was nothing I could do.'

'You said that you'd come for me, take me away from Massena. I waited, James. You didn't come.'

'Orders. There was nothing I could do.'

'Yes, you're a soldier, of course. Well, I'm used to soldiers. Remember? I'm married to one and the mistress of another.'

'How is Captain Lievremont?'

'What are you implying?'

'Nothing. I merely asked how he was.'

'As he was yesterday. And the day before. Agitated. Like an imprisoned beast, waiting to get out.'

'He may have a long wait.'

'You seem very interested in him.'

'No. Not really.'

'Could it be that you believe he and I are lovers? That you are jealous?' She smiled.

'No. Of course not.'

'Why "of course"? You know that we were, James – were lovers. And now you want me to tell you that I do not love him, that I love only you and I will never see him again. Well, I can't tell you that.'

Keane's heart sank.

She went on, 'I can't tell you that because I don't know what I feel. I don't know, James. I do feel something for you. But I feel close to Captain Lievremont. We have been through something together and that does not easily go away. Here I am, just realizing that I am still alive, when so many lie dead. And you arrive here. You walk back into my life and expect me to be what I was to you back in Almeida. And I'm not even sure if I know what I was then, if we really felt something for each other or if I was just being the whore that I am.'

He could see that she was crying and went to put his arm on her shoulder, but she brushed him away.

'No. Don't, please. That will just make it worse. If I do come to you, I will come in my own time. I don't think it's a good idea for you to come here.'

'Swear to me that you have finished with Lievremont.'

She stared at him. 'What?'

'Just tell me that you're finished and I will go.'

She shook her head. 'This is all about trust, isn't it?'

'I've said I'm sorry for leaving you at Almeida. I can beg for your forgiveness, if you want me to. It's all I can do. It didn't mean that I didn't want to come back for you.'

She laughed. 'Oh, really? I thought that Captain James Keane could do whatever he wanted to do.'

'Then you thought wrong. We're all in thrall to someone, Henriette. None of us is free.'

'Wise words. And now here you are. I have to confess, I was taken aback.'

'No more than I was. Am I right to hope that you might still care? Could you possibly?'

She smiled. 'What if I do? What would you do, in my place? How can I trust you again?'

'Perhaps you can't. And, if that is the case, then I would not blame you and we should say goodbye.' He paused. 'But I think you know that you can trust me. You want to trust me. Don't you?'

She shook her head. 'Even if I do, isn't this foolish, James? What can we hope for?'

'But I do hope. I have hoped every day since Almeida. I don't care, you know – about your husband, I mean. Or Massena.'

'You don't care that I'm French? That I'm married to an officer?'

'You don't love him.'

'You know that?'

'Yes. And he doesn't love you.'

'How do you know that?'

'How can he? How could anyone who really loved you allow you to go to Massena? I could never do that.'

'It was for the empire.'

'Rubbish. It was for the marshal. I'd have fought him, rather than that – called him out.'

'That's not my husband's way. Anyway, I had no say in it.'

'Sold off by your husband? I don't believe that, Henriette. I think you knew what you were doing. But I think it changed you.'

'You think I went to Massena from choice?'

Keane nodded and, as he did, her look became angry.

'Then we might as well stop talking now. We have nothing else to say . . . How can you think that?'

'Because I know what you're like. We're two peas in the same pod, you and me. We see a chance and we take it. That's it, isn't it? Massena might have been that chance?'

She looked away from him. 'No. Not at all. That's not how it was at all.'

'Then how was it? You're lying, Henriette. Don't lie to me. You saw your chance and then you realized what you'd done.'

'Why do you love me, James? How can you, after everything you've said? If all that is true, why would you ever love me?'

He said nothing for a moment, then, 'Because I see myself in you and I see a woman like no other I have ever known. You're beautiful, Henriette. But you're strong, too. You have a soul, but you have spirit. You don't give up. I saw you in the hospital yesterday, when it was all at its height – when, at any moment, all could have been up with us – and it told me all that I need to know, all that I've known from the start. You're one of us – like me and the men. Other people might look at you and sneer, call you the 'marshal's whore' and the rest. But I know you. You want something better from this life. Not just gold and good fortune. You want a real life. And that's what I want, too.'

'And what do you suppose we will do, James? Do you really think that you will carry me off back to England as your happy bride?'

Keane shook his head. 'You know that I don't think that. I'm an officer in the British army and you are a Frenchwoman with a personal history that would not do me any credit at St James's or at court. That's not my plan.'

'Oh, really? You have a plan?'

'When this war is over, we shall see. Perhaps France will give us a home. Ireland can be forgiving. I could purchase a small estate.'

She laughed, but he could see that she had warmed to him and that there was a spark of forgiveness, even of love, in her eye. 'You're dreaming again, James.'

'No, just planning. There's a difference. I don't bet on certainties, Henriette, but I don't bet to lose. I'm a gambling man. I play cards to win and, if I think I'm going to lose, then I'm quite happy to cheat. I don't intend to lose here. Not in this war and not with us.'

'Us? Is there an "us"?'

'I think so – if you want there to be. Do you?'

She said nothing and he thought that he might have gone too far. It was true, all of it. She was extraordinary: beautiful, headstrong, brave and feisty. She was as close to him as he had ever seen in a woman and, for that reason alone, he was not going to give her up.

'Can you wait? Will you wait?'

'I waited before.'

'Yes, but can we wait? I do believe that we will win this war. I believe that the duke will carry it off. But it will not be done speedily. This is going to be a long war, Henriette. Long and bloody. But if we make it through then we might just have a future – a new life together. Will you stay with me? Will you at least give me a chance?'

She looked at him and, for a while, said nothing. Then she nodded and, pulling him towards her, kissed him and held him there. At length, she pulled away.

'Now you had better go to Doctor Sobral. I'm sure we've kept him waiting far too long.'

He found Sobral downstairs, seated at a desk, reading, in one of the hospital's offices that had remained relatively intact after the sack.

'Captain Keane, how good to see you again.'

'How are you, doctor?'

'I am still in pain.'

'It was outrageous. That anyone would do such things to a man of your age and intellect!'

'I was lucky to escape with my life and all my faculties. What are a few broken bones to me? All I regret is that, in the end, I yielded. And for that they let me go. I can only count myself fortunate that one of their senior officers had mercy in him.' He looked at Keane and there were tears welling in his eyes. 'But only after I had betrayed you, captain. And for that there can be no excuse. Pain is a cruel master, Captain Keane. I had thought myself a better man. But I was wrong. I gave in. I betrayed you and your men, and I am heartily relieved that you managed to escape.'

Keane shook his head and patted the old man on the back as Sobral dabbed at his eyes with a handkerchief.

'Well, you are safe now, doctor. Or as safe as we, any of us, can be at this time.'

Sobral looked up and smiled. 'Thank you, captain. You saw her?'

Keane was taken aback. 'Yes. I saw her, doctor. How very shrewd you are.'

The old man smiled. 'Allow me to guess. You asked her about her feelings for Captain Lievremont.'

'How could you possibly know that?'

'Captain, when you are as old as I am, it's not much of a guess.'

He looked back down at his book but continued to speak to Keane. 'If it is any consolation, she told the French officer of her feelings for you yesterday.'

'Are you certain?'

'He told me as much.'

'He told you?'

Sobral nodded. 'I seem to attract the confidences of young men. Particularly young men such as you. I think you are troubled, captain.'

Keane said nothing.

Sobral continued: 'It is interesting when you come to the final years of your life that you seem to find those who, in some way, echo some lost part of you, some earlier you. I think that is what I see in you, Captain Keane.'

Keane looked at him and wondered how the man could think that he might understand someone whom he had only known for a few days.

'I have spent my life here in Coimbra. A life devoted to study. I began with humanities and, when I was acquainted with all that history had to offer, then I began to question the world around me. That is why I set up the chemical laboratory here. We need to know about our world, captain. Don't you agree? Only by knowing the world we live in can we hope to explain the great questions: who we are, why we are here and where we are going.'

'You were a teacher here? Yes, I knew that. A chemist, I thought.'

'Yes, I was a chemist. To be precise, I was director of the chemical laboratory, which had been built for teaching chemistry in the 1770s, when I was a student here myself. But I enlarged it. I made it what it is . . . sorry – what it was. What it epitomized to me was the spirit of the age – an age of hope. The Enlightenment, captain. What years! And what hope we had! I established the greatest centre in the world for the ideology of the experimental teaching of science.'

He paused and looked down, seemingly lost in thought. When he looked back again, his eyes were glassy with water.

'But, captain, ask yourself, what does that mean to be a chemist – a man who transforms materials from one thing to another, who can change the way something behaves, who can change the very way that we see and make the useless into the precious? So, yes, I am a chemist. But, you see, that is a very big word.'

Keane nodded. He did see. This man was much more than he had first appeared. He was not just a man of science and a teacher. He was a thinker, a philosopher. But he was more, too, than that. Doctor Sobral was a symbol – a totem of everything that the nation stood for. He was a symbol of hope, in particular, for the young men he had taught – those same young men who now formed such a vital part of Trant's militia.

Keane understood more than ever why they had done what they had to the French. This was not just about rape and pillage, about attacks upon peasant girls. This was about their hatred for men who would torture a man they revered – a man who, to them, was the very spirit of their country.

And there was another side to Sobral, too. One that, at this moment, was vital to Keane's purpose. Here was a man who knew every inch of the old city – every tunnel and catacomb, every library and lecture theatre of the university. He was sure that Sobral could find the book. Keane looked at him and saw in his returned gaze that Sobral was ahead of him.

'And, Captain Keane, I believe that we need to talk on another matter, do we not? I believe that you are searching for a book.'

'And I believe that you might be able to assist me.'

'I may be able to help you find it, but I doubt if even I will be able to translate its information.'

Keane smiled. 'I have a man – one of my own men – highly intelligent, name of Archer. He has an aptitude for code breaking. I think he might be able to help us, doctor.'

'Well, that may be so. But, to my knowledge, the book you seek has never been entirely understood. Nevertheless, he may be the man to manage it. I will do what I can to help him.'

They started towards the door and, as they did, Keane was aware of movement outside – footsteps. He opened the door quickly and shot a glance down the corridor, quick enough to see a flash of an orange-trimmed blue officer's uniform hurrying around the corner. Lievremont. Keane wondered if he had been listening at the door and, if so, how much he had heard. He wondered, too, about his motive. Surely he had not guessed about Keane and Henriette? But what other reason could there be? Keane dismissed the notion and turned back to Sobral. 'Sorry, doctor, I thought I heard someone. It was nothing. Now, shall we find that book?'

It was not far from the hospital to the great library and, on the way, Keane passed by the men's billet, where he found Archer. Then the three of them continued, slipping silently through the streets. Sobral knew every alleyway of the city and, under his guidance, they managed to avoid what might have been the troublesome enquiries of Trant's men, who had set up guard posts at the major road crossings to deter any French who might seek to leave the safe haven of the hospital.

Reaching the building without incident, they stopped before its two great doors.

Keane spoke: 'This is the great library.'

Sobral gazed up at the statues on the façade: on the right, Honour, and to the left, Virtue. 'Yes,' he said, 'this is the place.'

Together, they entered, pushing at the doors, which, standing already ajar, swung open. The place seemed to Keane just as he had left it. But Sobral stopped in his tracks and gasped.

'I'm sorry. I had forgotten how beautiful this place was. I have not been back in here since the French came. I have not yet had a chance to see what has become of it.'

Archer walked carefully across the marble of the atrium and further into the library and stopped before the second set of doors, staring at the piles of torn books and scattered papers that lay strewn all around the gilded hall. He shook his head. 'It's incredible, sir. Look at this. How can anyone do this?'

Sobral provided an answer: 'Alas, I think it is only too common. The French take everything. They destroy anything of beauty in their path or carry it away. It is almost as if it is planned as part of their strategy. It's what they have been doing for years. For Bonaparte, looting is a declaration of his triumph, just as it was for the Romans.' He turned to Keane. 'You're an educated man, captain. That I can tell. Think of Casear and Pompey.'

Keane smiled and shook his head. As bizarre as it seemed, for the second time in a week someone was talking to him about ancient history, Greeks and Romans. Things he had thought he had heard the last of years ago seemed suddenly to have taken on a new importance, a new value. Sobral had opened his eyes to something bigger than the campaign – the war, even:

Bonaparte was not just fighting a war, he was making a whole new world. That was why they had to stop him.

Sobral went on, 'It is a demonstration of his ideological goals. Napoleon imagines that he is founding a new empire to rival that of Rome. It is his goal to demonstrate the similarity and the superiority of Napoleonic France to ancient Rome.'

Archer nodded. 'Yes, of course. That is why he does this. Think about it, sir. Napoleon not only follows the Roman model of looting, but he seeks to seize the treasures of the Roman Empire itself. For Napoleon, conquering Rome meant conquering a symbol of power, and he took symbolic possession of its treasures. Imagine the savage eating the heart of his noble enemy in order to digest his powers. He believes that the rustic, boorish Romans, once an uncultivated race, only became civilized by transporting to Rome the works of conquered Greece. Now France will do the same.'

Keane nodded, impressed by Archer's eloquence and passion.

Sobral went on, bending to pick up a ruined book. 'Napoleon's armies purged Rome of its most treasured cultural objects. And now our country is to suffer the same fate.

'Five hundred paintings and sculptures from the Vatican, paraded through the streets of Paris. The Laocoön, the Apollo Belvedere, the Medici Venus and the Discobolus. The treasures of Venice, too. The horses of San Marco, the great bronzes that Venice herself had taken from Constantinople in 1204. Of course, Constantinople, too, had obtained them by violence. Think about that – how the beauties and wonders of our civilization are taken time and again.'

Archer spoke up: 'Napoleon doesn't want these things for their cultural value. He wants them as political tools.'

Sobral smiled. 'Quite right. And it's all done to order. This is no isolated looting by generals and private soldiers. Did you know that? He's systematic. Have you ever heard of the Commission Temporaire des Arts? It's a subcommittee set up after the Revolution to compile lists of works of art in countries where the Republican army would invade. Under Napoleon's specific direction, his armies seized thousands of works of art throughout the countries he invaded.'

'They take what the emperor orders?'

'And don't forget they have leave to destroy anything else they want to. They burnt my house, captain. Not only that, but they destroyed my library. My books, captain. Who would do such a thing? Destroying knowledge – the very essence of humanity?'

'And they tortured you, doctor.'

Sobral looked down at his hands and held them up before his face, as if he were looking at some beautiful object that had been damaged. Keane had noticed that they were bandaged and guessed what he was about to say.

'Yes. They broke my fingers.' He paused. 'My fingers. I suppose I will never play the piano again. It is but a small sacrifice, in real terms – compared with what is happening to my countrymen.'

Keane shook his head and touched the old man gently on the shoulder. 'Think nothing of it, doctor, please, I beg you. It is I who should be sorry and grateful to you for your resistance. Such inhumanity sullies the name of honour.'

'These men know nothing of honour, Captain Keane. They know only the way of the sword and the power of brute force. Bonaparte's empire might have been born from the Revolution, but his soldiers have long lost the roots of the spirit that fanned that great conflagration into flame.'

'Why should they have come for you so quickly? How did they suspect that you might know our whereabouts?'

'It was well known that I was sympathetic to the British and that I also had made gunpowder. When they were outside the city, and when they entered, the students and the citizens who were left fired at them using my gunpowder. That is why they hated me. I had become known as the "Master of Gunpowder."'

Archer turned to Keane. 'Remind me again why we're here, sir.'

'You're searching for a book, Archer. A picture book. The *Très Sainte Trinosophie*.'

'Sounds intriguing.'

'Doctor Sobral will explain everything.'

Sobral nodded. 'It's quite distinct. A triangular book with red calf binding.'

Archer looked around them. 'One book, among so many.'

'I'm sure that you'll find it,' Keane said. 'I'll leave you to it.'

'We'll do our best, sir.'

'Yes, I'm sure you will. You have to find it, Archer.'

Since the affair at the hospital, Trant had kept his distance and so it was a surprise for Keane to see one of the colonel's orderlies waiting for him outside his quarters.

'Captain Keane. You have a visitor.'

'A visitor?'

'Yes, sir – a Colonel Grant. He is with Colonel Trant now. Please, we will go to see him.'

They found Grant with Trant sitting outside the latter's billet; as usual, a bottle of rosé stood on the table. Trant took a long draught and poured himself a fresh glass.

'Ah, Keane. Colonel Grant here was just singing your praises as an exploring officer. Apparently, you're quite something; a talented artist as well as a linguist.'

Grant stood. 'James, good to see you.'

'Colonel, I'm surprised to see you here.'

'Oh, I'm everywhere these days, James. Quite the well travelled man. I was passing close by, en route to a rendezvous, and thought that I might see you both. Colonel Trant and I go back a long way.'

Trant laughed. 'Yes, you could say that, couldn't you, Grant? A damn long way back. Where was it exactly our paths first crossed?'

'I seem to recollect that it was in Egypt, Trant. Would that be right?'

'You might be, Colonel, you might be. You'll take another drink?'

'No, thank you, colonel. Not just yet. I'll join you presently. If you'll excuse us, I must speak to Captain Keane on a trifling, personal matter. My apologies.'

Trant nodded. 'Of course, of course. Old friends, Grant. I'll have a bottle waiting for you.'

He waved his hand at his servant and turned the bottle upside down to indicate that another was required.

As the man scurried off to fetch it, Grant motioned Keane to follow him and, together, they walked a little distance away from Trant, deeper into the overgrown gardens of the villa, where the scent of the bougainvillea flowers mixed with the more prevalent stench of ordure that seemed to haunt the city.

Grant clapped him on the back. 'So, how do you find my old friend, the colonel?'

'Shall we just say, sir, that he's an acquired taste.'

'And have you acquired that taste, James? Do you and he share "that taste"?'

Keane knew that, in saying it, Grant meant he was eager to know if Trant's particular brand of maverick personal interest, curiously aligned to duty to his commission, might now mimic Keane's own attitude. He shook his head.

'I have yet to do so. I am inclined more to pursue the orders of my commanders than the temptation of self interest.'

Grant laughed. 'Are you quite sure, James? Whatever your stance, that's a bold accusation.'

'I'm accusing no one, sir. I'm merely stating that I find Colonel Trant's very particular way of soldiering not entirely in keeping with my own.'

Grant laughed again. 'That's reassuring, James.'

'So what exactly is it you need to tell me, sir? This trifling matter?'

'You know as well as I that was a ruse.'

Keane nodded and smiled.

Grant continued, 'Well, James, the truth is, there's some good news and some not so good. Firstly, the Portuguese have had a change of heart.'

'I can't say that I'm entirely surprised.'

'No, not the common people. The regency. Just as we conduct our planned retreat to the lines, the Portuguese regency, despite having initially agreed to the peer's evacuation of their population and to his scorched-earth policies, has changed its colours.'

'Ah, I think I see.'

'According to Sir Charles Stuart, the Portuguese regent, Prince John – and also, I believe, his wife – have been terribly upset by the devastation being wrought in his country and the sacrifice expected of his people.'

'How very sensitive of him.'

'What it means, James, is that those bumpkins in St James's have suggested to the duke – suggested, if you please – that he should cease what they can only see as his retreat and fight a pitched battle against the French.'

Keane shook his head. 'But, sir, haven't we done just that at bloody Bussaco? And look where it got us. Here, to this god-forsaken place and among all this death.'

'My point exactly. There are even rumours going around that the British plan to abandon Portugal entirely to the French.'

'Impossible, sir. The peer would never do that. Would he?'

'No, never, of course not. You might not think so, James, but the peer has a genuine concern for this nation.'

Keane shook his head. 'I can't see much evidence of it, sir. Burning the country and abandoning its people to their fate.'

'I know it seems like that, but you must realize that, as a commander, he has to take such decisions. He has to sacrifice the few to save the many. It is a hard mantle to wear, James. You or I would not take to it. And, don't worry, he's putting up a brave show. It will take more than Major Cavanagh and his friends at court doing this to force the duke into changing his master plan. Shall we find a glass of something? I'm uncommonly thirsty.'

They walked back towards the table, where Trant was still sitting, and, as they did, Keane noticed that the colonel was now asleep, or at least he appeared to be, his great head lolling back on his shoulder. Grant lifted two glasses and the bottle from the table.

'I doubt he'll miss these now. Where was I?'

They walked away from the snoring colonel.

'You were talking about the Portuguese, sir. The regency.'

'Ah, yes. Well, you see, with their present attitude, and the duke being so set on his plan, we are more desperate than ever to get hold of the book.'

'The book – ah, yes.'

'We have other reasons of our own, now. We need some sort of glorious success to hold up to Prince John and his courtiers. A positive and verified report of the book would be the perfect thing. Keane, it is absolutely paramount that you obtain it.'

'We're doing our best, sir. But, you must understand, in a library of three hundred thousand books and with no apparent guide, even Archer and Doctor Sobral are hard pressed.'

'Yes, James, I can see that, but time is of the essence.' Grant took a sip of wine and Keane made use of the pause to take the initiative.

'Sir, may I ask what it is that really brings you here?'

Grant looked at him. 'Oh, you know, the usual business. Information, Keane. That's our business, isn't it? Intelligence.'

'Yes, sir, of course. But I believe – '

Grant held up his hand. 'You believe that there is some other motive and you are quite correct, James. You are very shrewd.'

'You mean to impart some new report?'

'Much has been discovered, James. Much that may impact upon the army and much that may impact upon yourself.'

'Go on, sir, if you will.'

'We have had intelligence from Massena's army. A rumour has been circulated among his men that all the Frenchmen left in Coimbra, the garrison and the wounded alike, have been put to the sword.'

'That's outrageous.'

'Quite so. And it has clearly been done quite deliberately. It's designed specifically to incite hatred against us. And, more particularly, against the Portuguese. This is the sort of thing that happened with the Spanish. Once it starts, it can't be stopped. One side does something in revenge and then the other follows suit.'

'They know that it was Trant and his men who took the city?'

'Yes. Never forget that they, too, have their eyes and ears.'

'By God, they'll be after his blood.'

'That they will. That, indeed, they are. And that of his men. But it's not just that. Massena was already unpopular with his men, as much as he is with the emperor. The feeling in the army was that he should never have left Coimbra. That was the soldiers' instinct. With this rumour, they will hate him even more.'

'So it wasn't Massena who put it round?'

'No, James, most certainly it was not.'

'Then who?'

'Perhaps Bonaparte himself? Or, more likely, someone who wants Massena out of the picture and who might himself have something to gain by it.'

'Another general? A marshal? Ney? Soult?'

'It seems not beyond the bounds of possibility. Or perhaps an agent provocateur out for his own gain and hoping, through helping to ruin Massena, to curry favour with the emperor in Paris.'

Keane shook his head. 'Macnab?'

'It seems more than likely to me.'

'That man would appear to be everywhere.'

'And it seems to me that it might be a priority to arrange for his removal.'

'I intend to manage that at the earliest opportunity.'

'Well, James, you might be in luck. He's bound to come here.'

'Macnab? To Coimbra? With Trant and his men here? Only a fool would do that.'

'A fool – or perhaps someone who believes himself to be untouchable. James, that man has such an opinion of himself to think that he can evade death. He's managed it four times at least thus far, to my knowledge.'

'Then I shall have to prove him wrong, sir. You think he'll come here in search of the book?'

Grant nodded. 'Think about it, James. He's ambitious. He wants— No, I should say, he *needs* to ingratiate himself with Bonaparte. What better way than to hand him, personally, something on which he has fixed his sights? In fact, just what Massena intends to do and for the same reason. But, at the same time as doing that, of course, Macnab would also discredit Massena. Take my word for it. If he doesn't have the book already – and I'll wager he doesn't – then Macnab will come to Coimbra.'

Keane shook his head. 'As usual, his plan is brilliant and infuriating in its completeness.'

'I also have reason to believe that he will pretend to Massena that he is coming here to obtain the book for him. That is the nature of the man. He trusts no one and is faithful to no one save himself.'

'He will never have the book, sir. You can be certain of that.'

It was a bold, hugely rash promise, but Keane couldn't help but say it. Grant was aware of his bluster, but secretly impressed.

'Take care, James, not to make too many promises.'

'I only ever make promises I know I can keep, sir.' More bluster, Keane cursed himself for it.

Grant smiled. 'As you will. I know you will do your best, James, and I fully expect to hear a report of his death. But do not allow yourself to be outwitted. I cannot afford to lose you.'

8

Like a murderer revisiting the scene of the crime or a dog drawn to its own rotting faeces, as hard as Macnab might resist, Keane knew that he would be sure to return to the places he knew in Coimbra. Just as Keane was certain that he must have revisited the ruins of his shattered billet in Celorico, where he had staged his own death the previous year in an explosion that had cost three good men.

So, for the last two days, Keane had kept a careful watch.

Sobral had told him that he had been tortured by Macnab in the city's old prison building in the lower town, and this, it seemed to Keane, might be the most likely location in which Macnab would make his new base. He had posted sentries, his own men, sharp eyed and trusted, at the key entrances to the prison.

But thus far there had been no sign of the man.

Over the same two days, Archer and Doctor Sobral had been hunting for the precious book in the university library and still they had not found it. Indeed, at times, Keane had begun to doubt its very existence and wondered if the whole thing might not be an elaborate ruse, dreamt up by the French to put them off the scent of some genuine prize or plan. But Sobral had assured him that the book did exist and he respected the old man's opinion. Sobral told him that he understood the classification system of the library, but, having searched in the places where it should be, neither he nor Archer had found the book.

Keane was well aware that to locate the book was of paramount importance and was considering putting more of his men on the search, even though he thought that they would quite probably miss it. And while he persuaded himself that this would be the case, there was another reason why the troop were not all in the library. For, in his heart, Keane had to acknowledge that the chance to encounter Macnab again took precedence over any mission and, for that reason, had stationed the men across the city in key positions with the instruction to keep a sharp lookout for the traitor.

And there was another thing. Ever since their meeting at Leiria, Keane had been troubled by a niggling doubt about Wellington. He had no cause to question the peer's military skills. It was in his handling of the Portuguese that he differed so much. Or perhaps it was, allied to this, the fact that the man seemed to want to deny his Irish roots in a way in which Keane would never have dreamt of doing. Most of all, though, it lay in the suspicion that Wellington might know the identity of his father. If this was the case, then why the devil had he not thought to suggest to him whom it might be? It had been something that Trant had said that had put the germ of the idea in his head and now he could not lose it. He had thought to probe Trant again on the subject, but the time had not yet arisen and, in any case, he wondered whether the colonel would be any more forthcoming in his answer than the peer. He wondered if they were teasing him, or testing him.

Either way, it annoyed him intensely to think he might be being manipulated. If there was one thing he had learnt over the last year, it was to always be one step ahead. And now, here he was – several steps behind, it seemed, in all things.

With the frustration on all these matters growing inside him, Keane sat on the terrace of the Bishop's Palace with Trant and drew on a slim cheroot as he watched the colonel's junior officers drilling their men in the afternoon sunshine on the plaza. He had picked up the habit of smoking the Spanish cigars from Trant and found it relaxing on the nerves – particularly when, as now, there was much on his mind.

He had avoided Henriette and had not even revisited the hospital since their last encounter. What, he wondered, might be the point? For, despite what Sobral had told him, he was still not convinced she had ended relations with Lievremont. After all, he told himself, hadn't she betrayed her own husband for Massena and then Massena for him? Why should she be loyal to anyone? But still a voice in his soul refused to be silent, telling him that she might just be his as he had hoped she would be. He exhaled and watched the blue smoke as it rose against the azure sky.

Trant spoke: 'Did you ever hear of a man in Salamanca – an Irishman – name of Curtis?'

Keane shook his head. 'No, colonel, I can't say that I did.'

'Oh, he's well known. Quite well known, if you know what I mean. He's a good friend of the peer. Father Cortez, they call him – Patrice Cortez – as if he was a Spaniard himself, when he's no more Spanish than you or I.'

He paused and blew smoke out before taking another drink.

'But perhaps, in your case, you might have some Spanish blood, Keane. Do you think?'

Keane stiffened. It was a direct reference to his father and, in effect, an insult. Although to have responded to that end would have not only insulted the Spanish but also been insubordinate.

He held himself in check. 'No, you're wrong there, colonel. I'm as Irish as you. And as the peer himself.'

Trant laughed. 'Now, there you have me. But I am aware, captain, of what it is that irks you. And I think that I might be able to offer some assistance. What we need to do is to have a sit down and have a good old talk. But we need time for that, don't we? I'd like to tell you more about Father Curtis – Don Patrizio, that is – and other matters. I believe that the old father might have the clues for which you're looking. But that will have to wait until we both have the time. For, I can tell, at the moment, you're impatient to be away.'

Keane shook his head. 'That's where you're wrong, colonel. I'm in no particular hurry.'

'Are you not? I was under the impression that the good colonel had given you a most urgent mission. Isn't that the case?'

'I have men working on it.'

'Oh, have you? Of course, the good doctor and that very clever boy of yours. What's his name? Archer, isn't it? The Scot. A disgraced doctor, isn't that right? A resurrectionist.' He pretended to shiver. 'Ghastly business. Clever boy, though. But have you not another matter in hand, yourself?'

Keane said nothing. Had he told Trant so much about Archer? Perhaps, in his cups. And how could the man know anything of Macnab?

'Another matter, colonel?'

'A matter of honour, isn't it? Which you must feel the need to settle.'

Again Keane was dumbstruck. He was at last about to say something when Trant began again, turning his glass in his hand as if observing the colour of the wine. 'Come, come, Keane. The French lieutenant. I know that you have a problem with his affections for Madame Lebreton. Can't say I blame you. Or him. Lovely girl. But I shouldn't get too carried away with her, Keane. You know where all that leads – only too well, I hear. Take my advice.'

More teasing. So perhaps Trant did not know about Macnab, but then what could explain his last comment? Did he know of the affair with Kitty Blackwood and her brother's death at Keane's hands? Grant had been in earnest when he had warned Keane to be on his guard around the colonel.

'I'll keep my own counsel, Trant, if you'll oblige me. But thank you for the advice.'

Trant smiled again. 'As you will. But don't say I didn't warn you. Now, I think that I must take my leave, much as I would love to stay and join you in your leisure. I have work to do. I must put my men through their paces, keep them battle ready. Sadly, we are not all able to enjoy the life of the "exploring officer".'

Keane bristled but managed to restrain himself; instead, he merely stood and smiled at Trant.

The comment had hit hard on a nerve. He continued to have doubts about his command and was aware that he might not be putting as much as he should into his present task. It was not like him and he knew it stemmed from a disaffection with what he had become – the more so since he had been in Coimbra. He longed to be back with his own regiment, the 27th, meeting the French in a firefight, urging his men on in an attack, there, on the field of glory, with everything to play for. This hiatus was unbearable and, coupled with all of his current frustrations, it amounted to no less than torture.

He was still sitting on the terrace nursing a glass of wine when there was a respectful cough from behind him. He turned to see Doctor Sobral and Archer. Keane leapt from his chair. 'You've found it? The book?'

But Sobral shook his head. 'No, sadly, we have not.'

Keane glared at him and thumped the table with his fist. 'Damn it, man. How the devil can you not manage to find it? The thing must stand out a mile, even in that place. Christ, it can't be that bloody hard, can it?' He rounded on Archer. 'How hard have you tried? The bloody thing must be in there somewhere. Macnab can't have taken it already. Can he?'

The question was really aimed at himself, but Archer answered.

'Well, sir, I'd dearly like to believe he has not, and – yes – I have tried my utmost to find it and so has Doctor Sobral, to the very best of his ability. Believe me.'

Keane stared at him for a few moments then looked back to the doctor. 'Good God, I'm so sorry, doctor. Please accept my apologies; what was I thinking of with such an outburst? Of course, I realize you're doing your best. It's just so infuriating. You understand?' He paused. 'A glass of wine? A seat?'

'I'll accept both from you, captain, and, don't worry, I do understand your situation.'

Sobral sat down at the table and Archer poured him a glass of the pale rosé wine from which he took a small, slow, dainty sip before continuing.

'The truth is, we simply cannot find it. We have looked in every possible location that it might logically have been placed, and even some more unlikely areas.'

Archer added, 'And we searched carefully all over the books on the floor and through the torn-out pages –'

'But it is nowhere to be found, captain,' Sobral interrupted.

'So he may have got to it first. But how on earth could Macnab have found it already, when you cannot, doctor?'

Sobral shook his head. 'You don't understand me, captain. I don't believe that he has found it.'

'Then who the hell would take such a thing? Who would want it, or even know about it? One of the students?'

Sobral shook his head again. 'No, I don't think so. They are too concerned now with fighting. They have forgotten their studies and cannot wait to leave this place to face the enemy. They swear allegiance to the university but they forget what that means. Besides, why would they take that book? They would not realize its significance.'

He took another short sip of wine and then, after wiping his lips on a small handkerchief, reached into his pocket. 'After we had searched the library for the fourteenth time, I returned again to the place where I thought I could recall having last seen the book. And I found this. I suppose I must have missed it before, not being aware that I was looking for anything other than a red-bound book. It might explain matters.' Sobral produced a piece of folded paper, which he handed to Keane, unfolding it.

Keane stared at the writing, squinting. After five minutes, he spoke. 'I can't make head nor tail of it.'

Sobral smiled. 'No, nor could I, at first.'

'What about you, Archer?'

'It's most definitely in some sort of code, sir. I'm still trying to crack it.'

Keane gave the paper to Archer and turned to Sobral. 'So you think it's a clue?'

'It was placed, quite carefully, in the location in the library which was the most likely for us to have found the *Très Sainte Trinosophie*. At least, it was the one place where I do remember having seen the book in the past. But that was some years ago, of course.' He smiled. 'You understand I am not in the habit of perusing occult manuscripts in unreadable hieroglyphs.'

'So it seems that it might be a clue. Do you suppose that it was left deliberately to guide anyone searching for the book?'

'Quite probably, yes.'

'But whoever in Coimbra would have done such a thing? Is there anyone left here except the French and the militia and us? Who would have taken it? Is there anyone else here who would want it?'

'No – or, at least, I didn't think so.'

Keane thought for a moment. 'But it's gone and we must conclude, I think, that, unless it has been destroyed, which is not impossible, then it is more than likely still somewhere in the city.'

Sobral nodded. 'That was my assumption, captain. As I said, I hadn't thought there was anyone else in the city.'

'So you think that there might be someone else here? Of whom we are not aware? They will have seen the city change hands and will now be concerned that the book will not be safe in the library. And, if someone went to the trouble to leave a clue – or, at least, an explanation – written in code for those who might be seeking it, then it is reasonable to conclude that both that person and the book must now be safe and still within the city.'

Sobral nodded. 'Correct again, I think.'

Keane sighed with relief. 'Thank God for that, at least. Archer, have you any idea at all what it means?'

The young man glanced up at him from the paper, which he had been looking at assiduously as they had been speaking, writing notes in a small book as he did so. 'I'm making some progress. Doctor Sobral has been very helpful.'

Sobral spoke: 'You recall, captain, that, when we first met, I mentioned in passing that the tunnels had been created by the Jesuits, who had originally occupied the university at Coimbra until they were suppressed?'

'Yes, of course, but has this something to do with the book?'

'Quite possibly it is a clue as to who might have taken it. Although they were suppressed, the Jesuits continued to thrive in secret. Not just here in Portugal, but in every nation in which they had been treated the same way. They infiltrated the highest levels of society. And, in revenge on the govern-ments of all those nations which had suppressed them, they determined to create division within and without states. They swore a terrible oath. Listen to this.'

He produced a small leather-bound book from his pocket and opened it at a marked page. He began to read: 'I swear to insidiously plant the seeds of jealousy and hatred between com-munities, provinces and states that are at peace, and to incite them to deeds of blood, involving them in war with each other. To create revolutions and civil wars in countries that are inde-pendent and prosperous, cultivating the arts and the sciences and enjoying the blessings of peace. To take sides with the com-batants and to act secretly in concert with my brother Jesuits, who might be engaged on the other side, but openly opposed to that with which I might be connected. I will do this only that the Church might be the ultimate victor in the end, and that, whatever the cost to humanity, that end justifies the means.'

Keane thought for a moment. 'That's a dreadful oath. A

promise to create wars and condemn millions to death, and all in the name of the Church?'

'Yes, it's chilling, isn't it? You see, for the Jesuits, the Pope was the ultimate ruler on earth, over all others. Tell me, captain, you are an intelligent man, what does that oath tell you about what their attitude might be towards Bonaparte?'

'Surely that, like all the other rulers, they would bring him down.'

'Yes, of course. But not before they had done their utmost to use him to create as much bloodshed in the world as possible. If they knew about the book and its importance to him, what do you suppose they would they do?'

'Give it to him?' He paused. 'Or keep it hidden.'

'Exactly.'

'So you think a Jesuit has hidden it?'

'Yes, that's my guess and I also think that the code is one of theirs, readable only by the Jesuit brotherhood. They often used ciphers – here in Europe and in South America. This is probably a polyalphabetic cipher. But that doesn't make it any easier for us. We still have to find the code. The rhythm.'

Keane paused for further thought.

'So, if I understand you correctly, what you're telling me, doctor, is that it's possible that Macnab is in league with the Jesuits and that he has an accomplice in the city?'

Sobral nodded. 'He may even be a Jesuit himself. Think about it. The brotherhood was banned in both France and Spain by the Bourbons – persecuted, even – and who was it that replaced the Bourbons after the Revolution? Bonaparte. And who was crowned, at his own insistence, by the Pope?'

'Wait, doctor,' Keane interrupted. 'You are telling me now that Bonaparte is a Jesuit?'

'Not exactly; though, for all I know, he may well be. The Jesuits fled to Corsica, among other places, and he is a Corsican. But, whether or not Bonaparte is a Jesuit, the fact remains that if Macnab is one then he will most certainly believe that, by getting the book to Bonaparte himself, he will be personally helping the Jesuit cause and will receive his just rewards not only on earth but in heaven.'

'You really think this is possible?'

'I believe that it is, captain. This country is full of strange beliefs. I am a man of science. I believe in what I see and what I am able to prove. But there are many who are not like me, who hold beliefs that I cannot fathom.'

Keane nodded. 'Yes, I know. I've seen it – here and throughout my life. In Egypt, with their gods and temples, and, God knows, not least in my own homeland. The things men will do in the name of God back there beggars belief. I'm like you, doctor. Though I don't pretend to have your wisdom and knowledge. I'm a simple man. I know where I put my faith: in a sharp sword, a well balanced gun and the hope that some greater power, if one exists, might spare me from the bullet that bears my name. I have no business with this mumbo jumbo. But, by God, I've seen its effect on others.'

He reached for the bottle and poured a glass of wine, which he drank fast to calm his nerves while Sobral took another sip.

Keane went on, 'So, let's say that you're right, that some Jesuit fanatic working here in Coimbra took the book to a place of safety for Macnab to collect and left a note for him in code. A note which we now have.'

'Yes, that's about it.'

'And if we break the code, then we will also find the book before Macnab?'

'We've beaten him to the note.'

Keane turned to Archer. 'Anything?'

'Sir, you must understand, to break any cipher takes time.'

'And time is precisely what we don't have.'

Archer spoke: 'Sir, I think I have it – the cipher.'

Keane sat up. 'You have? How? What does it mean?'

'Well, Doctor Sobral was right. It is really very simple, after all. It's a polyalphabetic cipher consisting of six rows of cipher alphabets, each having a regular alphabetical sequence, but excluding the letters J, K, V and Y, with different starting positions. To encipher it, you have to start by looking for the first letter to be enciphered in the first row and taking the number above the letter as the cipher for the letter. The second letter is enciphered with the second row, and so on. To encipher the seventh letter, the first row is used again.'

He paused. Keane nodded, blankly. Archer continued, 'Proper switching of the six rows is essential to get the right meaning. If a row is repeated or skipped, the resulting cipher will simply be – well – undecipherable.'

'That sounds good, Archer. What hope have the French when we have you? So, what does the note say? Where is the book?'

'I've translated the note, sir. Here, see what you make of it.'

Archer handed the paper to Keane.

Keane read, 'Friend, I have taken the book which you seek to keep it safe. If you wish to possess it, you will find me in the crypt of the college of the eleven thousand, where our late masters prepared their mission. Note well, I will be there only at a certain time. At that time after the orb reflects the world and before the moment of St Peter's denial.'

Keane shook his head and handed back the paper.

'It's gobbledygook. I'm no clearer. You might as well have

left it in code, Archer. What the devil does it mean? Who are the eleven thousand and what on earth is the mission of our masters?'

Sobral smiled. 'Allow me to explain. The college of the eleven thousand refers to the Jesus College, that is the College of the Eleven Thousand Virgins. It was founded in 1542 for the Jesuits – the first Jesuit college in the whole world and the largest in Coimbra.

'Its role was to prepare missionaries. When the Jesuits were expelled in 1759, the college became part of the university. Its church became the New Cathedral and in 1775 it was converted to house the Museum of Natural History. That's where our friend has the book. Simple.'

'That's extraordinary. Well done, doctor, and well done, Archer. Now we'll get that bloody book.'

Archer shrugged. 'Unless Macnab beats us to it.'

'How can he do that? We have the note.'

'But you're forgetting, sir. He's Macnab, isn't he? He has ways of finding out.'

'Nonsense, Archer. The man's not some mysterious magus. He's just a man, like us. All this occult rubbish is getting to you.'

'If you say so, sir.'

'Doctor, tell us when we should go. Explain the timings to me.'

'It's exactly what I was expecting. It's Jesuit iconography, captain. The orb refers to an emblem book written in the seventeenth century by the Jesuit, Willem Hesius. The *Emblemata Sacra de Fide, Spe, Caritate*. In the symbol called "Capit Quod Non Capit", a winged boy, a symbol of the soul, is shown holding a sphere reflecting a cross and the sun. So, as I see it, he is telling us he'll be there "after sunrise". St Peter's denial, of course, is from the Bible, when Christ told Peter that he would deny him before the cock had crowed three times. So I think he means after sunrise but before cock crow. It's a slim window.'

Keane looked at him. 'You are astonishing, doctor.'

Archer spoke: 'Sir, what should we do now?'

Keane smiled. 'We go to the college when he tells us he will be there, and then we can be certain that we will find the book.'

The sun had just touched the crest of the hills to the east of Coimbra when, with his men following, Keane led the way through the quiet streets of the city. They moved in silence into the narrow street outside the Bishop's Palace and walked the bare hundred yards that led to the western entrance of the old Jesuit College, now the Museum of Natural History. The building had a towering baroque façade in which four niches carried statues of Jesuit saints, so Sobral had said. There was a huge coat of arms and, atop everything, a massive stone cross. Clearly, it had been designed to impress and intimidate. And it certainly served its purpose. It was not, however, through this façade that Keane now entered the building, but through a modest side entrance. Sobral had, of course, wanted to accompany them, but Keane had ordered him to remain behind with Gabriella. It was almost certain that Macnab would be waiting for them and, if that were the case, who could say how many men he might have with him?

Keane had also considered the possibility that the writer of the note might not be a quiet cleric, as described to him by Sobral, but rather a fanatical Jesuit, armed to the teeth. Either way, Sobral stayed.

Keane had managed to find a French officer's coat to fit him from the many at the hospital. Doctor Sobral had helped him, having access to the stores. He had put this on and, over the top, now wore a grey cloak. The French were still confined to the hospital and he didn't want to risk an encounter with any of the Portuguese.

His men wore their brown uniforms. They were to remain concealed behind him and only to intervene if he was discovered.

Keane tried the iron handle of the door and was surprised that it opened with ease. He looked behind and waved his hand in an indication to keep silent, then he entered.

They found themselves in a low atrium of cool stone, with a vaulted ceiling. Sobral had told him that this was the safest way to enter the church and that to go through the apse was the only way to gain access to the crypt. On the opposite side of the room was another door. Without hesitating, Keane walked across the tiled floor towards it and, after listening at it for a few minutes to ensure no one was beyond, pushed it open. Walking through, he had to stop for a moment to take in the sight which met him. He was standing in a magnificent, soaring church.

Pushing in behind him, Silver let out a gasp. 'Oh, my good God.'

Keane reprimanded him with a glare.

'Sorry, sir.'

But he could hardly blame the man. The interior was huge – a great cathedral of white stone with coffered ceilings sixty feet high and everywhere gilded wooden decoration.

'Where's the door to the crypt, sir?'

'Close to the dome, Sarn't Ross. Follow me, all of you.'

The nine men moved as silently as they could along the wall

of the church until they were standing beneath the great dome. As one, they looked upwards and were rewarded by an ornately painted ceiling eighty feet above them on the interior of the dome, showing Christ in triumph, surrounded by the saints.

Ross spoke first. 'That's what they do best, sir, the papists. They love their art, they do, sir.'

'If you say so, sarn't.'

Gilpin gasped. 'I never saw the like; it's like . . . like they're all actually alive, isn't it? Up there, Jesus and all the saints.'

Silver nudged him. 'Hark at him. "Jesus and all the saints." Careful, Sam, you'll be turning into a bloody believer next.'

Gilpin rounded on him. 'Who says I'm not already? I know what I believe in, and, anyway, what business is it of yours?'

Keane turned to them. 'Quiet, both of you. You'll have the whole bloody establishment on our tails, whoever's here. Now where's that damn door?'

Martin saw it, sharp eyed as ever. 'Over there, sir, behind that pulpit.'

Together they moved past the elaborate baroque pulpit, towards a low door in the wall.

'Yes, that's it. Right. I'll go down first. Follow on, but keep twenty yards or so behind me. I'm meant to be alone. I'll make a signal if I need you.'

Keane pushed the door and it creaked open; then, entering, he found himself at the top of a spiralling staircase of stone steps, descending into gloom. He turned to Ross. 'Twenty paces, sarn't.'

He took the first step and began to walk down, his eyes becoming accustomed to the light as he went. The treads of the steps were worn away and he had to go carefully, holding on to the central pillar of the staircase as he went.

At the foot of the stairs was an oak door. Keane turned the handle and pushed it open.

Entering the room, he was surprised at how light it was after the gloom of the staircase. It was lit from above by a shaft of light from a lofty cupola, and Keane waited for a second time as his eyes adjusted, aware only that he was surrounded by tombs and grave steles. He noticed another door to his left, firmly shut, and then a shape appeared before him, which he realised was a man, and that he was moving closer. Instinctively, Keane's hand tightened on the grip of his sword.

The man spoke – only a single word: '*Apostoli*.'

The password. Thank God, he thought. Sobral had been right about that. He prayed that the doctor had also been right about the correct response.

Keane took his life in his hands. '*Magister*.'

The man smiled at him and offered his hand. 'Welcome, Colonel Macnab.'

9

Keane stared at the man. He was not sure what a Jesuit fanatic was supposed to look like, but this man seemed – at first sight, at least – to be an unlikely candidate. He smiled at Keane and spoke in a cultivated French accent.

'My dear colonel, it's very good to meet you at last. I apologize for my complicated measures. We have to guard our secrecy, as you know so well.'

Keane mustered his best French in reply: 'Of course, monsieur. But I do not know your name.'

'And nor shall you now, I'm afraid. I find it better to remain anonymous – even from members of the fellowship.'

'Of course, I understand, monsieur. You have the book?'

'I do.'

'May I see it?'

'Of course, colonel.'

The man turned and went to the tomb in the centre of the room. It was the sort Keane had seen in English churches, its top adorned with the sculpted figure of a knight in armour, hands folded in prayer, a shield across his legs and, at his feet, a lion. He touched a finial on the left side of the coffer and it slid aside to reveal a hole beneath the effigy of the knight. The man thrust his hand inside and drew out a cloth-wrapped bundle. This he took across to Keane and, laying it carefully down on one of the many stone grave steles, unwrapped the cloth, with an air of occasion, to reveal a book, triangular in shape and bound in red morocco leather. It was embossed in gold on the cover with an eye set within a triangle and sur-rounded by the rays of the sun.

The man stepped back with a flourish. 'There, colonel; behold, the *Très Sainte Trinosophie*. Exquisite.'

Keane was uncertain whether or not the man wanted him to open the book or merely stare at it in awe.

'Ah, yes, what a treasure indeed. May I?'

It appeared to be the right response. The man nodded and smiled, and Keane turned the cover and opened the book, not knowing what to expect.

After such a search and effort to get hold of the book, to actually see it and hold it surprised him as something of an anticlimax. The inside title page was richly decorated with painted symbols. There was the triangle with the eye and the sun again, beside it an Egyptian beast of a type he had seen in Alexandria and, beside that, a pair of red wings. He turned another page and found an image of a naked man being beaten with a rod while his hand rested in a burning pyre. It was, he thought, strangely disturbing, but hardly as revelatory or shocking as he had been led to believe.

Keane wondered what he should say. He tried to imagine how Macnab might have reacted. 'Wonderful, it's really won-derful. The emperor will love it. To own such a thing will be a triumph for him. A book of such extraordinary power.'

'The emperor will possess the book?'

'The emperor, yes, of course. Isn't that to whom I'm taking it? A present for the emperor?'

The man squinted at him. 'Yes, but not the real thing. You know that, colonel. You had agreed to make a copy for Bonaparte. You know that the original should never be allowed into his hands. Remember, Bonaparte is no more than a puppet. He is not a true member of the brotherhood.' He paused. 'You do remember, don't you, colonel? You do know what it is I'm talking about? You do know, don't you, Colonel Macnab?'

Keane was about to reply, but he guessed that it might already be too late, that his blunder had exposed him as an imposter.

The man drew a sabre from his side and gave a shout. '*Aidez moi, amis de Jésus!*'

The door Keane had noticed when he entered the room flew open and four men entered. All wore the uniform of the French dragoons and, to Keane's alarm, each of them was armed with a drawn sabre.

The man called to them, 'Seize him! He's an imposter. He must be a spy.'

With a swift action, Keane drew his sword and took up the en-garde position. The dragoons advanced towards him and, deciding that now was surely the moment, he yelled towards the door, 'Sarn't Ross, Silver, to me! Now, for God's sake!'

The door through which Keane had entered opened and Ross and Silver fell into the room, just as the lead dragoon, a junior officer, went for Keane. In the seconds it took Keane's men to adjust to the light, the other dragoons had turned towards them, but not before Martin and Gilpin, too, had followed the others in.

Keane parried the dragoon officer's clumsy thrust to his

chest and riposted with a quick cut, which connected with
the man's chin and drove up into his throat. Keane whipped
the blade free and the dead dragoon fell to the floor.

While the other French soldiers were engaged with Keane's
men, he looked around for the Jesuit, but the man was nowhere
to be seen, and neither was the book.

Keane supposed that the man must have left by the door
through which the dragoons had entered, that being the only
other means of exit. Leaving the rest of his men to deal with
the remaining dragoons, he ran to the door and, praying that
there would be no more French behind it, went through.

The corridor beyond the door was dark, but not as dark as
that through which they had come from the church, for torches
in brackets had been lit every fifty yards along its length and
it was bathed in an eerie orange light from their flickering
flames. He listened for a moment and heard ahead of him the
distinct sound of running footsteps.

Keane began to run and was soon sprinting along the corridor, at the same time wondering where it might take him. He
was quickly aware of descending a shallow slope and knew that
he was now well below ground level. Ahead of him the light
began to grow stronger and, unsure of what or who lay ahead,
he stopped. The footsteps had stopped, too, and he wondered
if the Jesuit had heard him.

Slowly, Keane walked along the tunnel in the direction of
the light. There was no sound from behind him, now, and
none, either, from in front. The only noise was a heavy panting
and that, he knew, came from his own mouth. He could see,
ahead of him, a room bathed in light, and, as he grew closer,
he realized that it was a high chamber painted with signs
similar to those he had seen in the book: staring eyes and

globes, creatures with wings and fiery heads and a hanged man. Around it stood a number of stone plinths, carved with the same symbols he had seen in the room. It had evidently been the work of some centuries and Keane knew he was somehow in the presence of something other than the everyday world he had left behind, above him, in the light of day.

Through the middle of the atrium flowed a sluggish stream, some three feet wide, of green, fetid-looking water. The place stank of sewage and Keane rightly presumed that the stench was rising from the stream.

The atrium appeared to be deserted. Keane looked around for a door but saw none. The place appeared to be a dead end. He presumed that it might have been some sort of water supply for the college when the place was built, but since then it must have been sealed up, apart from the entrance he had used.

For a few moments, his heart rose as he thought that the Jesuit must still be there, somewhere. Then, looking more closely at the watercourse, Keane saw that it disappeared from the atrium through a low stone arch. The gap above the water was hardly visible and certainly not possible for a man to pass through without completely immersing himself. It was just possible that the Jesuit might have made his escape that way. But, if so, then he would have had to completely enclose the book to prevent the water from ruining it. That, Keane supposed, was what must have happened, for there was no sign of life in the stinking cavern. The book was lost and, with it, for all he knew, the war.

Utterly disheartened and not knowing what he might do, he was about to turn and walk back up the tunnel when the sound of running feet came from behind him and, turning fast, he saw the Jesuit. The man was running towards him, barefoot on the stones, an expression of hatred and fury across his face.

Closing on Keane, he lunged at him with a pearl-handled scimitar of a type that Keane had often seen used in Egypt and which had since been carried by officers on both sides. Its razor edge connected with his leg, slicing the skin like a piece of fruit. But the man had not reckoned on Keane's reactions and the blow, while painful, was not serious. Keane jumped back and prepared for another attack, which came at lightning speed as the man flew at him again, the scimitar raised this time in a cut at his head. Keane parried it with his heavier blade and then dropped his sword down, ready to make his riposte.

The Jesuit jumped back to avoid Keane's blade and, at the same time, swept the scimitar round in a curved action intended to lop Keane's head from his body. Keane ducked and the blade flew over his head by a couple of inches. After it had passed, he rose and went again for the Jesuit. This time, his blade struck home and drew blood from the Jesuit's upper thigh. The man let out a yell and Keane saw the fury in his eyes. Apparently impervious to the pain and the blood coursing down his leg, he shouted as he made ready for another attack.

The two men circled each other and Keane was aware, now, of the pain in his own leg. He tried to ignore it and stared at the Jesuit's eyes.

The man spoke, deep voiced: 'Give up, Englishman. You're lost. You know you are. Your men are being cut to pieces by mine. And I have more of them. Many more. They will be here soon.'

Keane shook his head. 'How? You're wrong. This place is full of Portuguese and my men are more than a match for those green coats. Give me the book and surrender yourself.'

The Jesuit spat and wound a piece of cloth around the wound in his leg. 'What do you know of the book? You're a fool, heretic. You deserve to die.'

He cut at Keane's head with a skill that Keane had rarely encountered. He dodged the blow, but only just, and, from instinct, made his reply – a short lunge at the man's stomach, which just touched him.

Realizing that the only way to win against such a fanatical opponent was to go on the offensive, Keane went to make another attack on the Jesuit, who had retreated and was standing by one of the plinths. This time, though, the man did not move. He stood and stared at Keane, almost daring him to advance. Keane was uncertain what else he could possibly do. He ran towards the Jesuit and, as he grew closer, saw that the man was pushing at the plinth. He thought that he should stop himself, but it was too late now, the momentum was too strong and, as he grew closer, he could only watch as the stone toppled towards him. It hit him on the upper arm, knocking him to the ground. And, as he fell, the stone continued to fall, too – directly on to his right arm. Keane yelled and grabbed at his arm, but it was pinned beneath the stone. The pain seared through him, but he flexed his fingers and knew that it was not yet broken. He pulled at it, desperate to get it free. But all he did was rip the skin from his forearm. He shrieked in pain and, as he did, he was aware of the Jesuit standing over him, peering down – smiling.

Keane's head was reeling with the pain and, as the man spoke, the words seemed slow. 'You fool. To think you could win against me – against the truth. And now you will know how all heretics must die: by the sword or by the flame.'

Keane watched in horror, and in desperation began pulling

again at his arm. The man raised the scimitar high above his head, preparing to bring it down in a move that would surely sever Keane's head from his body. The Jesuit grinned and spoke again: 'For the glory of God, Christ Jesus and the true faith.'

Keane stared, incredulous to apparently be witnessing his own death. Almost in slow motion, the sword began to fall and, as it did, the chamber was filled with a tremendous noise – a thunder clap – the unmistakable sound of a gun firing. Keane found himself staring directly into the Jesuit's furious eyes and, as he did so, they adopted an expression first of surprise, then of anguish and, incredibly, the man began to fall. He toppled sideways, away from Keane, his hand still tight on the grip of the scimitar, and then the sword was falling with him, away from Keane's head.

Keane tried to raise himself up, desperate to watch the man fall, but the slightest movement sent red-hot pain searing through his trapped arm. He fell back, but was aware of the Jesuit still falling, and then he heard a loud splash and pre-sumed that the maniac had slipped into the watercourse. He turned his head in the direction of the shot and saw a shadowy form grasping a gun.

'Who's there? Who are you?'

'It's me, sir. It's Will Martin. He's dead, sir. I killed him.'

Then, in the matter of an instant, there were men pulling at the stone on his arm, dragging it off his limb.

Keane managed to focus on them: Ross, Garland and Silver. He sat up and clutched at his arm. Amazingly, he thought, it did not appear to be broken, although several layers of skin had been flayed from the upper part of his forearm where he had pulled at it in his attempt to break free. Silver took a rag from his neck and tied it round the oozing wound.

Keane staggered to his feet, feeling again the pain of the wound in his leg, which hadn't troubled him during the fight. Looking down, he noticed it had soaked his overalls in blood.

He looked towards the stream. 'Where is the body?'

Ross pointed to the stream. 'He's over there, sir. He won't be getting up again.'

The Jesuit lay face down in the fetid watercourse, which Keane saw was running red around the body. The scimitar lay a few feet away from him, where it had fallen from his dying hand.

Keane could see the gaping exit wound in the man's back, where Martin's bullet had left the body. 'Thank you, Martin. This is becoming something of a habit.'

Martin grinned and patted the gun, Keane's own. 'I wouldn't have done it, sir, except you seemed to be in a bit of difficulty on account of the stone. And I couldn't have done it without her.'

'You could say that. The gun's yours, Will. You know that.'

Archer walked across the room from the door and took hold of Keane's damaged arm. 'You can move it, sir?'

'Yes.'

Archer flexed his captain's fingers and then his wrist. Keane winced.

'I don't think it's broken, sir, but God alone knows how.'

A sudden look of alarm clouded Keane's features. 'The dragoons?'

Ross answered, 'Dead to a man – all of them. We're all fine, sir.'

Another panicked look passed across his face. 'Christ, the book! The book – do you have it? Sarn't Ross?'

'No, sir; we thought you must have taken it.'

'No, that maniac still had it.'

He looked across at the dead Jesuit, whose body was now drifting slowly along the stream towards the mouth of the tunnel.

Holding his injured arm, Keane ran across and, with Martin and Archer, using his left hand, managed to drag the man's body from the stream. Ripping open the dead man's coat, he searched its pockets, but found nothing.

'Where the devil did he put it? All of you, spread out and look all over the room. Look in every corner. Everywhere. It must be here somewhere.'

They spread out and began to hunt around the vault. Keane, finding it hard to move from shock and fatigue, stood watching them, shouting out occasional commands. The atrium was a vast room, its soaring vaulted ceilings emphasizing its size, but there were surely few places in which the Jesuit might have hidden the book. Or perhaps, Keane thought, there was another twist – some other hidden place that they would never find. He walked across to where Ross was looking, but saw nothing but a wall of stones.

The torchlight flickered, casting huge shadows on the walls. The pain was searing through him now and he peered into the gloom, desperate to find any possible hiding place. He had begun to lose hope when, feeling faint from the pain, he stretched out his hand and placed the palm against the wall for support. The stones felt cold and damp. But then he was aware of another sensation on his hand – something that was not stone, was not as cold. He peered at the wall, digging his finger deep into a crack in the mortar. And then he felt it: soft, like skin. Like leather.

'It's here. I've found it. Help me.'

Keane scrabbled with his fingers at the space between the stones and the mortar began to fall from the gap. Others were with him now, clawing at the cement. Ross pushed his great thick fingers into the hole and immediately something began to move. It fell to the floor and Ross retrieved it, smiling. 'Sir, would this, by any chance, be what you're looking for?'

Keane looked towards him and saw that, in his hand, the sergeant was holding aloft a red morocco-bound book in the shape of a triangle.

Keane smiled. 'Well done, Sarn't Ross. Forget what that madman said. You're my bloody saviour. I'll stand you a bottle in the sarn'ts' mess.'

Silver piped up, quietly: 'Not that you're ever likely to find yourself in one again.'

Keane turned to him. 'Sorry, Silver? You had something to add?'

'I said that, when you did it, it would be a big one, sir.'

Keane said nothing.

Archer had made a sling from Silver's neck rag and was now busy tying it around the injured arm.

Keane winced. He had, in fact, heard Silver's comment perfectly well, but chose to ignore it. He knew that the men were not happy here in Coimbra, just as they were not convinced about the importance of the mission to get the book for Wellington. There had been an unsettled air about them since he had brought them back here and he sensed that it was getting worse. They seemed to be convinced that they would not make it back to the main army. He had never known them to be like this and wondered what combination of factors might have brought it about.

He knew that, if they were to function properly as a unit, it was absolutely fundamental that they should not only believe in their objective, but be able to act together as one, with a concerted will. They were a small band of brothers, each of them with his own quirks, his own virtues and his own failings. The fact that there were so few of them, and that they necessarily operated in situations of extreme danger, required an absolute belief in one another. And he was now seriously worried that closeness, that camaraderie, was slowly being eroded. In some cases, he thought it might be in danger of vanishing entirely.

In particular, he had been watching Heredia. For the last few minutes, the Portuguese trooper had been standing a short distance away from the rest of them, having arrived in the vault with Archer, shortly after Martin had shot the Jesuit. Now he said nothing, but walked across the vault and gazed down at the body as it lay, face up, at the side of the stream.

Keane noticed his movement and wondered what, in particular, was troubling him. Archer finished his sling and Keane walked across to Heredia.

'Ugly bugger, wasn't he? Damned good fighter, though. Damned quick with a blade.'

'He was insane. How can you fight a madman?'

'He was a fanatic. Now he's a dead fanatic.'

'He almost killed you.'

'What exactly are you trying to tell me, Heredia?'

'This mission, sir. I know it will end badly. I know it. These people – this one, here, and the other, your friend, Doctor Sobral – they are not good people, sir. Trust me. They do not understand my country.'

'I grant you this fellow, but Doctor Sobral is a scientist, man. He's intelligent and forward thinking. But it is his country, too, isn't it? And he has your country's good in his heart. How can he do wrong to you?'

'He has his own ideas and they may be too much for my people. He is trying too hard to make us modern. Portugal is not like this. And this book is dangerous. We should not be dealing with it.'

Keane shook his head. 'I didn't think I'd hear this from you. You really believe all this mumbo jumbo?'

'I don't know if it is what you call mumbo jumbo. For many of my people it is very real. I only know what I have learnt and that I do know good from evil. That book I know for certain to be evil.'

Keane shook his head and brandished the book. 'God above, give me strength! It's a book, man! Nothing more than a book of pictures. The truth is that Bonaparte can use it to create a code – a code that we will never be able to break and which will lose us the war. That's why we have to have it. Not for any other reason. Certainly not because it has magical properties. It's just a bloody book. Nothing more.'

'Well, if it's just a book, sir, may I say that it must be a very powerful book to have caused you so much trouble and pain. Think about what it has already made you do.'

Keane, with the pain from his arm pounding away, finally lost his composure. 'Well, if that's really your opinion then there is no place for you in this company. You're a good man, Heredia, but you're out of place here, with us. I need men with intelligent, independent minds, but it is not your place to question my orders or my motives. In fact, I'm of the opinion that you would be better suited to being back with a troop of horse . . . of your own countrymen, as soon as possible. I shall arrange it as soon as we regain the lines.'

Heredia nodded and strode away towards the entrance. The others stood watching in an uneasy silence.

Eventually, Ross said, 'Sir, do you not think we should get away from here? I can't say I really like this place.'

Keane rounded on him. 'Good God! Not you, too, sarn't? Christ! How many more superstitious buggers do I have to deal with? It's just a bloody book and this is just a bloody cellar.' He paused and winced as another pain shot through his arm. That had been a foolish thing to say. 'I'm sorry, Ross; yes, we should leave here.'

Keane tucked the precious book under his left arm and began to walk towards the entrance which led back up to the church. After a few steps, he turned. 'Gilpin, Garland, heave that bastard into the stream and let him rot in it. Collect his sword, will you? It's as nice a piece of kit as I've seen of late. I've half a mind to use it myself.'

10

Keane could not recall ever having been so impatient and so frustrated. Sitting in the colonnade of the palace, he drummed the fingers of his left hand on the table and looked with disgust at his right. It was not broken, but it had been severely damaged by the weight of the plinth and Doctor Sobral advised him to keep it in a sling for as long as possible.

He had tried to persuade Keane to have it looked at in the hospital by one of the two French doctors left by Massena. But Keane had refused. He had not wanted to meet Henriette again so soon. He was still unsure as to how to play her. Of one thing he was certain, however: he did not want her sympathy. He wondered, though, if she had heard of his injury and perhaps might come to him.

For two days, he had done nothing save sit in this shady colonnade. It did not come easily. Keane needed to be on his feet and, had it not been for this damned wound, he knew that, even now, he would have been riding to Wellington at Torres Vedras with the news that they had the book, before presenting him with the source of their troubles. As it was, he was loath to let it out of his sight. Of course, he had allowed

Archer and Doctor Sobral to have it for the better part of the last two days. But he had insisted on being with them, and that it be returned to him overnight.

Sitting there, he opened it again and flicked through its pages, looking at it intently, as he had done for the past two days. He could still make little of it, although, during that time, he had learnt something about it from both Sobral and Archer, to whom he had given the task of copying what they had deemed to be the most important of its pages.

One image, in particular, haunted him and seemed to appear whenever he opened the book. It was of a man in a cuirass and helmet – a soldier – carrying a white sword, standing alongside a naked woman. Both of them were under the gaze of an all-seeing eye. He had no idea what it meant, but, for some reason, every time he saw it, it disturbed him and it had begun to appear in his dreams. Worse than this, the book itself troubled him. He had become obsessed with its safekeeping and its worth. He felt compelled to open it, yet, when he did, it was with a curious sense of revulsion. It seemed to possess an aura and he could not help thinking it might be cursed. Of course, that was nonsense – the sort of superstitious twaddle for which he had berated his men. Unusually, he also felt that he was not in control of the situation. The episode of the Jesuit had unsettled him and, used to being the watcher rather than the watched, he now felt vulnerable. The answer, he knew, was action. But until his arm healed that was impossible. So, meanwhile, all he could do to lay his demons was to resort to logic.

Aware that he should send a report to Wellington, he had written a full account of the encounter with the Jesuit and had emphasized the fact that French dragoons had been with him. He had also not omitted to describe the way in which the Jesuit had reacted with astonishment to the news that Bonaparte was to have the book.

He had been worrying, too, about the men. In particular, about Heredia. The decision to dismiss him had been taken on the spot and, ever since, Keane had harboured uncertainties about his decision, born as it was in the heat of the moment, under pressure and in pain. It was stupid, un-soldier like. Yet, from pride as much as anything else, he could not bring himself to rescind it.

Most of all, he wondered where Macnab might be.

Since their return from the crypt, Trant had been incessant in his questions. Who was the enemy? Was it Macnab? And, if not, who? Did he have the book? Why was it so important? Keane was heartily sick of it. Yet, from what Trant had hinted at, he knew the colonel was the brightest hope of his ever discovering the identity of his father and so he tolerated the questions and fielded them to the best of his ability. The thought of finding his father fuelled his impatience and, once again, absent-mindedly, he opened the book at the illustration.

He was jolted from his thoughts by the arrival of Doctor Sobral.

'Captain Keane.'

'Doctor?'

'You asked me to come.'

'Of course. Yes, please take a seat.'

Keane clapped his hands and a Portuguese servant appeared, on loan from Trant following Keane's return with his wounded arm. Keane ordered a carafe of wine and, turning to the doctor, pushed the book across the table towards him.

'I need your help again, doctor. I need you to tell me again what you found and to answer a question.'

Sobral shrugged. 'I have told you all that I know. Before you came, I had looked into the book only once or twice. I had never troubled to sit down and try to decipher the codes. Fascinating, in their way, but not my main field of research. I had thought that I might save it to investigate at a time when I had fewer students to teach. Clearly, now is that time.' He laughed and went on, 'I can tell you, captain, that, in all my experience, I have never encountered such ingenious codes and methods of concealment as are found in this manuscript. And Archer agrees.

'In only a few instances are complete phrases written in the same alphabet; usually two or three forms of writing are employed, with letters written upside down, reversed, or with the text written backwards. Vowels are often omitted and, at times, several letters are missing with merely dots to indicate their number. Every combination of hieroglyphics seemed hopeless at the beginning, yet, after hours of dissection, one familiar word appears. The texts are written in Chaldean Hebrew, Ionic Greek, Arabic, Syriac, cuneiform, Greek hiero-glyphics, and ideographs.

'I believe that Archer will break at least one of the codes before long. He's a talented young man, captain.'

Keane nodded. 'Yes, you're right. Tell me, doctor, what do you know of this picture?' Picking up the book, he turned the pages until he found the image of the armoured man and showed it to Sobral.

'From what I know of such emblems, the woman is Isis and the man is what we might call a pupil. Don't forget, the book's original purpose was as a teaching text for initiates into a cult. This man, this soldier, is just such a man and, in this image, he has reached his goal. The goddess leads him to nirvana. He has found everything he sought – his past, his future, his love – everything. Why do you ask?'

Keane smiled. 'No reason, really. I was just curious.'

He looked at the book again as it lay open on the table, and now it seemed less sinister. Here was an image of hope. Not some arcane curse, but hope for the future.

He closed the cover and, being careful not to move his damaged arm too much, stood up before picking up the book and tucking it into his inside coat pocket.

'And now, doctor, allow me to accompany you back to the hospital.'

'You're coming?'

'Yes, I thought that I might visit one of those French physicians to whom you would have me submit myself.'

'And perhaps Madame Lebreton?'

'Perhaps, yes.'

They stepped out from the shade of the colonnade and, as they did so, it occurred to Keane that something had changed. Sobral's interpretation of the picture that had troubled him so much had put him strangely at ease. The past and the future resolved. It was all that he could hope for.

Rather than taking the route that he would normally have chosen, Keane decided, on a whim, to walk on a lower system of streets, which took them on a longer road. Knowing that he might well encounter Henriette, he wanted more time to think as he went and was attempting to put together some sort of speech for Henriette when he became aware that they were being followed.

It was nothing new to Keane and he had a well-honed routine for dealing with such situations. Not turning immediately, and gently encouraging Sobral not to, either, he carried on

along the street for a while before ducking down a narrow lane
that led off to the left. They found themselves, as Keane had
supposed they might, in a close, which sloped down the hill,
alternating sequences of steep steps and sloping cobblestones.
Keane walked slowly with the doctor, deliberately onward for
some twenty yards and then, very quickly, turned.

There was no one else in the street. Sobral said nothing.

He wondered whether his mind might be playing games
with him. Certainly his nerves had been on edge. Yes, he told
himself, that was it. He had just imagined the shadow. It was
all in his mind. Rounding a right-hand bend in the close, they
took another turning to the right, which led back on to the
main street. But, just as he reached the junction, he was aware
again of someone or something behind them. Keane stopped
and listened. But he heard nothing. Nothing, save the sound of
his own heartbeat and Sobral's heavy breathing. Keane turned
and thought that, just for an instant, he might have seen the
flash of something – a coat tail, or the glint of a button – something so subliminal.

This was becoming tiresome. Moving fast, back on to his
original route to the hospital, he put the idea from his mind
and began again to compose his speech to Henriette. He would
ask for her pardon, apologize for having been so rude and
ungentlemanly, praise her for all she was doing in the hospital.
But how, he wondered, could he include some derogatory comment about Lievremont without it seeming too pointed? Yet he
knew that he must do something to persuade her away from
the man – whatever Sobral had told him.

They were close to the hospital, now, still on the lower road
and downhill from the university buildings and the great college
of the Jesuits. Walking uphill, Keane found his arm beginning

to give him pain and stopped to massage it. He motioned to
Sobral not to speak and, as he did so, he chanced to look down
an alleyway. What he saw at the end made him freeze. For there,
staring straight at him, perhaps fifty yards distant, stood Macnab.
He looked leaner than before and had more hair on the side of
his face. He wore a dark blue civilian coat, white breeches and
short hussar boots. So this had been the shadow. He had not
been imagining it. Knowing that he would be unable to draw
his sword, Keane had stuck a loaded pistol in his belt beneath
his coat and this he now reached for with his good, left hand.
He saw that Macnab, too, had a gun and, as Keane went to cock
his own, he realized that the spy had already done so. Instantly,
Keane pushed Sobral away from him, into the shadows of a
building. Macnab raised the gun and Keane – who, as a veteran
of many duels, was used to such things – braced himself for the
shot. He sensed Macnab squeezing the trigger.

And, at that moment, a door opened directly in front of
Keane, blocking his view of Macnab as half a dozen of Trant's
student militia poured drunkenly from a cantina and fell into
the street. There was a bang and one of the students fell, blood
gushing from a wound in his neck. Keane stood and watched
and, as he did so, one of the students caught sight of him and
began to yell.

'He's got a gun! He did it. I saw him.'

Keane knew there would be no point in denying it. He moved
sideways to look past the door for Macnab, but knew what
he would find and, of course, the man had gone. Lowering
the lever on the pistol and tucking it back into his belt, he
moved away quickly from the crowd of students, who now
stood around their dying comrade, and then, grabbing the arm
of Doctor Sobral, who had remained in the shadows, he ran.

Both men ran as fast as they could towards the hospital and, behind them, almost before they started, Keane could hear the shouts of the students. It was scarcely credible, he thought, that, having survived the onslaught of a crazed religious fanatic, he should now be running from Trant's own militia, implicated by Macnab, of all people, with a shot meant for himself.

They ran into the hospital courtyard and paused at last outside Sobral's office. The doctor was doubled up, gasping for breath.

'Doctor, you have to get word to Trant. Tell him that one of his men is dead and they think I did it, but that it was Macnab.'

'Macnab? That was him?'

'Yes. Now, please, get word to Trant. And find my men.'

With escape in his mind, he suddenly realized that the hospital might not be such a good idea for a refuge. For one thing, it was a dead end, and the last thing that he wanted was to find himself cornered in a ward. For another, it was still filled with Frenchmen and, given their previous attitude, he wondered, should they not find him, whether the students might not exact a revenge by proxy on some of the patients. He ran from the office and, leaving the hospital just as the students rounded the corner of the street, made for the university. There was one place for certain that they would not find him now. He could still hear the clamour behind him as he ran through the streets. They would know that he was making for the university, but would surely have little idea of to what building he was headed.

He entered the Natural History Museum by a different door to that which they had used three days before – a similar entrance, on the east side of the building, that gave into a beautifully painted entrance hall. Once inside, he shut the door behind him, bolted it top and bottom and made straight for the church.

It was empty and exactly as he recalled it and, once in the nave, the door to the crypt was easy to find. It was unlocked and there was no key to be seen. It was with a feeling of no little unease that he returned down the staircase towards the room where he had first encountered the Jesuit. To reassure himself, he pulled the pistol from his belt and cocked it again.

The end of the staircase came more abruptly than he remembered and the door at the bottom was tight shut. With a feeling of some trepidation, Keane turned the handle and entered with his pistol carried at chest height, ready to fire.

But the room was empty. Sunlight entered through the high cupola and bathed it in light. The bodies of the dragoons had gone, although there were several telltale bloodstains on the floor and walls. Keane crossed the room and found the other door, which was also closed. He turned the handle and it opened to reveal the corridor. This time, however, no torches had been lit and the tunnel was pitch black. Keane reasoned that the students would never find him here, that there was no need to go any further. But something within him urged him on with a niggling desire to revisit the vaulted chamber. It was, he realized, a similar obsessive desire to that which he had suggested Macnab might pursue – to revisit the scene of the crime. Although, in his case, there surely was no crime. This place was rather a scene of near catastrophe.

Keane walked into the darkness, feeling his way along the corridor, sensing, once again, the vertiginous feeling of descending the slope. And then, faster than he recalled, he saw the light ahead and soon emerged in the atrium. He could hear the stream now, something that he had missed in the fury of his fight with the Jesuit, and he caught, too, the smell of the place – rank and fetid and with something of death about it.

He walked slowly across to the stream and noticed the blood stains where they had laid the body of the Jesuit. Of that corpse there was, as he had expected, now no sign and Keane presumed that it had washed down the stream and finished wherever the foul watercourse had taken it. That was not his concern. He would wait down here for an hour, he thought, and in his mind began to count off the minutes, allowing for pauses of thought.

It was an extraordinary room: a massive chamber filled with wall drawings of terrifying and indecipherable images, which remained in his mind as he walked back up the corridor, still holding the cocked gun in his hand. He was feeling more at ease now, although the encounter with Macnab had shaken him up. He presumed that the students would, by now, have given up the chase and that Trant might have them under control. Either way, it was, he concluded, relatively safe to leave the crypt.

On emerging into the antechamber, however, he was aware at once that something was different. On the tomb in the centre of the room, in the middle of the knight's shield, there now lay a human hand.

Keane stared at it in horror and the first thought that came to him was, to whom had it belonged? This was swiftly followed by the question as to whether it had been placed there with the intention that he should find it. He walked across to the table, aware that someone, possibly Macnab, might be close by – could even be watching his reaction. Nearing the table, he looked at the hand. The bloody wrist was not running wet and the blood was dark and beginning to congeal. It had been severed, he thought, perhaps within the last hour.

It was a gruesome sight and brought back to Keane the full horror of the fight with the Jesuit and the curious, mind-numbing power of the 'mumbo jumbo' which he constantly accused his men of believing. For an instant, he was consumed by fear – a fear which he could not recall feeling since he had stood, as a boy, on his first battlefield and felt the rush of the shot as it passed over his head. Desperate to get out of the room, he ran to the door and, to his relief, found it unlocked. Leaving it open for maximum light, he began to make his way up the staircase.

He was halfway up the stairs when the door at the bottom slammed shut, enclosing him in darkness. Fear again consumed him. He wondered if the killer was on the staircase with him or back in the room. Either way, he was not going to find out. Hurrying through the darkness, he ran up the stairs and pushed at the door at the top. But this time it was locked. Keane turned and shouted into the darkness behind him, 'Who's there? Who are you? Show yourself! Macnab, if that's you, I know you're there. Don't be a coward.'

Nothing. He half turned to the door and tried it again. It was stuck firm. Keane banged on the door. 'Help! Get me out of here! Help! For God's sake!'

There was a noise on the other side of the door – a scratching at the lock; no key, but someone was picking it. Keane turned to face whoever it was, the pistol cocked in his hand.

The door swung open to reveal the figure of Sergeant Ross, a picklock in his hand.

'Christ, sir, we wondered where you were. You look as white as a sheet.'

'You have no idea what I've just seen.'

'Well, you'd better be ready for bad news.'

'What? What is it?'

'Gilpin, sir. He's dead.'

Keane shook his head and then spoke in a low voice, 'And – don't tell me – his right hand was severed.'

Ross gawped. 'Yes. That's right. How could you know that, sir?'

'Because I've seen it. That's what I've just seen. Gilpin's hand. It's down there, in the room where you fought the dragoons. Christ, this is a bloody mess. Where is he?'

'We found him in the street, sir. Close to the billet. He was looking for you.'

'How do you know that?'

'He told me, sir.'

'You mean he was alive when he lost his hand?'

Ross nodded his head. 'Yes, sir. Bloody barbaric, if you ask me. It's torture.'

'How was he killed?'

'Been shot in the leg, sir. Clever shot. Just to bring him down. Then stabbed twice in the chest and had his hand off.'

Keane said nothing for a few moments, then, 'No one does that. Not to one of my men. If I catch whoever did it, God forgive me for what I'll do to him.'

'Who do you think would have done such a thing, sir? Is it to do with the book? Some sort of heathen practice?'

'I don't know, sarn't. But I suspect it was meant to scare us – to frighten us away from something – which, if I'm right, means that we are getting close to something that certain people don't want us to discover.'

'Close to what, sir?'

'The truth, perhaps.'

*

They found the others in sombre mood at the men's billet. They had laid out Gilpin on the table in the kitchen. Gabriella had closed his eyes and wound a handkerchief around the stump of his arm. Keane winced when he saw him.

The three wounds were evident. Two ugly gashes that went deep – deep enough to kill – and the wound to the leg from the shot that had brought him down. Even at a cursory glance it was evident that they had been made by an expert.

Ross looked at the body. 'Poor bugger. No one should have to suffer like that.'

Silver spoke. 'It's this place, sir. I knew something like this would happen here. There's something bad about it. All this stuff.'

For once, Keane said nothing. After his experience on the staircase, he was shaken. He was right. They all were. There was something strange about the city – an air of unreality. For a moment, he half considered that it might be on account of all the innocents who had been slaughtered there. But he shook himself. He was as bad as the peasants, having such thoughts. Superstitious nonsense. Even so, though, he did share some if their unease.

Eventually, Keane spoke: 'Yes, I know it's bad. I have no wish to be here any more than the rest of you. But I have orders and I have a job to do that must be done. And, although it is unpleasant and dangerous, that is what I will do. I'm . . .' He hesitated. 'I'm sorry about Gilpin. He was a good man and he deserved better. We should toast his life. Silver? You're a resourceful fellow. You'll have a bottle. What can you offer us?'

Silver held up two bottles of the local red. 'I've nothing but this filth, sir.'

'Then that'll have to do. Everyone, get yourself a glass.'

Keane waited until each of them was holding a full glass of the wine, then intoned, as he looked down on Gilpin, 'We stand here to honour Sam Gilpin – soldier and comrade. Sleep well, Gilpin.'

They all repeated the words and drank of their glasses in one.

'We'll stand a vigil, bury him in the morning. Two of you stand watch. I don't want him touched. Silver, more wine for everyone, if you please.'

They all drank and, as they did, Martin approached Keane. He spoke quietly. 'There's something I think you should know, sir.'

Keane looked at him and saw the anxiety in his face. 'Yes, Will? Tell me.'

'Well, sir, you see, it wasn't just Sarn't Ross as found Gilpin. I was with him, too, and when Sarn't Ross was turned away for a moment, Gilpin said something else.'

'He did? What? What did he say?'

'He just said, "Macnab", sir. That's all; just the name.'

Keane nodded. 'I knew it. Thank you, Will. That was more important than you know. You're a good lad. I'm sorry about Gilpin. Truly sorry. I hope you don't think it was my fault, like some seem to.'

'No, sir. I know it wasn't your doing. It's just war, sir, ain't it?'

'Yes, Will, it's just war. That's exactly what it is.'

At last, Keane felt himself relax. It was, after all, just war. And it was just Macnab – if that could ever be a blessing. But, to Keane, at this present moment, it most certainly was. He realized that, for a short while, contrary to his usual clear head-edness, he had embraced superstition on the same level as so many of the people whose country he was fighting to liberate.

And he realized, too, that he had been manipulated. Macnab

had had him jumping in all directions. Chasing after shadows. How had the man got into a locked building? Why had he killed Gilpin and left his hand? The thought infuriated him – that and the atrocity that had ended poor Gilpin's life.

He spoke again to Martin. 'You know, Will, that I won't rest until I find the man who did this to Gilpin. And I'll kill him.'

He turned to the others. 'You all know that, don't you? That I won't rest until I have killed the man who did this. But, make no mistake, all of you, and remember this: this was the work of a man, albeit a man with no soul and no humanity, but a man nevertheless. There is no spectre, no spirit, no ghoul. It was a man who did this to Gilpin. And I know who he is. And I will kill him.'

Silver looked at him. 'It was Macnab, sir, wasn't it?'

'Yes, I'm sure of it. It bears his signature: cruel to the point of a perverse enjoyment and calculated to have the maximum effect upon our minds. He's playing with us all – playing with our minds – trying to scare us away.'

Martin spoke: 'But he won't win, sir.'

'No, he won't. But we must all be on our guard until he's taken or killed. You especially, Gabriella. Silver, look after your wife. This man is capable of anything. Who of you have seen his face?'

Ross and Silver nodded.

'Tell the others what he looks like. He's wearing a blue frock coat and white breeches. Looks like a staff officer. Or he did when I saw him. Oh, and he's grown whiskers, too. Don't move about on your own. Always make sure you go in pairs. Three of you, if possible. Stay on your guard at all times. We have something he wants.'

Garland, who was usually markedly quiet at such moments, now spoke up. 'The book, sir. Could we not just give it to him?'

'I wish that I were able to do that, Garland. I honestly do. And then we might gain the upper hand and be the pursuer rather than the quarry. But it is in my specific orders to take the book to Wellington and that is what I must do.

'So, no, we cannot give Macnab the book. But perhaps we can turn that very fact to our advantage. He thinks he has us scared, that he is running the game. But I intend to turn the tables on him. I will use the book to draw out Macnab. There is only one course open to us. We must avenge Gilpin. If we do it properly, the book that caused his death will be the instrument of his killer's downfall.'

An hour later, Keane left the billet, taking Garland and Martin as an escort, and made his way back to his own quarters. They said nothing, but in the gathering twilight of the pleasant autumn evening, every shadow seemed to offer the promise of danger.

As they rounded the corner of the road on which the Bishop's Palace stood, they were met by the sight of a score of horsemen. Most were dismounted, but a few remained in the saddle and, in their hands, they carried long, wicked-looking lances, topped with red and yellow pennants. Keane recognized them instantly as a particular band of Spanish guerrillas and immediately his heart lifted. He walked faster across the square, followed by the others, and there in the garden of the palace, seated at a table, sharing a bottle and a cheroot with Trant, he spotted the man he had hoped he might find.

'By the stars, Don Julian Sanchez! Colonel Sanchez, it's good to see you here.'

The man turned and smiled at him. 'Captain Keane – James Keane – I had heard that you were here. How are you, my friend?'

The newcomer was a man in his forties with dark eyes and wrinkled, wind-burnt skin. Colonel Don Julian Sanchez smiled at Keane, his white teeth showing bright against the sallow skin of his face. He had a shock of curly black hair, a moustache and extravagant side whiskers. He was dressed, as was his custom, in the uniform of a French hussar, with a dark blue short tunic trimmed with gold frogging and red facings, matching overall trousers and a pelisse of the same colour, trimmed with brown fur and gold braid. His headgear consisted of a French hussar's shako on which he had wittily turned the emperor's brass eagle upside down.

As Sanchez looked over at Martin and Garland, his eyes fell straight to the gun in Martin's hands. He grinned. 'And how is your gun? Your beautiful gun, Captain Keane?'

Sanchez had persuaded Keane to include the gun in a deal made with the guerrilla captain, but Keane, being Keane, had won it back from him at cards.

Trant smiled. 'This sounds fascinating. You have a gun, Keane?'

'It's not much, colonel, just an old game gun that belonged to my father. Martin carries it now, but Don Julian has his heart set on it.'

Martin chimed in, 'It's a fine gun, sir. It's an honour to use it.'

'Well, it's saved my life more than once in your hands, Martin. I can't think of a better custodian.'

Sanchez grinned, 'We'll see, captain. You can never tell how things will turn out.'

'What brings you here, Colonel Sanchez?'

'I have information for Colonel Trant – fresh information; very good information – taken from French prisoners. And I have prisoners.'

'We have enough of those here already, colonel, haven't we, Colonel Trant?'

'Indeed we do, captain, and may I say that I was appalled to learn of the death of one of your men.'

'Thank you. It was particularly horrible.'

Don Sanchez looked inquisitive. 'Really?'

'Yes, one of my men – you may remember him – Gilpin – a clever fellow, talent for voices – he was killed. Tortured. Maimed, while he was still alive.'

Sanchez shook his head. 'This war is filled with such horrors, Keane – some of them necessary, some just done for pleasure. This war is making monsters of us all.'

Keane nodded, but he thought, not quite all of us. Not, in particular, Don Julian Sanchez. He was not like other guerrilla leaders whom Keane had encountered. There was a humanity to Sanchez which raised him above the more usual methods of extracting information and exacting revenge upon the Frenchmen who had occupied his country. Keane admired him for that restraint, for the belief that men could still speak to each other as human beings in a war which, as he had remarked, too often descended into barbarity.

'What information do you bring, colonel? Or might that be for Colonel Trant's ears alone?'

Sanchez looked at Trant. 'No, my news is for the good of all. You are a spy, like me, Captain Keane. It is your duty to find information, yes?'

'Yes, colonel, if you say so. Although, a spy . . . ? Of that I'm not so sure.'

Trant banged on the table and laughed. 'Well, whatever you call yourself, Keane. I am a simple man. I don't understand the clever use of words.' He clapped his hands and shouted and his servant scurried out from the house, bearing another bottle of wine – red, this time. He continued, 'Colonel Sanchez, here, has some most interesting news, which I think we should all know. Colonel?'

Sanchez took a long draught from his glass. 'As I said, we captured a French patrol about four days ago. They were company strength, but we killed half of them.'

Keane shrugged. 'So you took – what? Forty men?'

'Thirty, to be precise. They were under strength. Well, of course, they were only too happy to talk to us.'

Keane smiled. 'Very funny, Don Julian.'

Sanchez raised an eyebrow. 'No, seriously, captain. It was no great problem to make them talk.'

'You made them talk?'

'Yes, of course.'

'May I ask how?'

'Captain Keane, you have seen me at work. You know my methods.'

'Yes, colonel, I have. And I know that you prefer to use fear and threat rather than torture. Isn't that the case?'

'I'm sure I don't know what you mean. You know that anything I do is only done with the best interests of the cause in mind.'

'That's a very curious reply. Are you telling me that things have changed? That you have changed?' He paused. 'How many did you kill?'

'I told you, Keane, we killed half of them.'

'In the fight, yes. Half. So how many do you have with you now, here? How many are left?'

'We have an officer and four men.'

'That's all? What happened to the others? The other twenty-five men?'

'I told you. That's all we have.'

Keane shook his head. 'I don't believe it. You're telling me that you killed twenty-five men during interrogation?'

Sanchez said nothing.

Trant intervened: 'Might I suggest, Captain Keane, that Don Julian's methods are not for us to question? We are all aware what the guerrillas will do to extract information and we are also well aware that the French do exactly the same for their part. Good God, man, a French spy just cut off the hand of one of your own men and tortured him to death and you bother to question this man about his methods?'

Keane nodded. 'Yes, is that so wrong? Surely we need to maintain some sort of civilized conduct, here?'

'Captain Keane, you amaze me. Don't you understand, after all we have said these past days? There is no "civilized conduct" any more. The rules of war have been torn up and thrown to the winds. Your civilized attitudes are outdated. I had thought that you and I understood each other.'

'I think we understand each other very well, Colonel Trant.' He turned to Sanchez. 'Colonel Sanchez, tell me what it was that you managed to extricate from the twenty-five Frenchmen, before they died.'

Sanchez looked, for just a moment, slightly compromised. 'You must see, Keane, it is our duty.'

'Oh, I see that perfectly well. Just tell me, colonel, what was so vital that it resulted in their deaths.'

'They had information about Marshal Massena. Apparently he is carrying with him, in his baggage train, a huge quantity of gold.'

Keane shrugged. 'That's generally the case with the French,

when their armies are on the march – as you and I know only too well.'

'Gold, Keane. Doesn't that mean anything to you?'

'I suspect that it means trouble.'

Trant chimed in: 'Don't be obtuse, Keane. It means an opportunity, and you know it. We need that gold. Wellington needs that gold.'

'You're right about that. Wellington is desperately short of funds. Not just to pay the army, but to pay for the services of his informers. Of course I know that.' He shot a glance at Sanchez. 'Are you proposing that we should somehow take this gold, colonel?'

Sanchez nodded. 'That is exactly what I am suggesting. Why not? We have a formidable force, do we not? Colonel Trant has his militia, just spoiling for a fight. I have my men, and you will be impressed, captain, at the way my little army has grown. And, of course, you have your team. In truth, I should value your expert help. I have worked with you before, Keane. Your men have special skills we would value.'

'Thank you for the compliment, colonel. But I'm afraid that, at present, I am engaged on another mission.'

'Yes, of course. I presumed as much. But whatever it is can surely wait. Why not come with us?'

Keane shook his head. 'I'm sorry, colonel. It cannot wait while I go off on some hair-brained scheme to take French gold from a vastly superior force.'

Sanchez put his hands together and looked hard at Keane. 'I'll be blunt with you, captain. I'm desperate. I managed to get some information from my prisoners, but only that Massena has the gold. No one has yet told me where it is exactly and when it might be moved. It is for that that I need your skills, captain. I have seen you at work before. You can work miracles. You are able to get information that any amount of torture cannot.'

Keane smiled. 'Ah, now I see. I must say that I'm pleased you are beginning to realize that brute force is not always the way. But, to be frank, Colonel Sanchez, I do have a vital mission from the duke. A mission of duty.'

'More important than gold? More gold than you or I could imagine? I find that very hard to believe, colonel.'

Sanchez moved closer to him and looked deadly serious. 'I am not joking with you, captain. This is a chance for all of us. For the three of us – you, me, Colonel Trant – and, not least, for the duke himself.'

Keane said nothing.

Trant spoke up: 'Captain Keane will need to think about it, colonel. But you're not in a hurry, are you? Here, have a glass with us.' He turned to Keane. 'James, why don't you have a think about it? Let's leave the colonel here to enjoy his wine. I think, perhaps, that we should have a little chat.'

11

Trant and Keane walked together away from the palace and into the street that led towards the university quarter.

As he had directed to the men, Keane was accompanied by an escort; in his case, Garland and Martin, armed with the game gun. They walked a few paces behind the two officers and out of earshot.

Trant spoke: 'Whatever your feelings, Keane – and, believe me, I do share many of them – we must cooperate with Sanchez. You do realize that, even if we don't work with him on this scheme, he will still go ahead with it. If that should happen and he should succeed, then we will have lost out on an opportunity. We will both be the poorer and so will the army. If he should fail, then we are likely to be accused of non-cooperation with our allies. We could be disciplined. We will most certainly be on the end of a sharp reprimand.'

Keane stopped and looked at him. It irked him to admit to himself that there was some truth in the colonel's words. He tried for one last time: 'I meant it in earnest, sir. As soon as my arm is sufficiently healed, and I think that might be at any time now, I have a duty to get the book to the duke. I intend to take it myself and that precludes my involvement in any scheme.'

'You could just interrogate the Frenchmen.'

'Yes, I could, but, as I see it, that will provide information which will enable Sanchez to get his hands on the gold. If I don't help in any way, he might not be able to find it.'

'You're being most unreasonable, Keane. You admitted to me yourself that you need the money. Just as I do – that I freely admit. Now, let's be honest with each other. Isn't it more than likely that the gold, if and when it is moved – which is when we will be able to take it – will still be in the proximity of Massena's army?'

'Yes, that's true.'

'And where is Massena's army?'

'You know as well as I do, colonel. It's pursuing our own army and probably very shortly attempting to besiege Wellington when he reaches the lines of Torres Vedras.'

'And to get the book to the duke, where do you and your men have to travel?'

'To the lines and to the army. Yes, I grant you that. Very well, colonel, I admit that we would be travelling in the same direction. But I intend to ensure that the book makes it through to Wellington. That is my priority. For any of us to be involved in an unnecessary action, with the possibility of losing it, would be extreme folly.'

'Keane, I presume that you are still anxious to learn more of your father?'

'You know that I am. Why?'

'You will, perhaps, be aware that I am in possession of a few facts regarding his identity?'

'You have led me to believe as much, yes.'

'Shall we just say that there are certain people to whom I could direct you who might be able to furnish you with more substantial information regarding many things.'

'You would do that?'

'Of course, for a brother officer. But I would have to be able to rely upon that officer to stand by me at all times and to place his belief in my judgment.'

'You are saying . . . ?'

'I'm merely saying, Keane, that if you wish to learn more about yourself, then perhaps you might begin by becoming a little more amenable to my suggestions.'

'In other words, if I help you and Colonel Sanchez with this scheme, you will give me the names of people who can help me discover the identity of my father. And if I do not help you?'

'When you get to my age, Keane, you will discover quickly how fickle the memory can be. How many years in the field can addle your mind, make you forget things which would otherwise tend to be imprinted on your memory. It's curious how that can happen.'

'If I don't help you, I can safely assume that you simply won't tell me who those people are – ever. Is that it?'

Trant nodded. 'Is it so much to ask? Simply to ask the French a few questions and then help us retrieve the gold?'

'That's blackmail.'

'Oh, Captain Keane, I wouldn't call it that. That's a very ugly word. Very ugly. All I'm asking for is a little cooperation. Give me that cooperation and I'm sure that my poor old, addled mind will be able to recall what it was I was going to tell you.'

Followed discreetly by Garland and Martin, Keane walked away from Trant and stood alone for a few minutes. He needed space to think, to consolidate his thoughts. He had the book – that was the most important thing and he had almost died for it. He knew, too, that they should leave here immediately. Macnab was still out there somewhere and, for all their vigilance, Keane feared for the lives of his men, and for Gabriella.

Trant was right about one thing. He had struck a raw nerve. Keane was desperate to have anything that might lead him to his father. As for Sanchez, well, a cruel guerrilla captain was nothing new, although Keane was disappointed in a man whom he had reckoned greater. The gold was a bonus and, if they could take it, would be welcome for them all.

And there was more than that. The men were disaffected and, much as he would have liked to believe that they would do their duty for him, if not for Wellington, he knew they would have a new surge of loyalty and enthusiasm for the cause once they each had a bag of gold livres in their haversacks.

Against all this, he weighed the possibility of losing the book. And then a thought struck him. What, he wondered, if they could deliver the book to Wellington and then go on to take the gold, wherever it might be, on their return journey to Coimbra?

For, if they were to undertake this task, Keane was determined to return to this city, with all its horrors. In all of the complicated equations in his mind, there was one that he had so far omitted, but most certainly had not forgotten. Henriette was in Coimbra. And of one thing Keane was now sure: he would return for her.

He turned to Trant. 'Very well, colonel. I'll do it.'

Trant smiled. 'That's the way. Excellent! I knew that you would see sense.' He placed what felt uncomfortably like an almost avuncular hand on Keane's shoulder. 'The first thing you must do is speak to Sanchez's Frenchies. I hope they're in a fit state to talk to you, poor buggers.'

Don Sanchez had had his men lock his surviving prisoners in a damp storeroom of the hospital, close to Doctor Sobral's office, and that was where Keane found them an hour later. Leaving Garland and Martin to stand guard outside, he went in.

The officer was sitting on the flagstones in a corner of the room, a distance away from the few miserable survivors of his company. All of the men were staring at the ground, although not at anything in particular.

The officer looked up as Keane entered and stared at him for a moment, uncertain of his uniform. Then he resumed staring at the ground. The other men did not move.

Keane walked across to the officer and the man drew back and gazed at him.

Keane addressed him in French: 'Captain? I'm English. I'm here to help you.'

The man shrugged.

'Listen to me, captain. I'm here to help you. I need you to answer a few questions for me.'

The captain stiffened. 'Questions? The Spaniard asked questions. A lot of questions. But my men did not answer. And so they died. I won't answer your questions. Why don't you just kill me now and be done with it?'

'I'm not going to kill you, captain. I'm an English officer. But I am here to plead with you.'

'You will plead with me?'

'Yes. In fact, I'll go so far as to beg you. And them.' He pointed to the other ranks in the corner, who were now staring at them.

'I don't understand.'

'Do you know what we have in this hospital?'

'I know something of it. You have French prisoners of war.'

'Yes. Do you know how many?'

'I think that you did have a good many.'

'We have five hundred patients and two hundred marines of your emperor's Imperial Guard, along with their commanding officer.'

For the first time, the man looked Keane in the eyes and Keane could see the surprise on his face. 'Seven hundred men? We heard that the Portuguese had massacred most of the prisoners. Perhaps all of them.'

'That was a lie, spread among you deliberately by your senior commanders. You can come with me and see the prisoners, if you wish. I promise you, captain, they are very much still alive.'

'Yes, I would like to do that. My soldiers will remain here.' He muttered something to the men, some of whom nodded and murmured, and then, with Keane, he left the room.

Followed by Garland and Martin, they walked past Sobral's office and the doctor raised his head and smiled as they passed. Ascending the staircase, they began to come across some of the patients and, looking down, the captain stopped as he saw some of them sitting out in the gardens.

'I can see that you were not lying. You do have a great many of our men.'

'Yes, come on. I'll show you. There are many more.'

Still climbing, they reached the first ward and entered through the large doors. The place was lined with men, some on beds and some on the floor. And there, at the end of the room, ministering to one of them, stood Henriette.

The captain nodded. 'Monsieur, I owe you an apology. You

were not lying. Thank you. Clearly, it is we who were lied to. Sometimes the high command have a strange way of doing things.'

Hearing voices, Henriette looked up and, seeing Keane, looked down once again.

The French captain noticed her. 'Ah. You have a nurse, there, a *vivandière*?'

'Yes, she has been wonderful. Have you seen enough, captain?'

'Yes, I think so. But I still don't understand why you want to beg anything of me.'

'Why don't we find somewhere to talk? Shall we start with our names? Captain James Keane, 27th foot.'

'Henri Dussitot. Captain, 105th line.'

'That's better. Now at least we know each other.'

They returned down the staircase and Keane knocked at Doctor Sobral's open door, staring in to find the doctor. 'Doctor, may we borrow your office for a moment? We shan't keep you long.'

Sobral smiled and invited them in, before leaving. With Garland and Martin posted outside, Keane closed the door behind him and began to speak.

'I'm afraid that your situation is very grave, Captain Dussitot. I beg you to tell me more about the shipment of gold with Marshal Massena's army.'

'I have said nothing and nor will I do so now, captain, even under your charming persuasion.'

'All I need to know is its location. That's all. Is that so very hard when lives depend upon it?'

'Lives? More lives? Is there to be more killing?'

'You have seen Colonel Sanchez's men at work?'

The captain nodded. 'Of course. You know that.'

'I have it from his own lips that, unless we discover the location of the gold, he will kill every one of the prisoners we hold. Just as he killed your men.'

The captain shook his head. 'It's a bluff. He wouldn't. There are too many of them. Besides, you are here to stop him – the British army.'

'We are but eight men, captain.'

'But what about Colonel Trant? He is your countryman. He commands a brigade.'

'A brigade of Portuguese, captain. And it was some of these men, the regular militia, who killed so many of the prisoners before Trant stopped them. Given a command by Sanchez, I don't think they would be so considerate.'

Dussitot said nothing. He paused for a few moments and then looked Keane directly in the eye. 'I would need a reassurance from you, captain. A guarantee.'

'You would have it, from me. And, with it, my word as an officer.'

'If I tell you what you want to know – and be aware that this is information which may well by now be out of date and so, in effect, it may be wrong; be aware of that – if I tell you, I need an assurance that everyone in the hospital – patients, marines, the *vivandière* I saw, and myself and my men – that everyone will be unharmed. All I ask is our safekeeping.'

Keane nodded. 'You have it, captain. On my honour. You have my word that no one here, no Frenchman or woman will be harmed, as long as we can prevent it.'

Dussitot smiled. 'Very well. In that case, I will tell you what you want to know.' He paused. 'The French army is divided. Marshal Massena is unpopular – as I'm sure you are aware.'

Keane nodded. 'We have known that for some time. Your generals are fighting one another.'

'Your intelligence is impressive, captain. But for one thing you are wrong. Not all of them are fighting one another. Some, yes. Some are not happy with Massena. Marshal Ney, in particular. He was much affected by news of the massacre here. If he only knew the truth that you have shown me – '

'But he won't, will he? So the truth changes nothing. Please go on, captain.'

'In his fury, Ney – he has a terrible temper – rebelled against Massena. He wants to move his command back here, to Coimbra. He believes that Massena should never have abandoned the city.'

'Ney plans to move his corps back here, to Coimbra?'

Dussitot nodded. 'Yes. He's adamant about it.'

'This is very good information, captain, for which I am much obliged to you. But I cannot yet see how it has relevance to our desire to find the gold in the marshal's train.'

'Yes, I can see that. But the fact is that, quite apart from intending to move his corps back here, Ney also has plans for the gold.'

'He intends to take Massena's gold?'

'Not exactly. He believes that the gold will be taken by guerrillas.'

'Well, in that he's not wrong, is he?'

'That's merely his justification. The truth is, according to my sources, that Ney believes that Massena intends to take some of the gold, if not all of it, for himself.'

'His love of riches is as well known as his love for women.'

'Ney seems convinced of it and, one thing is certain, Marshal Ney is loyal to the emperor. In his eyes, the gold belongs to

Napoleon. If you want my honest opinion, captain, I think Ney believes that, if he saves the gold from guerrillas, it might improve his standing with the emperor – over that of Massena. Ney is a fine soldier, captain. The finest and the bravest of the brave. But he is ambitious and he loves the emperor almost as much as his career. He's out for all he can get.'

'He's a shrewd general.'

'He is, captain. He knows that Massena is bound to end up being sent back to France with his tail between his legs. Bussaco was a farce. Massena sent the men in, up that hill, and they were mown down by your musket fire. And did you know he had a mistress out here? Brought her all this way from France. She's married to a hero of France. His troops resented her presence. It's become a scandal and the emperor doesn't like it. Not at all. Massena's desperate to find favour again.'

'Yes, I know.'

'You do? Truly your intelligence is impressive.'

Keane said nothing about Henriette. How, he thought, could this man, intelligent as he was, possibly understand?

'Do you know when Ney will take the gold, and where?'

Dussitot nodded his head. 'Yes, I know that. My brother-in-law is an aide in Ney's headquarters. He tells me everything.'

'Useful man, your brother-in-law.'

'I suppose that I might even thank him for saving my life.'

'You may, although I wouldn't count on it yet, captain. You need to tell me the time and the place.'

'I can do better than that, captain. I can show you on a map. You have one?'

'Yes, and I'm willing to wager that it's a damn sight better than anything you'll have in your army.'

Dussitot smiled. It was common knowledge that Wellington's

mapping officers had worked hard to create new maps of the entire country and, even now, every day, were out in the field about their duties.

Keane opened the valise he had been carrying hung around his neck and drew out a map, which he unfolded and placed on a table that stood in the centre of the room.

Dussitot nodded. 'Yes, you're right. We have nothing like this.'

Keane drew his finger over the map, close to Coimbra. 'Can you show me by which route Ney intends to approach the city?'

Dussitot pointed. 'There. Ney's column will come through there. From Santarém, here, they will march to here, at Pombal, then to Redinha and then to Condeixa.'

'You're certain of this?'

'Quite certain, captain; I am talking for my life. I would not lie to you. Not just my life, but all the lives of the Frenchmen in Coimbra depend on the fact that I am telling you the truth. If you go to find the gold and this is not true, then we shall all die. Why would I lie?'

Keane looked at the map. 'How long would you say between Santarém and Coimbra?'

'Ten days, perhaps, do you think?'

'Yes, that was my thinking exactly.'

He looked at the map again, but said nothing; yet, in his mind, he had already decided where it would be best to meet Ney's men. The town of Pombal lay some twenty-five miles south-west of Coimbra. And it was there that they would take the gold.

They rose together from the table and Keane folded the map and replaced it in his valise before leading Dussitot, together with Garland and Martin, from Sobral's office, out of the hospital and up the hill towards the palace.

They found Trant and Sanchez sitting on the terrace. Seeing
Keane approaching them, both men rose. And both of them
froze when they caught sight of Dussitot.

Keane spoke first. 'Captain Dussitot has been most helpful.
He has offered me significant information, which I have no
doubt will enable us to make contact with the enemy and
secure the shipment for the allies.'

Sanchez coughed and drained his glass.

Keane continued, 'I have given the captain my assurances
and my word as an officer that neither he, nor his remaining
soldiers, nor any of the French in Coimbra will be harmed. And
I intend to keep it.'

Again Sanchez coughed and shook his head. But Trant looked
directly at Dussitot and nodded. 'Captain, thank you. Would
you care for a glass?'

Dussitot said nothing. He ignored Sanchez, who was now
standing slightly apart from the others, and turned away from
him before speaking to Keane and Trant. 'I prefer not to keep
company with murderers, gentlemen.'

Keane frowned and went on, 'Are we agreed, gentlemen?
That no harm shall come to any Frenchman in Coimbra? I need
your best assurances.'

Trant nodded. 'Yes, of course, I will swear to it. Just as you
say, Captain Keane. You have my word.'

Sanchez stared at them all and then, after a few moments,
spoke: 'Very well, gentlemen. I do not understand your way of
doing things. It is not my way. But you have my word. My men
will not harm any Frenchman in Coimbra.'

Dussitot smiled and Keane was not certain whether it was
because he was aware of the irony in the fact that Sanchez
had harmed so many Frenchmen to date, or if he simply did

not trust the man. For his part, Keane could not abandon the hope that Sanchez might revert to the humanity of the man he had known before.

Keane went on, 'And I require immediately that Captain Dussitot and his surviving men be released from the room in which they have been confined till now and allowed to find comfortable billets in the hospital, among their own.'

Trant waved his hand. 'As you wish, Keane. The captain may go on his way.' He called to his aide, 'Lieutenant Romero, release the other French prisoners that Colonel Sanchez brought in. Send them with Captain Dussitot to the hospital. Oh, and you'd better give them an escort. We wouldn't want anything unfortunate to happen to them.'

After Dussitot and the aide had gone, Keane spoke once more: 'So we are decided?'

Trant nodded. 'Yes. As you say. What are the details?'

'Marshal Ney intends to march against Coimbra. He will send a column of five thousand men, infantry with cavalry support and light guns, to take it from you, Colonel Trant. And with them he will send a portion of Massena's gold.'

'Five thousand. We could hold them off here, I think. But I would guess that isn't your intention.'

'No, not at all. Nor yours. You intended to attack the convoy and that is what we will do. We have Colonel Sanchez's men. How many do you have, colonel?'

Sanchez smiled. 'As I said, captain, my force has grown since we last met. I have seven hundred and seventy men, captain, and fifty-one officers, all in uniform. You have seen them, no doubt? We are organized in sixteen companies. And I have infantry, too. How many do you suppose, captain?'

Keane shrugged. 'I have no idea, colonel.'

'I have over a thousand men in six companies with twenty-eight officers. And we have two cannon. What do you think of that?'

Keane smiled appreciatively. 'Very impressive, colonel. Are they trained?'

'Of course they are trained. Trained by me and my officers. But they know the ways of the hills, anyway. They don't need to stand in line to lose their lives, like the British soldiers.'

'So you have around eighteen hundred men to face Ney's column of five thousand.'

Sanchez grinned. 'I will need only the lancers. Seven hundred can deal with five thousand in ambush – if we have the right ground.'

Keane nodded. It was true. A few companies of the lancers armed with carbines could pin down the French in a gorge or valley. And then, when panic set in among the column, the rest of the horsemen, armed with their lances, could push in from each end of the valley and deal with what remained of the desperate enemy. Just as the guerrillas had dealt with the grand convoy in the bloody massacre at Salinas, back in 1809. It would not take long.

Keane looked at Sanchez. 'You will need to know your ground, colonel, and use it well.'

'Have you ever known me to do anything else? Can I ask you, captain, when and where you propose that this will happen?'

Keane reached into his valise and, unfolding the map, spread it on the table between them, weighing it down at the corners. He pointed with his finger to the town of Pombal, which lay in the Serra de Sicó.

Sanchez nodded. 'Pombal, yes. That is good ground. They will pass through Pombal?'

'Captain Dussitot swears to it.'

'I know the ground. The Serra has several places where we can take them. It's as good a place as any to kill Frenchmen. It will do.'

Trant, who up till now had said nothing, looked at the map and shook his head. 'No, I'm sorry, colonel. It's not enough. You need more than the lancers for this. What if anything should go wrong? What if the ambush should not succeed and the action should become a firefight? We need to be certain of finishing the column and getting the gold. You will need the infantry.' He turned to Keane. 'Do we know what men Ney is likely to send?'

'My agents sent me a full order of battle for Massena's army before Bussaco. Ney has the 6th corps. It's my guess he'll send three full regiments – one light, two line – along with one of cavalry. The lancers can deal with those.'

Trant shook his head. 'But there's no doubt of it. You need the infantry, Don Julian.' He turned to Keane with a faint smile. 'You will go with them, Keane, won't you?'

'It was my intention.'

'Then you will also need men – more, at least, than you have at present. You can take the students. My students.'

'The students?'

'The Coimbra militia. They're good lads. Handy with a musket.'

'Good lads they may be, but they're hardly experienced troops, colonel.'

'Oh, I'm sure you can work on them, Keane. You know what to do. And it's a sizeable force. Foot and horse together. There are just short of five hundred of them.'

'And we leave you with . . ?'

'The militia. I can hold this place with them. A thousand good men.'

Keane thought for a few moments. 'Very well. It's agreed. But I have one condition: you both must agree that I be allowed to make contact with Wellington before we attack the column and not afterwards. That is vital.'

Trant, who had ordered another carafe of wine, drank half a glass in his impatience. 'Yes, yes. If those are your conditions, Captain Keane, then yes we agree. Do we not, Colonel Sanchez?'

'Yes, Colonel Trant. Of course. Captain Keane may have his rendezvous with Lord Wellington and then we shall find our gold.'

Keane, with Garland and Martin walking close beside him, made his way down from the palace towards the men's billet. In retrospect, he thought, things had gone none too badly. He had been a little surprised at Trant's offer of the student regiment, but he was happy with the challenge of training them up.

Of course, it went without saying that he did not trust either Trant or Sanchez. The latter he had dealt with before and Trant filled him with doubt.

He knew that, when they had dealt with the column, in the likely event that they beat off the French, Sanchez might well attempt to take more than his share of the gold. Trant, of course, would not be there in person, but Keane was well aware that part of the reason for him having been given command of the student militia was so that they could claim Trant's share, or perhaps more. They would have to be watched.

Keane entered the door of the tavern that was the men's billet and found the same weary atmosphere in which he had left the place.

'I have some news.'

Silver, who was throwing a cup of dice on a table, spoke under his breath: 'If it's about that bloody book, I don't want to know.'

Keane ignored the insubordinate comment. 'As I said, I have some news, and no, Silver, it's not about the bloody book. It's about gold.'

Silver looked up from his game and the others turned towards Keane.

Gabriella walked across. 'Gold?'

'We have a slight change of plan. We're taking the book to headquarters, as were our orders. And I can't say that I shan't be glad to be shot of it. But then we're coming back here.'

There was a groan, not least from Silver. 'Not back here, sir – not again. Not to this godforsaken dung heap.'

Keane continued, 'And, on the way back, we are going to ambush a French convoy.'

There was a murmur among them, which Keane took for approval.

Ross nodded. 'Would they be carrying the gold, sir?'

'That they would, sarn't. We're going in with Don Sanchez's men and I've been given command of the student militia.'

Silver shook his head. 'The guerrillas are all right – good fighters – but those boys? The students? That's not a command, sir. They need a wet nurse.'

'Well then, Silver, that's what you'll be.' The others laughed. 'I intend to train them. There's not a man alive who can't be trained to fight.'

Garland spoke up: 'Well, I don't envy you, sir; no, I don't.'

'Well, you won't have to. You're going to help me.'

'What, sir?'

'I'm giving each of you one company of the students. I want them battle ready in two days. Heredia?'

The Portuguese cavalryman, who for the past few days had not spoken a word to Keane, walked forward from the shadows. 'Yes, sir?'

'I'm putting you back on the strength. Effective immediately. I need a troop of the students properly led to fight on horseback. I know that they're already good horsemen with their own mounts. I want them ready to fight. Can you do it for me?'

'I can, sir.'

'And will you do it?'

The man nodded. 'Yes, sir. I will.'

'Good. Then that's settled. The rest of you, you're all infantrymen, originally. You know the drill. They all have muskets – British ones – and they use the same ammunition.'

Ross asked the question that was in all their minds: 'How long do we have, sir?'

'I have information that the column will be setting off in four days' time. We have to be ready to meet it at the appointed place in six days.'

Ross whistled. 'Blimey, sir. Six days to train a platoon. They had better be good.'

Garland spoke: 'I hope they learn well.'

Silver turned to him. 'Learn well? They're bloody students, you dimwit. Course they'll learn well.'

Keane continued, 'Oh, I can promise you they're clever. They're all from the university here.'

Silver shook his head and muttered, 'Four days to train a bunch of students to fight. What next?'

Keane went on, 'And, for the duration of the command, I'm raising all of you to the rank of acting sergeant. Apart from you, Sarn't Ross; you can be the regimental sarn't major. Silver and Archer, you're senior sergeants. We meet our new recruits in the morning.'

There was one more thing left for him to do.

He entered the hospital and found Henriette washing out bloody bedclothes, up to her elbows in milky, red water. Seeing him, she looked away. But Keane stood close and touched her arm. 'Can we talk?'

She smiled and stood up, wiping her hands on a fragment of cloth. Then she walked with him to the end of the ward and spoke softly. 'I'm sorry. We can't really talk here. The lieutenant.'

'Do you care for him?'

'He's been very good to me.'

'But what I asked was if you cared for him.'

'I don't know. Yes, perhaps. I need to get back to the men.'

'Do you want to stay here?'

'Here? Yes. Why? I'm busy, you can see.'

Keane shook his head. 'Not now. To stay here, in Coimbra. With Lievremont.'

'What choice do I have?'

'You could come with me.'

'Where?'

'To the lines. To Torres Vedras. I have to leave here soon, but I'll be back. Will you wait for me and come with me then?'

She looked away.

'Henriette, I have the book – the book for Wellington. I have fulfilled my mission. But there's more. Trant wants me to go with Sanchez and take a French convoy – a convoy of gold. Some of it will be for the guerrillas and some for Trant. Most

of the rest of it I will take to Wellington. But some of it I will
give to my men and some of it I will keep. We could be rich. I
might even be promoted.'

He touched her arm again and drew her towards him.

'Tell me. Do you care for me?'

She looked at him. 'Yes, of course. You know I do.'

'Well then, wait here while I'm away and then come with
me. I won't be long.' Keane looked at her and their eyes met.
He pulled her closer. 'Come with me.'

She looked at him. 'And be a soldier's wife?'

'Isn't that what you'd have with Lievremont? What you've
always had?'

'I don't want that.'

'With him? Or with anyone? All your life has been spent with
soldiers – your husband, Massena – why not me?'

'You're asking me to marry you? I don't know, James.'

He let go of her. 'Then don't marry me. Just come away with
me. Live with me.'

She said nothing. From the ward, someone called her name.

'I have to go.'

'At least will you think about it?'

She nodded. 'Give me time.'

'I don't have much time. Only five days. We leave in five days.'

'Then that's the time I'll need. Five days.'

The following morning, Keane's recruits began to arrive. He
had asked Trant to send them to the plaza at the university
and they came ambling along in twos and threes, as if, he
thought, they might be on their way to a lecture or a tutorial.
They wore the curious uniforms he had noticed on his arrival
back in the city.

The horsemen were somewhat less unkempt. In fact, they were splendidly turned out. Undoubtedly, he thought, they had furnished their own mounts and came from aristocratic families. He wondered how they would take to Heredia's command.

It took a good half hour for the students to assemble. They stood in groups and Keane supposed that these were either the platoons and companies to which they already belonged or simply their friends. Either way, he decided to keep them together. It was easy to pick out the officers among them by their gold epaulettes and elaborate hats and, as soon as ten of these were evident, he walked across to one of them.

'Captain Keane. I've been placed in command of you for the next few weeks.'

The young man, a good looking youth in his mid twenties, stood straight as he replied, 'Captain Francesco. Yes, sir. Colonel Trant told us that, and that your men would be joining us.'

'Good. The idea is to train you to act and fight like British soldiers. We need you to be able to beat the French in a firefight.'

'Oh, we can do that now, sir. We took back the city from them.'

Keane smiled. 'In all fairness, captain, that was not what I would call a firefight. You had the element of surprise and most of the French were blind drunk.'

The captain said nothing.

Keane turned and walked to the edge of the square, where he had drawn up his own men. Then he turned back to face the assembled regiment. 'Right, all of you. Listen carefully. My name is Captain Keane and I'm your new commanding officer. These are my men. They are your new sergeants. We have a job to do. We have to train you to fight. I'm not saying that you can't fight already, that you won't fight. What we are going to do is train you to fight properly, to fight so you can defeat the French. You're going to fight like British soldiers do. And we're going to do this in four days.'

There was a general murmur from the crowd, most of whom, it seemed, were able to understand English.

The officer who had spoken to Kean stepped forward.

'Captain – Captain Keane. I'm sorry. You want us to be like your infantry?'

'Yes, precisely. That's it.'

'No, I'm sorry. Your soldiers are driven by the lash and brute force. We are not like that. We will not be beaten.'

'No, captain, you misunderstand me. I do not intend to punish you. I merely want to make soldiers of you.'

The officer said nothing, but looked at Keane. 'How will you do that?'

Silver spoke up: 'The same way we make any man a soldier, sir. By working him hard – bloody hard. You'll learn to fire four rounds a minute, sir. It'll be hard at first and then it'll come like second nature. That's how you make a man become a soldier, sir.'

12

Five days can seem like a very long time. Particularly, thought Keane, if you have a mission to complete but, instead, are compelled to stand out on a parade ground and watch a bunch of amateurs being made into a fighting unit.

Even worse, of course, if you're one of those men, with some bastard of a sergeant screaming commands at you in a foreign tongue and making you fire a musket until your shoulder is numb from the pain of the recoil and your finger is bleeding from squeezing the trigger.

For five days, the students of Coimbra had been put through their paces. They had been drilled in the art of musketry on the very square where once, in another life, they had passed their time, between academic studies, in carefree conversation. Now, an aggressive little man with red hair and a strange accent was shouting at them, telling them that they were worthless, that they had to fire faster, had to learn to kill the enemy with every volley. Tear, spit, ram, present. Tear, load, ram, present. That had been their litany these past four days and the walls of the *departamento de ciência* bore testimony to their firepower. Its whitewashed walls were pitted with rounds – some, remarkably high; some, horribly low. Most, though, had gone in at about chest height, or, better still, the height of a man's head – the right height, at any rate, to kill a Frenchman.

And, through all of the four long days, Keane had watched them, had seen them grow from nothing more than a mob with muskets into a disciplined unit. He'd watched as their ragged volleys – snapped off too soon, or rattled off too late – had become a thing of precision, a thing, dare he say it, even of some beauty.

Silver had been right. You could teach a man the art of war. Any man. In just five days, the boys of Coimbra University had become proper fighting men. And his men had done it – his bunch of jailbirds, as Grant liked to call them. He was proud of them, more proud than he could say, certainly more proud than he would ever admit to them. Apart from the effect they had had upon the students, the exercise had done wonders for the men themselves. It had restored their faith in themselves and somehow had reaffirmed everything they were fighting for. Keane knew that none of them had a great moral drive. None believed that they were engaged in a crusade. But somehow there was an unspoken bond between them, which was driven by the desire to rid the world of Boney – and, above all, by the wish to get back home.

He watched now as the young officer with whom he had spoken on the first day marched to the front of his company, ordered there by Sergeant Ross. The young man, Captain Francesco, who, up till now, had been firing in the line with his men, handed his musket to Ross and took position on the right of the front rank. He had done his work as a soldier. He had learnt how to fire his musket like a British soldier and now he was going to learn to give commands like a British officer.

Under Ross's watchful eye, he repeated the commands for the musket drill. 'Tear, pour, ram, present.' Finally, he yelled, 'Fire!'

Fifty muskets spat flame and again the shot poured into the whitewashed wall. The captain smiled and, as Sergeant Ross surveyed the pattern of the balls, waited.

Ross turned to him. 'Very good, sir. Well done. A good volley.'

Turning, Francesco caught Keane's eye and, in that instant, Keane knew that the students would do.

It was approaching six in the evening when Keane set out for the hospital. He did not need treatment. His arm, though still painful, was free of the sling now. There was another reason for his visit.

He had not thought that he would feel so anxious about Henriette's decision, but at this moment his stomach felt as empty as it did when he was facing a column of advancing Frenchman or standing under an artillery barrage. Everything seemed to be coming together. The gold, or his share of it, would give him security and a future. Trant had promised more information about his own past and his father, and he really felt that he might be about to get close to the truth. And, above all, the book was in his possession. He kept it with him at all times now, tucked carefully into an inside pocket of his coat. Perhaps it might lure Macnab to him. He had sworn vengeance against him and he meant to keep his date with the double agent. Martin always went with him and he had posted the men around the old town with orders to report any strange movement on the streets. Macnab was canny, with an unnerving ability to slip through the shadows undetected. But Keane knew that if anyone could pick up his scent then it

was his own men. Wherever the book went, Keane suspected
Macnab would not be far behind and, when the moment came
for him to show himself, Keane would be ready.

But, even with all of these potential successes and triumphs,
Keane knew that happiness lay elsewhere. If Henriette were to
turn him down, then everything else might seem practically
worthless.

He felt the hollow feeling in his stomach again and quickened his pace. Without thinking, from instinct, he ducked
down one of the smaller side streets, taking what he had discovered to be a short cut through the old university quarter
to the hospital. The street doubled back on itself and then
emerged in the muffle of a flight of steps among the student
lodgings, the old medieval *republicas*, before coming out again
directly before the hospital.

Keane rattled down the steps to enter the last of the streets.
And it was only then that he realized he was being followed. It
was nothing as loud as a footstep, nor even a moving shadow,
but merely a sense that someone was watching him.

He turned and looked to his rear, but saw no one. And it
occurred to him that he had lost Martin. He cursed himself for
his foolishness, for having hurried ahead in his urgency rather
than keeping the boy close to him. He called quietly into the
evening shadows, 'Will! Will Martin? Are you there?'

There was no reply and, around him, the streets were silent.
He had not thought it would happen again, but here he was in
this accursed place, hunted for a second time – and most surely
by Macnab. The majority of the houses in this part of the old
city had been abandoned when the French sacked the place, and
none of the French or the Portuguese had any desire to occupy
them. These streets had seen some of the worst violence. There

was too much death here and, after nightfall, the rats roamed free. The tall, close-packed houses stood open and desolate, their windows gaping like empty black eye sockets, framed by tattered curtains or broken shutters.

Keane turned back to his route and, listening briefly for any footsteps, began to move on. Where the devil could Martin have got to? For a moment, he thought of Gilpin and his mind raced with an image of Martin taken by Macnab. But he banished it. It was his own stupidity that had brought him here alone. The boy would be searching the streets of the upper town, even now, desperately trying to find him. For a moment, Keane thought that it might be better to retrace his steps. But then, realizing that the hospital was only a few yards away, he set out at a faster pace. Again, he was aware of someone close by. He stopped abruptly and stared up. That was the trick, the soldiers' trick that no one ever thought about. People looked at their own level while, all too often, danger was lurking over their heads. But now Keane saw nothing.

He walked on a few more paces and then was certain, this time, that he saw movement in an upper window. He paused at the door and drew his sword before entering, feeling the smooth ivory hilt of the Jesuit's Egyptian scimitar and catching sight of the wickedly honed, curved blade. The door creaked on its hinges and revealed the wreck of what had once been a beautiful and treasured house. Possessions lay across the floor and the air stank of mildew and decay. There was a creak above his head and the noise of something moving. It could, he thought, be rats or a dog. But within him he knew that it was not.

Slowly, Keane began to climb the stairs, but each step brought a new creak. There was no point in caution. The best way was to rush whoever was above. He scrambled up the staircase and, at the top, came to a door, which was ajar. He kicked it open and swung into the room. Macnab was standing in the corner beside the window. He was wearing the same blue civilian frock coat that Keane had seen him in before and now it occurred to Keane how, curiously, it made Macnab appear something like the duke himself. In fact, it was precisely the costume favoured by Wellington.

A smile played across Macnab's face, which now turned to a sneer. 'Captain Keane, I wondered how long you would take to get here.'

Keane had not heard Macnab speak before and was now surprised by the voice. It was soft, almost like a woman's, and with a gentle touch of Irish, which gave it an oddly reassuring quality.

'Macnab.'

'Colonel Macnab will suffice – if that is the name by which you know me.'

'I've been waiting for this moment.'

'And I, likewise, Captain Keane. I must say, I'm intrigued to meet you. Honoured, too, that you should have taken the trouble to seek me out.'

'I thought it was you that was chasing me.'

'On the contrary, captain. You are the hunter; I am the prey. But it seems that now the tables are turned.'

Macnab drew his right hand from where it had been hidden behind his back and Keane saw that it held a pistol, cocked and ready to fire.

'And now, captain, if you please, I believe that you have something: a piece of my property – or, should I say, the emperor's property – which I shall very soon have returned to him.'

'It was never your property, and it is most certainly not the property of Bonaparte.'

Macnab winced. 'Oh dear. How it pains me to hear the emperor called that. The man who brilliantly took command of Europe when all the prancing fops who called themselves her kings were ruining their own countries, betraying their own peoples. Napoleon is a saviour, captain. The saviour of Europe. Of the world.'

He recognized the same passion he had seen in the Jesuit and knew at once that Macnab was that very worst of foes: the man who utterly believes in the truth of his cause.

'You murdered one of my men and you killed my best friend.'

'Oh, come, come, Keane. I don't think that even you, by any stretch of the imagination, would describe Captain Morris as your best friend. Not after what he did with Miss Blackwood.'

Keane half made to rush at Macnab, but stopped himself. 'You won't provoke me, Macnab. I know who Tom Morris was – the sort of man he was – and I know all about him and Kitty. He was my friend and you killed him. Just as you did Gilpin.'

'No, there you're quite wrong. Captain Morris was shot on the battlefield, fair and square. Gilpin – was that his name? What a curious name. Gilpin.' He tossed the word around on his tongue. 'Him, I killed in cold blood. And, let me tell you, it gave me huge satisfaction. You should have seen his face as I took off his hand. Exquisite.'

Keane felt his hand tighten on the sword grip. 'You will die, Macnab. You know that.'

'Yes, of course I will, inevitably. But I suspect that it will be at an advanced age, sitting in a dressing gown in my rooms in the Doge's Palace, or even the Vatican. You see, Keane, I have no plans for eternity quite yet. And now, if you please, the book. Of course, I could make it easier and kill you first. But that would be tiresome and also potentially harmful to the precious object. Who knows where my ball might land or where you have hidden it.'

'Fire away. You'll not make me give it up willingly. You'll have to take it from me.'

Macnab presented the pistol and pointed it directly at Keane's head. 'I warn you, Keane, I'm reckoned to be a fair shot. I should have liked to have killed you with at least some degree of finesse. Unfortunately, as you are being so uncooperative, it seems as if my only option is to separate your brains from your head. Adieu.'

The words had hardly escaped him when there was a crack of gunfire. Keane winced, expecting at any moment to feel the burn of the ball as it hit him. But instead he heard another shot as Macnab's gun exploded, firing flame and pistol ball into the floor. The man screamed and grabbed at his shoulder. The bullet had hit him high and had not penetrated the torso. But, nevertheless, the damage was considerable – certainly sufficient to stop him for just long enough.

Keane grasped the moment and leapt towards him as Macnab reeled backwards, overcome by pain and surprise.

As Keane lunged at him, Macnab moved sideways, away from the window through which the shot had come. At the same time, his left hand dropped down to his side and drew a sword from its scabbard, ready to meet Keane's. Steel rang against steel and Keane could see the pain in Macnab's eyes. Yet the man continued to smile at him and that was enough to stir his hate. He made another move towards Macnab, but his sword, the curved blade, with which he was pleased so far, was lighter and moved faster than his old sabre and he overestimated the distance, cutting the air beyond Macnab's face. The spy took his chance and went for Keane again, catching him a blow on the arm that drew blood through the cloth of his brown coat. Keane sprang back and Macnab, playing to his advantage, went after him with another savage cut, this time to the torso. But Keane was too fast for him and the curved Egyptian blade whistled upwards towards Macnab's face. Instinctively, Macnab went to protect himself with his left hand and, as he did so, the scimitar struck two fingers, the pinkie and the ring finger, shearing them cleanly from his hand.

Macnab screamed and, clutching at his bloody hand, dropped the blade as the two severed digits fell to the floor.

Keane snarled, 'That's for Gilpin. Two down, three to go.'

Macnab was bleeding heavily from his hand and Keane sensed the panic that now gripped hold of him. There was a chance, he thought, if he was able to keep his head, that he could finish him there and then. He crouched low, waiting for his moment, watching Macnab's face drain of colour. The spy made another lunge, clumsy now and overshooting Keane. He tripped and fell to the floor, his blade clattering from his hand. Keane leapt back and looked down. Macnab was lying face down on the floorboards. He did not move. Surely, he thought, the man can't be dead? A shoulder wound and two fingers? This was a ruse. The man was playing with him.

Keane moved away from Macnab. 'Get up, you coward. Get up and fight.'

There was no reply. He tried again: 'Get up, you bastard! Fight for your bloody book and your pathetic emperor. Fight for Bonaparte.'

That, he thought, must rouse him. But still there was nothing. Slowly, Keane drew closer, and that was when he noticed it:

a pool of blood around Macnab's head. It was fresh and black and flowing. Christ, he thought, he had hit his head. Perhaps he was really dead.

He stood motionless, trying not to breathe, trying to detect the merest hint of breath and life in Macnab's body. But he saw nothing. The back was not rising, nor the rib cage. The fingers did not twitch, as they might in a wounded man. The feet and legs lay prone where they had gone from under him. It certainly looked as if Macnab must be dead.

There was a commotion beyond the open door and footsteps on the stairs, and there was Martin. He stared down at Macnab. 'Christ, sir. Is he . . . ?'

'I'm not sure. But well done. It was a good shot.'

'Not good enough, though. I should have killed him.'

'Looks as if he might have done the job himself.'

Both men looked down at Macnab. Keane, tempted at last, poked him in the back with the tip of the scimitar – gently at first and then harder. He looked up to Martin. 'Do you know, Will, I do believe he might be – '

But his words were cut short. With a single, swift movement, Macnab spun round on the floor and, now facing up at Keane, grabbed the blade of the scimitar with his good right hand, around which he had wound the sleeve of his coat. He pulled the sword away from his chest to the right, just as, instinctively, Keane tightened his grip on its hilt. It was what Macnab had predicted. Now, pushing up his left leg, he kicked Keane hard in the groin and, keeping the leg straight and stiff, used it as a pivot with which to propel him forwards, over his head, towards Martin. Keane, carried on by the force of his own weight and in agony from the savage kick to his groin, left the ground and hit Martin in the solar plexus with his head, winding him and sending him reeling backwards down the staircase. Macnab let go of Keane's blade and threw it to the floor. Then, losing no time, the blood still gushing from his maimed left hand, he threw himself on Keane and ripped open his coat from behind. He began to probe desperately with his remaining fingers until he found what he wanted. He pulled the book from Keane's pocket and stuffed it into his own. Then, as Martin reached the top of the staircase, the gun still in his hands, Macnab ran towards the window and leapt through it to the street below.

Keane pushed himself up with his arms, crouching in agony, and shook his head to clear it. He saw Martin.

'For Christ's sake, man. Shoot him!'

Martin ran to the window, but saw that Macnab was already crossing the street. By the time he had primed and loaded, it would be too late.

'He's too quick, sir. No time.'

'Then go after him. Get that bloody book back.'

Martin didn't need telling twice. He turned and clattered down the staircase. Keane was on his feet now and, moving towards the window, looked out. But it was as he had known it would be: there was no sign of Macnab, only the sight of Martin, running along the deserted street.

The boy stopped and looked up at the window. 'He's gone, sir. Didn't see which way. Sorry, sir.'

Keane walked back into the room and, massaging his groin, retrieved the bloody scimitar from the floor, where it lay close beside Macnab's two severed fingers. One of them, the smaller, wore a gold ring. Keane stooped and picked it up, looking at the engraved seal.

For a moment, he was frozen. The symbol on the ring was a

hand, palm facing out, beneath which, quite discernible, were drops of blood. Keane stared at it and began to wonder what it meant. Was it some strange reference to Gilpin's horror?

He was no expert on heraldry or family crests, but he reckoned that someone might have an inkling of to whose arms it belonged. And then, he thought, they would have a proper clue as to the true identity of Macnab, the double agent.

Keane's news was not well received and Gabriella had not finished treating his wounds when Trant walked into the room in their shared billet. Sanchez was close behind him.

'You were wounded?'

'Yes. But not badly. I told your man, the lieutenant.'

'And Macnab got away with the book?'

'Yes, damn him. It was not what I had expected.'

'He seems to be master of the unexpected.'

Keane delved into his pocket and, bringing out the signet ring, which he had carefully removed from Macnab's severed finger, laid it on the table.

'It belonged to Macnab. I took off two of his fingers. Do you recognize that seal, colonel? I thought it might be Irish.'

Trant picked up the ring and looked at it closely. 'No, I can't say that I do. Very distinctive, though. A severed hand.' He looked at Keane. 'Why, it might be a representation of your poor dead man's own hand.'

'Yes, the thought had occurred to me.'

Trant looked at it again, but, as before, his face betrayed nothing. 'No, I'm afraid that I don't know the family.' Continuing to examine it, he appeared to find something on it – blood, Keane presumed. 'So, you took off two of his fingers. It must have been a desperate fight.'

'Let's just say it wasn't easy. The man's good, colonel. He's a real fighter.'

'A fighter, it would seem, who knows what he wants, and who tends to get it.'

Keane looked away. He was ashamed that he had lost the book, that Gilpin's life might have been given in vain. He was also determined to recover it.

Trant shook his head. 'You must be furious. To have lost that book! How did he manage it?'

'I told Lieutenant Romero, sir, and Martin can bear witness, the man feigned death and then overpowered me.'

'It's too bad. Just as well that you will have something to give Wellington, with the gold.'

Keane stared at him. 'I intend to recover it.'

'I dare say you do. But it cannot affect our resolution to get the gold, surely?'

'It was the purpose of my mission – the sole purpose, as far as Wellington was concerned.'

'But you said yourself that the gold would be vital to Wellington. He needs it for the troops and not least to keep the guerrillas in his hand.'

'Yes, colonel, but the book is an even greater need.'

Sanchez had been listening. 'The book. You speak so much about the book. What is it, other than just a book? The gold is gold. Gold, Keane. Doesn't that mean anything to you? I thought you and I were the same, had the same needs, the same desires.'

Keane smiled. 'I don't think so, Colonel Sanchez. Perhaps in some things. But not everything.'

'But a book, Keane? I ask you. A book?'

Trant took up the call. 'Tell me, Keane, how much does the book mean to you?'

'Sir?'

'Is it worth, say, a hundred thousand livres?'

'I dare say it might be. I don't think it can have any real tangible value.'

'I see. So what would it be worth? Where would its value lie? Perhaps in the intangible. Would you say that, for instance, it might be worth to a man the sum of knowledge of his own history?'

Keane looked at him. 'By which you mean . . . ?'

'By which I mean, is it worth the information you need to discover the truth about your own background? Is it worth that, or worth more or less?'

'That's blackmail.'

Trant shook his head. 'Not at all, Captain Keane. I am merely suggesting that, should you choose to set off to recover the book rather than go, as agreed, to assist Don Julian in taking Marshal Ney's gold, that it might be less advantageous for you in terms of attaining the knowledge I am aware that you seek.'

'As I said, more blackmail.'

'Call it what you will; the offer remains.'

Keane turned away and said nothing. His mind was reeling. The fight had drained him. What had seemed to be so clear cut, a steady and almost certain route to everything he had longed for, was now muddied and unsure. He was on the horns of a terrible dilemma, faced with a choice that most certainly would affect the rest of his life. He had lost the book, had failed in his mission to Wellington and Grant. His duty as a soldier was surely to retrieve it. But what then of the gold? That, too, would please Wellington and would prove vital in assuring the continuing loyalty of the guerrillas. It would also please Henriette and ensure their happiness.

And then there was the question of Trant. Keane knew now that the colonel held the knowledge that would lead him to his father. And he knew that he would only impart that knowledge if Keane did as he wished and led the students he had trained with Sanchez's men to take the gold.

Trant had told the students that they would find glory in killing the French, but Keane suspected that they were actually to be used as cannon fodder. Sanchez had persuaded Trant to do it, to spare his own men; there was, thought Keane, a certain logic in that. Sanchez's men were hardened veterans, the kind of experienced fighters who would eventually liberate this country, and Spain with it.

But it stuck in his craw that he should be involved in throwing the students into a death trap to enable Sanchez's men to live and take the gold. That was why he had done his best to train them to fight. He knew that they would not, could not, ever win in a firefight against French infantry. But he hoped that he might have given them what was needed, if they made the best use of the ground.

He wondered if he really had a choice any longer. If he were to pursue Macnab towards France, which was where he was sure to take the book, then he would lose everything else. Trant, he was sure, would go after the gold with Sanchez. He would take the students himself and, without Keane's guidance, the boys would throw themselves against the French and be massacred for certain. The gold would not be his and neither would anything that Trant could offer him as to the reality of his past. And, more than this, he would, he was sure, lose Henriette.

She would remain in Coimbra and, surely, Lievremont would come to dominate her. And then what? Exchange for Portuguese or British prisoners and transport back to Paris? And what fate, he wondered, awaited her there? Massena would be discredited, in all likelihood, and she would forever be known as the marshal's mistress. Her husband would shun her and she would find no favour at Bonaparte's court. She would be ostracized. He saw her tramping the streets of Paris, broken, used and ruined.

He turned back to Trant. 'You drive a hard bargain, colonel.'

'But you'll accept? You will go with Colonel Sanchez? You will attack the convoy and take the gold?'

Keane nodded. 'Frankly, I don't see how I can rightly do anything else. The loss of that damned book may have ruined my career, but at least I will have a life. And perhaps the pages copied by Archer and Sobral might prove useful.'

'That's good. We will drink to it. Don Julian, join us! We must celebrate our alliance. The three of us as one, in search of Ney's gold.' He clapped his hands for his servant and called for wine, but Keane shook his head.

'No, thank you, colonel. I have business to attend to. You may take it, though, that I am with you, whatever the cost. And I expect my commitment to be honoured in kind, as well as in substance.'

Trant nodded at him. 'Of course, Keane. I am a man of my word. On your return, we shall talk at length and then I will help you all that I can.'

Keane walked away from them and, seeing his own men standing on the opposite side of the plaza, he approached them and found Ross and Silver.

He spoke quietly. 'Well, that's our fate as good as sealed, and that of those poor buggers.' He pointed at the students. 'Remember what I told you. When we go into action against the French, wherever Sanchez decides to take the convoy, look after them. I expect to lose most of them, but I want them kept as safe as we can. They're good lads and they don't deserve to die fetching someone else's fortune.'

The two men nodded.

'Oh, and one more thing: tell everyone to keep their eyes sharp on Sanchez. I used almost to trust him, but now I'm not so sure. I'm going for a walk.'

He walked across the square, past the students, who saluted him as he passed. He smiled at them. Whatever tomorrow held for them, he thought, they were lucky. No responsibility. No men to command. No mission, no secrets, no damn spying.

He climbed a flight of stairs that led up the outside of a tower to a parapet and walkway on the old medieval ramparts and, turning, gazed out over the city.

The sun was sinking slowly, lighting the white walls and marble terraces with a soft orange glow. He watched his men in the plaza below him, laughing with one another. Garland had joined them. He cracked a joke and one of them, Silver, shoved him back. Keane watched and thought of all that they had been through together – of their meeting and of how he had taken them from the Lisbon jails and made them a fighting unit. His unit. He thought of Oporto and Bussaco and Sanchez and the German hussars. And then he thought of Gilpin and an initial sadness was overtaken by anger and a desire for revenge. He turned and looked out at the setting sun. Macnab would not escape him. He would have justice, but he would also have gold – and the book, if he could. The last rays of the sun touched the horizon and Keane wondered what destiny lay in store and how many more sunsets he might see. From the square below came the noise of his men laughing at another joke and of the students singing as they tried to return to their old lives and to that vanished time, before the French had come.

13

The night was unbearably hot. Keane lay awake, sweating, naked beneath the thin cotton sheet on his bed in the shared billet of the Bishop's Palace, and listened to the chirruping of the cicadas in the garden through the open doors to the balcony. His arm was giving him pain and his side ached. He had been bandaged where Macnab's blade had hit, but the pain was endurable, not least on account of the fact that, by his side, sleeping quietly, lay the girl whom he loved.

He would go with Sanchez, would take the students to the French and liberate the gold from Ney's column. Then, once he had delivered a portion of it to Wellington, he would return to Coimbra for Henriette and would take her back to the lines. It would be too late, of course, by then to start a pursuit of Macnab. In any case, by that time, the book would most probably almost be in Paris with Bonaparte.

Keane would report to Wellington without the book. But, instead, he would take the general another prize: gold. A good quantity of it, which he hoped would make up for the loss of the book. He prayed quietly in the darkness that Wellington would somehow understand, that, given the gold and the fact that Keane was working hand in hand with Trant and Sanchez, neither the peer nor his new superiors would have cause to question his lack of success. Keane realized that he would not gain the promotion he desired, but he would have money and the girl he loved, and he would win back the faith of his men. And, moreover, he thought, he would learn more about himself through Trant. It was a bargain with the devil, for that was what Trant most assuredly was. But it was a bargain that Keane knew he had to make.

It was three hours later, with some time yet to go before dawn crested the hills around Coimbra, that Keane awoke to find Ross standing over him. Startled, he sat up and, looking to his left, saw, to his relief, that Henriette was still beside him, sleeping peacefully.

Ross spoke with some urgency: 'The French, sir. They're in the billet.'

'What?'

Keane leapt up and began to pull on his clothes and his boots.

'They're attacking our billet, sir – a score of them – the marines.'

Keane pulled on his jacket and grabbed his sword belt.

Henriette was awake now. 'James, what's going on?'

'The unthinkable. It's Lievremont – he's attacking my men.'

He pounded down the stairs after Ross, fastening his sword belt as he went. Emerging into the street, the two men ran towards the men's lodging in the lower town. As they made the corner, there was a shout from their rear and Keane turned to see Trant following them. He, too, was wearing just his boots, breeches and shirt, and held his sword in his hand.

'Keane, what's happening?'

'The French, colonel – the marines – they've broken the truce. They've attacked my men.'

Trant caught them up and, together, the three of them raced through the narrow streets, arriving at the house to see two of Keane's men standing in the street, firing shots at three marines who were making their escape round the corner. Four marines lay dead in the street and, as he reached his men, Keane noticed that Martin had a cut on his left arm and that Garland was sitting on the ground, holding his side.

He looked at the men; did a headcount. Martin, Garland, Ross, Heredia, Leech. No sign of Silver or Archer.

He turned to Heredia. 'Where are the others?'

'With the French. Silver's chasing them. They took Archer.'

'Took him?'

'Yes, sir. They came in and took him.'

Keane turned to Ross. 'Sarn't, tell me what happened.'

'They just appeared, sir, out of the night. We were all sleeping.'

'Who was on picket?'

Ross shrugged. 'I hadn't posted one, sir. Didn't seem to be any point, sir. I thought we were all friends here. We saved the French from the Portos, didn't we? Doesn't seem right, now. Sorry, sir.'

'Too late now. Too bad. What happened?'

'First thing we knew about it was Archer – yelling at the top of his voice, he was, sir. Two of the French had got him and were dragging him down the stairs. We were up first – Silver and me – then the others. Got hold of them before they could get out. Silver had one of them with his knife. The other one wouldn't let go of Archer. I cut him and he let go then, all right. But then more of them came in – twenty of the buggers, at least. And that lieutenant with them.'

'You're quite sure Lievremont was with them?'

'Yes, sir, bold as you like. Kept shouting orders, pointing to Archer.'

Why, Keane wondered, would Lievremont want to take Archer? What did he have that the French could want? He was one of them – a guide, a spy – but, as far as Keane was aware, he had no special information that the others did not have. So why him, in particular?

And then it struck him. It was Archer himself that they wanted: Archer, the doctor; Archer, the intellectual; Archer, the code breaker. They wanted Archer so that they could break a code. But who knew of Archer's talent? Doctor Sobral, most certainly, and the rest of the men, of course. And Colonel Trant. But Trant was no traitor, whatever else he might be. Lievremont – the lieutenant had overheard his conversation with Sobral. Lievremont knew that Archer was uniquely talented. And Lievremont had turned against him. Perhaps the whole plot had been Lievremont's doing. Surely it was? He must have met with Macnab. With his connections, it would not have been difficult – an officer of the Imperial Guard seeking to speak to one of the emperor's spies. And he'd done it, Keane concluded, in revenge for having Henriette taken from him.

Keane thought fast. What messages could they have found that had been sent here? Certainly, he had received nothing and he wondered if Trant might have.

'Colonel, have you received any intelligence or orders recently?'

Trant shook his head. 'Aside from those of which you are privy to, from the duke and Colonel Grant, no, nothing.'

Keane thought again, wracked his brains for a reason, and then it struck him. The book. Macnab had it now, but what use was it without a means of understanding the encodings? It was a key to the code that might win them the war. Archer was the key – Archer, the code breaker. Keane knew that there were others in Paris. Bonaparte had a team of such men working constantly on decoding and encoding. Grant had told him that he had intelligence that the French were working on a great code, a *grande chiffre*. But Macnab would not want to be seen to have to use any of Bonaparte's hirelings. That was not his way. It was Macnab's intention to present the book to his beloved emperor as a fait accompli with which to win the war in Spain. And what better than presenting him with the book of codes and, along with it, the man who might actually be able to decode it?

He was disappointed in Lievremont – had thought better of the man. Perhaps, he wondered, it had been Macnab who had made contact with him. The man seemed to have eyes and ears everywhere and he must surely somehow have learnt of Keane's liaison with Henriette. Keane thought back to the overheard conversation with Doctor Sobral in which he had mentioned not only Herniette, but Archer. Lievremont, already furious, would have been an easy target for Macnab's persuasive tongue. It was a better conclusion than his initial supposition of Lievremont's treachery, and Keane chose to believe it.

A figure appeared at the junction of the streets and headed towards them.

Silver was limping and Keane could see as he drew closer that he had a wound to the left leg, low down, near his ankle. He half hobbled, half ran towards Keane and, when he was close enough to speak, his words came in panted breaths.

'They've got Archer, sir. Taken him.'

'Yes, I know that. You're hit.'

'Nothing, sir. Bullet grazed my leg. We've got to get him back.' He straightened up. 'Why would they take him, sir? I don't understand.'

'He has something they want. Something they need.'

'I thought they were with us – the marines. We never had any trouble with them and we saved them from the Portuguese, didn't we?'

'That we did, but some things are worth more than loyalty.'

'Why have they taken him, sir? What does he have?'

'It's the book. Archer is the key to the book. If anyone can read the codes it contains, he can. Macnab knows that. That's why they've taken him and it's my bet that, right now, he's on his way to Paris.'

'Paris?'

'To meet Boney himself, if I'm not mistaken.'

Silver gave a whistle. 'We have to get him back, sir. Don't we?'

'Yes, we do. But the question is, how?'

'We can do it, sir, if we go now. We've good horses, well rested. And we can all fight.' He looked at his leg. 'This is nothing. We're all fit. We should go now, sir, or we'll lose him.'

Keane shook his head. 'You're a true friend to him, Silver. Don't you realize, if we are to go after Archer and Macnab, then we have to abandon everything else?'

'Sir?'

'The gold. If we help Archer, then we can't possibly go with Sanchez to take the gold.'

Silver said nothing for a moment, then, 'What do you think, sir? What should we do?'

Keane was not entirely sure that he knew what he thought. He had gone to sleep sure in the knowledge that he was making the right decision in abandoning the book and going after the gold. But this one unexpected action had changed everything with a single stroke.

How, he reasoned, could he possibly leave one of his men to the mercies of Macnab? More than this – were Archer to go to Paris, he would undoubtedly be forced to talk, either once there or on the way. Keane could not imagine the unspeakable ways in which Macnab would achieve this, but he knew that achieve it he must.

Archer would talk. He would be forced to decipher the codes hidden in the book, and then Bonaparte would have at his disposal one of the most impenetrable codes ever created. Armed with this, he would have the power to communicate with his generals in the field, no matter what the guerrillas did or however many dispatches they intercepted. Not only this, but he would have Archer at his disposal, with all that he knew and with his agile mind. There was nothing for it. Despite everything that hung on the possibility of taking the gold, there was now only one option open to Keane. They would have to ride to Archer's rescue.

He would not tell Sanchez or Trant of his change of plan. Instead, he would ride out of the city as planned, taking the students with him. Then, when the column had travelled a few miles, at a prearranged place, Keane and his men would turn off the path and lead only the mounted students away in pursuit of Macnab. He would tell the student commanders his plan and imply that they had to keep it from Sanchez. He imagined that they would respond to the idea of rescuing the book. Trant, like Sanchez, must remain in the dark.

He found Trant talking to Martin.

'What price this, Keane? Who would have thought that the

marines would act like that? It seems that they wanted one of your men. A most extraordinary occurrence! Can you think why they might have taken him?'

'I can only think that they might have instructions to gather intelligence. Although how Lievremont might have received such orders is beyond me. I had my suspicions of Lievremont from the beginning.'

'Really? I always thought him a decent sort, for a Frenchman. What will you do?'

'What can I do? I cannot follow them; who knows where they have gone and by what route? To Massena, I presume. Perhaps we might find them when we go to meet Ney's convoy.'

Trant looked at him. 'Don't tell me you weren't tempted to rescue your own man.'

'Of course I was. It's something I swore I would never do – abandon one of my own. I'm sure you know the same feeling, colonel. But sometimes, particularly when there is as little hope as this, one has to think of the greater good.'

Trant smiled. 'Yes, I thought that you might say that. You see, Keane, you see, you and I are somewhat alike, are we not?'

Keane smiled, more secure in the knowledge that Trant was wrong. If there was one thing of which he was certain, it was that the two of them were not and would never be alike.

Keane cursed himself and he cursed Macnab. Of course, it was quite possible that Macnab knew that, in taking Archer to Paris, he would put Keane in an impossible situation. If anyone knew about the gold shipment and Ney's intentions, it was Macnab. So it followed that he would also know of the plan Keane and Sanchez had made to take it. In playing on Keane's moral high ground and forcing him to decide between the gold and Archer, Macnab would, in all probability, divide his men and make some of them turn against him. Such was the role of the agent provocateur. And that was what Macnab most certainly was. And he did it incredibly and infuriatingly well.

He walked back to their lodging, leaving Trant behind him, and found Henriette, dressed and sitting downstairs, sipping at a bowl of coffee.

'James? What is it?'

'One of my men – Archer – Lievremont's taken him.'

'Jean-Michel? Why? Where?'

Keane shook his head. 'You don't understand. Lievremont has helped the French spy take Archer.'

Henriette stared at him. 'No, he wouldn't do that.'

'He did. There's no doubt of it. His men attacked mine. They saw him.'

She looked down and said nothing.

'He must have turned against me because of you.'

'It's my fault. I'm sorry.'

'Not as sorry as I. I thought he was a good man.'

'Where do you think they will have taken him?'

'It's my guess to Paris. They have the book and the means to decode it. Deliver both to Bonaparte and their future is assured.'

'What will you do?'

'What can I do? What would you do? I have to save Archer – or, at least, to try. He's one of my men, my own.'

She was silent for a moment, then looked at him again. 'It's that damned book. It's cursed.'

'You're starting to sound like Gabriella.'

'But everything it touches, it ruins, James.'

'It's nothing to do with the book. It's the war. I have to do this. I'm sure that we will find Lievremont and Archer and I will come back for you.'

'You don't mean that. I don't believe you.'

'I believe it, and I mean it. I will come back.' He kissed her and turned to go, hoping that she might come after him, but knowing that she had turned away.

Keane walked to the door and didn't look back. The truth of it was he had begun to wonder how much of it he really meant. Did he really believe that the war would be lost if the book was decoded and used by the French? Did he really believe that no one but Archer could read it? Did he really think that they would catch up with Macnab and that he could then kill him? Did he really love Henriette?

One thing he did know: he believed in his men. That much was certain.

He was out on the street now and began to walk away from the billet, towards the nearby mews where his horse was stabled. There was much to do. And it must be done carefully in order not to make Trant and Sanchez suspect his true intentions.

He found Captain Francesco already awake and supervising the students in assembling their kit for the march. Keane drew him to one side. 'A word, captain, if I may. Your men seem ready.'

'They cannot wait to be at the French again, sir. And, with your training, we have a chance of really giving them more than a bloody nose.'

'You're very kind, but my men would agree that you cannot do anything if you do not have the right raw material. Your men were always good fighters, captain. And now they are good fighters who can fire four rounds a minute and kill more Frenchmen. I need to talk to you – in private.'

The two men walked away from the barracks and found a quiet spot against a wall in one of the old covered streets.

'This will do. What I have to say to you must not be related to anyone. Understood?'

'Of course, but what is so secret?'

'When we leave this place in a few hours' time, we will all ride out together, yes?'

'Yes, of course.'

'I have a change of plan. When we reach a certain place, I need you and your mounted men – only the horse – to come with me, away from the main column.'

'I'm not sure I quite understand.'

'Don Sanchez will be in front of the whole column, at its head. That is his way. He will ride at the head of his lancers, five hundred of them. Behind them will come the remainder of his brigade, the infantry and the guns. Then will come your infantry, under my command. But I shall ride with most of my men, on horse and with your mounted troops. When I give the signal, I want you and your horsemen to come with us.'

'Where are we going?'

'I have a secret mission, under orders from Lord Wellington himself.'

'Does Colonel Sanchez know of this?'

'No. Colonel Trant knows of it, but you cannot speak with him about it. Sanchez's men are everywhere.'

Francesco looked grave. 'I see. Can you at least tell me what it is, this mission?'

'The French have taken something that we need – an ancient artefact from the university.'

'Yes, I'd heard that they had plundered the libraries. Barbarians, all of them.'

'We need to recover this item – a book. We cannot allow it to fall into Bonaparte's hands.'

'But why do we need to keep this from Colonel Sanchez?'

'Colonel Sanchez, captain, is a law unto himself. He is not an educated man like you and I. He is a farmer who has risen to his current position by guile, bravery and ruthlessness. He is loyal to the British. But the chief source of his loyalty is coin. Let us just say that I consider it politic to keep the nature of the mission to ourselves.'

'And are we to rescue your man, sir? The one taken by the French.'

'You know of that already?'

'Of course; who doesn't?'

'Yes, they also have Archer. But that's not the reason. The book is the thing. Can I depend upon you, captain? We are looking for trustworthy men on the allied staff. I'm sure when I inform Lord Wellington of your help he will be most impressed and most generous.'

Francesco smiled. 'Yes, of course. You may depend upon me to the end, sir.'

The clock was striking five in the morning when Keane stretched out the map on the table of the men's lodging and, with Ross, Silver and the others around him, began to work his finger along the road south from Coimbra towards Pombal.

'What's their strength, Sarn't Ross?'

'As far as we know, he has a score of marines, sir.'

Martin chimed in: 'A score, less the ones that we did for, sir.'

Keane smiled. 'Yes, of course. Although, I wonder whether Lievremont might not have taken more of his men with him. We should be prepared for that. They will be mounted, how-ever many there may be. They took some horses from the militia. But they're not horsemen, these soldiers, any more than they're real sailors. They're just French infantrymen.'

Heredia spoke: 'They're Imperial Guard infantrymen, sir. Don't forget that.'

'That's as maybe. The main point is that we can ride and fight – we're trained for it, used to it – they can't.'

'The students are handy on a horse, remember, sir.'

'Yes, Silver, I do. And we've all that's left of them, less the horses taken by the French. How many's that, sarn't?'

'A hundred of them, sir; almost a full squadron.'

'There you are: a hundred horsemen and us. That should be enough, even to deal with Macnab. But we still need to be sure. We need surprise and we need to use the ground and numbers to our advantage. So what we have to do is take them in an exposed place where they can't dismount and fire on us. I want a cavalry battle. And I want Macnab.'

'We'll leave him for you, sir.'

'If you would, Garland, I'd be most obliged.' The others laughed. Keane continued, 'We'll need to be quick, if we're to do it properly. I don't want any slip ups.' He paused. 'I'd like to say something, to all of you. I know that you respect Archer and he's one of us and that you would do anything to get him back. But I also know what this means to you, that, by coming with me to rescue him, you're passing up the chance to get your hands on Massena's gold. I know it's an order and that you would never let me down. But I thought I might take the opportunity to say thank you.'

There was an embarrassed silence. Ross spoke for all of them: 'No need to thank anyone, sir.'

Heredia scowled at him and shook his head.

Silver spoke: 'What about Gabriella, sir? Can she come with us?'

'No, I'm afraid she'll have to remain here. I intend to come back here after we've dealt with Macnab. I have unfinished business here myself. I suggest that she hide in the tunnels until we return. We'll come in through the passages. I can't think Colonel Trant will be best pleased to see us. She'll be safe in the tunnels.'

He returned to the billet, but of Henriette there was no sign. The sun had risen now and was beating down on the pantiled roofs as another day dawned on Coimbra. But this morning was different. Trant had ordered a guard on the hospital and had barricaded the doors so that the remaining marines and the patients were unable to get out. Keane presumed that was where Henriette would be now, among her own people. He had not given up with her and had meant what he had said. He did have unfinished business here and, as soon as Archer and book were safe, he was determined to return and take her with him.

Outside, Martin had saddled his horse and, with some difficulty, owing to the sword cut to his side, Keane managed to hoist himself up. It felt strange, at first, to be back on a horse after so long in the city, but it also gave Keane a sense of much needed confidence. He knew that their task was not as clean cut as he had made out and he suspected that the men knew as much. This would be a game of cat and mouse. Macnab and Lievremont must have guessed that they would be followed, and would be taking every precaution. It was going to be a question of whoever could gain the upper hand in surprise. And Keane was determined that it would be him.

Pulling hard on the right rein, he drew his horse away and, with a click of the heels, trotted into the plaza. It was an impressive sight. The column stood ready to move. Pre-eminent were Sanchez's lancers, their red and yellow pennants fluttering in the morning breeze. The guerrillas looked less splendid, but the student battalion, five-hundred strong, was as well turned out, he thought, as many at a Shorncliffe or Blackheath review.

Seeing Sanchez, Keane rode towards him. 'A fine morning for it, colonel.'

'Yes, captain. Your charges look well; your cavalry, too. A true legion of them.'

'Thank you, and I might say the same of your lancers.'

Keane had already noted that the variety of Sanchez's men's uniform included a number which had originally belonged to the lancers of the Imperial Guard, along with green lancers of the line and Poles in blue and yellow *czapkas*.

Sanchez grinned. 'Yes, you see the variety of our enemies and, from the condition of their uniforms, how careful we are when we dispatch them. It would be a crime to waste such wonderful clothes. Such a shame that your men wear brown.'

Keane had thought that this comment might have been coming, and had prepared his response. 'Yes, although, in point of fact, I have been considering changing our uniform. I think we should wear red. After all, we are British soldiers.'

'And you are also British spies, captain. A spy in a brown coat is still a spy. If you wear a red coat, you may be shot in the field as a soldier, but at least you won't be shot as a spy.'

Keane laughed, but he had had enough of Sanchez's teasing and it gave him satisfaction to know that, within a few hours, he and his men would have left the column and would once again be operating on their own, as they liked to do, whatever the colour of their coats, behind enemy lines.

14

The weather, which had been growing steadily colder through the time they had remained in Coimbra, had not revealed itself in its full autumn colours. It constantly amazed Keane how a country so oppressively hot from May through to September could, in the space of a few weeks, become so intensely cold.

The roads, which had previously been baked dry by the sun, were now washed into mud by the rain. And what rain! thought Keane. It was nothing like the rain of England or Ireland. This stuff fell in sheets from a black sky, the huge drops bouncing off the ground.

They had come some ten miles in the first few hours of the march and, as Keane pulled his cloak around his shoulders and tried to push his face down into it against the weather, he realized that the rain, while dire in every other sense, would now actually be of some service to them. It was getting close to the moment at which they had agreed to pull away from the column and he knew that, when that time came, the rain would help to shield their departure, both visually and by the din of its constant drumming, drowning out the jingle of the

harnesses as they veered off from the rear of the column along
the road that would take them to the north.

Keane knew this terrain of old, had travelled it many times
in the past two years and he had an understanding, too, of how
the weather could affect it. The rain, if heavy, could make certain roads impassable. He wondered whether Macnab had such
knowledge and decided that he probably did not. The man was
many things, but he did not have Keane's breadth of experience
out in the field, where the duties of the exploring officer, as
defined by Wellington and Grant, included just such a knowledge. Playing this hunch, he had decided on two possible places
at which he thought they might intercept Macnab's party.

The French had no more than a few hours' advantage on
them, six at the most, and he had also reckoned that they
would be hindered by Archer. Most likely, he would have been
tied to a saddle and, while Keane and his men would be able to
travel at a comfortable canter or gallop, even through the rain,
Macnab's party would have to keep pace with their prisoner,
who would not be able to manage more than a trot.

He knew from the map that they were now close to Condeixa,
some ten miles south-west of Coimbra, and with another thirty
to go to Pombal, the place where he had originally decided they
would meet and destroy Ney's convoy.

Macnab would have had to take one of two roads out of
Coimbra. One ran due north and then branched east at
Mealhada to pass through Mortágua and Viseu before heading
north again towards the coast and the French territory. That
was the easiest way to France, and the safest. But Keane, trying
to read Macnab's mind, concluded that that would not be the
way he would choose to go. No, suspecting that he might be followed and taking no chances, Macnab would almost certainly

go by the second road. This went south first, before curving round, back up towards Guarda, following the line of the river Alva.

Keane, studying the new maps recently provided by the Royal Engineers, maps to which he knew that Macnab could not have access, had found the perfect place to effect an ambush. Close to the little village of Pombeiro lay a bridge: the Ponte de Murcella. That would be their ground. He knew the land, had seen it the previous summer. It was flat enough for horse to manoeuvre easily – a low-lying river plain in the lee of the Serra de Estrella, along which they had travelled last year. Good country.

They were almost at the junction of the roads, now, and Keane raised his arm as a signal. Behind him, Francesco saw it and did the same to indicate to the students to slow down. Slowly, the rear of the column began to distance itself from the men in front, the centre of the column, where the remainder of the student militia marched on foot, making the pace. Exactly halfway to Condeixa, he saw the road branching off to the left. Keane raised his hand again and, followed by his men, he led the way to the junction and left the column. Behind Keane's men, Francesco raised his hand and drew his cavalry away, and then, quite suddenly, they were alone – Keane, his six remaining men and the squadron of a hundred students – trotting silently through the rain, heading due south.

After they had gone what he considered a safe distance, Keane turned to Ross and called him forward.

'Sarn't Ross, ride to the rear and bring up Captain Francesco.'

The captain arrived at a gallop and pulled in close to Keane, followed by Ross, moving into the pace of their canter. As always, his eagerness was evident. 'Yes, sir, what are your orders?'

'Tell your men we'll carry on along here to where the route breaks with a left turn. That's our road. And well done, captain. I think we managed it. We shouldn't be discovered for a while.'

After Francesco had ridden back to his men, Ross turned to Keane. 'He's a good one, that one, sir. Keen as anything to be at the French.'

'Aren't we all, sarn't? Or, shouldn't I say, sarn't major?'

Ross laughed. 'You know what I mean, sir. Those boys, they're clever lads. Of course they are; they would be. But look at what the Frenchies have done to their country.'

'Look at what we've done, yet they take commands from us.'

'That's because they know that we're their only hope, sir – if they want the Frenchies out.' He paused. 'Do you think we'll catch him? Macnab, sir?'

'I'm rather counting on it.'

'And get Archer back?'

'That's all that I want. Archer and the book.'

Ross shook his head. 'The lads are sick to the teeth of the book, sir – if you'll excuse me saying so. They're desperate to kill Macnab, but the book? That's another thing. They'd rather have the gold, sir.'

'Perhaps it might surprise you to learn, sarn't, that that book is worth more than all of Massena's gold. More than all the gold in Portugal and Spain combined, in fact.'

'Is that right, sir? Then it must be a very fine book. It would be lost on me, though, for I'm not a reading man. Not so you'd notice.'

They trotted over a narrow bridge and, once across, Keane picked up the pace again to a canter. Ross turned to him. 'How long do you think we'll take to catch up with that bastard?'

'Over this river and we've six miles before we take the road to the north and then another forty to the bridge. That's where we'll take him, if I'm right.'

It was just as Keane had said. After four more miles, they crossed another river and then, a little after that, they came to the place where the road turned sharply to the north-east. The rain had slowed to a drizzle now, which was, if anything, even more unpleasant than the earlier heavy downpour, soaking through their coats and shirts until the garments hung limp and heavy on their bodies. Close to the village of Foz de Aronce, they recrossed the river for the third time and rode deeper into the valley of the Alva.

As they rode, Keane looked for traces that might suggest he had been right in his conclusion that Macnab had come this way. At first there was nothing and he began to fear that his hunch had not been correct. But then, as the road began to climb on to a ridge of hills, he saw what he had been hoping for. Ahead of them, to the left of the road, lay a black object. Keane was the first to spot it through the drizzle. Spurring on, he rode across to where it lay and saw at once that it was a shako, a bell-topped shako, of the French pattern. He dismounted and picked it up, then turned it round to face the front. There, on the centre, was a gold eagle in relief and, above it, a tricolour cockade. Around the top of the shako was an orange band, with another above the peak. He turned and held it up for the others to see.

'That's it. It's a marine's shako. This is the road they're on.'

They continued to climb steadily and Keane knew that, when they reached the crest of the ridge, he would know if the operation would be a success. For up there, he remembered from their operations scouting here earlier in the year, they would be able to see across the whole valley beyond: to the east, as far as Galizes and Seia, and to the west, over the Mondego and across to the battlefield of Bussaco.

They passed another discarded shako and other pieces of equipment and were quickly at the top of the road. In the churned mud of its surface Keane could make out the impressions left by a score of horses' hooves. The rain had grown heavier again and, as they reached the top of the hill, Keane cast a glance towards Bussaco and was rewarded by little more than a wall of grey cloud. His idea of a view was not to be. He reined in his horse and, keeping his silence, stared across the valley. Ross, Silver and Martin were beside him now. At last, Keane spoke as he reached for his telescope: 'Do you see anything, any of you? You, Martin – you've keen eyes.'

Martin squinted into the rain. 'No, sir, can't say as I can.'

Keane put the glass to his eye and adjusted the focus. 'No, nor I. Nothing. Damn this rain.' He steadied the telescope. 'Wait, what's that?'

He looked more closely and saw movement in the distance, on the road below them, perhaps two miles distant, but still on their side of the bridge. 'There is something moving. There.' He pointed.

The others stared and it was Martin who saw them first. 'I've got them, sir. Moving shapes. Down there. Men and horses. That's them. That's Macnab.'

Keane looked again through the eyeglass and saw them more clearly now, despite the rain. Men on horses, clearly discernible. He had no fear that they would see his party. They would not look behind through the rain.

He turned to Captain Francesco, who had come riding up. 'We've found them – down there. Look.'

As the others stared through the rain, Keane refined his

plan. 'We'll take them from two directions. My men – all of you, save Heredia – stay with me, here. Heredia, you go with the captain and half the squadron and ride as fast as you can to the right. There's a ford down there over the river. You can hardly see it, but it's there, trust me. You may remember it.'

Heredia nodded.

'Take your party across there and ride back along the bank towards the road. You can surprise them in the right flank while we're tying up their rear. The rest of you – I'm taking half of the troopers – we're going in from their rear. Straight down this road.'

With no time to waste, Heredia and Francesco led their troop away and down the hill to the right of the road.

Keane turned to the remaining fifty men, 'All of you, load your carbines. Keep them loaded and in their holsters. Then draw your swords and be ready.'

As quickly as they could, the students loaded with powder and ball and returned their weapons to the holsters. Then, as ordered, they drew the curved light-cavalry sabres with which Trant had issued them. Ross barked a command: 'Shoulder swords!' And the flats of fifty sabres smacked against fifty right shoulders.

Keane raised his hand and waved them forward, and they began to advance down the road in threes. The earth road had been churned to mud by Lievremont's men before them and, as they went down, the horses began to slither. Keane, desperate to prevent panic and the whinnying that would come with it, turned to Ross. 'Tell them to go down sideways, three quarters on to the hill.'

Ross explained to the students, most of whom were accomplished horsemen who had provided their own mounts, and

in moments they had taken his advice and were edging their
horses carefully down the hillside.

The slope – steep at the top, on the ridge – became more
gradual as they descended and, as they neared the flat ground,
Keane gave the order to form into line. He drew to a gentle
trot and watched as the troopers came up from the rear to
form two lines, each of some twenty-five men, their sabres still
shouldered. The troop continued to trot, edging ever closer to
Lievremont's men. Keane could see them now through the rain,
perhaps three hundred yards away and nearing the bridge. He
knew that soon they would become aware of them and, sure
enough, within seconds, he saw one of the figures turn and a
hand raised. There was a shout from their midst, barely audible
through the rain, and then others were turning towards them.
They were two hundred yards away now and the figures were
more visible.

Keane turned to the line and gave the command, 'Canter!'
The sergeant repeated it and the troopers pushed on towards
their target. At a hundred yards out, Keane shouted again:
'Gallop, charge!'

The students, who had been trained for this over the months
by Trant, removed their sabres from their shoulders and held
them, straight armed, in front of them, the points towards the
enemy. They were yelling now, caught in the moment. Ahead of
them, Keane could see fifty, perhaps sixty marines. So he had
been right in supposing that Lievremont would have more men
ready to take to the road. He reckoned this must be an under-
strength company. He could see an officer, perhaps Lievremont,
shouting at the men and trying to get them to form a line and
move in a counter attack. But it was no use. Keane and his
troop were almost upon them now and, through the rain, he

could hear the pounding of the horses' hooves, and the heavy breathing of his own mount, mingle with the huzzahs from the troopers and those of his men. He was closing fast, just a few yards out and then, with the sudden acceleration of the last moments, the line crashed into the marines.

Keane's sabre struck home with full force and pierced through the chest of the marine in front of him, driving in up to the hilt. His body jarred with the shock. He tried to remove his sword from the dead man's chest, but, realizing that it was impossible, gave up and abandoned it, leaving the ivory hilt protruding as the marine toppled from his horse. He drew his carbine and, facing another of the Frenchmen, pointed the gun at his head and pulled the trigger before the man had a chance to strike. The ball hit the marine in the forehead, penetrating first his shako, then his skull and brain, and exiting in a gout of blood through the back. Keane, now without a weapon, had the quickness of thought to reach for the dead man's sabre and, snatching it from his hand, he turned to see what was happening around him.

To his left, Martin was cutting and slashing at one of the marines and, beyond him, Keane saw one of the students take a cut to the head, which almost severed his neck. To his right, Ross and Silver were in the thick of the melee. He saw Ross cut at a marine, only to be parried and respond with an uppercut to the neck, which took off the man's face. Silver, like Keane, had lost his sabre and was fighting with a slim French sword. He parried the attack of a marine and drove home to the heart.

Keane knew that timing, now, was everything. He pulled back for a moment from the fighting and cast an eye to the east. He was rewarded by the sight of Heredia's troop riding down the river, hell for leather towards the bridge and the newly turned French rear. The marines had seen them, too, and, with Lievremont shouting commands, a dozen of them began to turn to face the new threat. As Keane watched, the men dismounted. So, he thought, they intend to stand and fight as they ought, like infantry. The marines pulled their carbines from their saddles and took position, like any line regiment – the front rank kneeling, the rear at the present. Lievremont stood beside them, ready to give the command. Keane watched as the students with Francesco and Heredia quickened their pace. They were at the bridge now and the marines were still loading, for, unlike his men, they had not come to the battle primed and ready to fire.

Keane watched and tried to calculate the odds of the marines being ready before the horsemen reached them. He needn't have worried. Heredia's men broke across the bridge, fanning out as they did so, and the French had just brought their weapons to their shoulders when the wave of horsemen crashed against them. He saw Lievremont shout a command and there were three flashes from the line of infantry. But that was all. The wall of marines dissolved in front of Keane's eyes into a welter of blue-coated bodies as the silver sabres rose and fell. As he watched the slaughter, it occurred to him that he had not yet seen either Macnab or Archer. Using the moment, Keane scanned the enemy ranks and, within seconds, he had found both men.

With Archer positioned a few paces behind him, flanked by two marines, Macnab was sitting on a black horse, slightly to the rear of the action. He had on a black bicorne hat, worn fore and aft, and a brown topcoat over his uniform. Keane wondered what nationality it was beneath – French or English? Or perhaps, today, even Portuguese. He was gesticulating madly, pointing in all directions, attempting to take control. And, watching him, Keane realized that this was no great, invincible man, after all. In fact, he was not much of an officer. He seemed to have no power of command in such a situation. The man was in a funk – out of his depth in the front line. At last, thought Keane, I can see where we differ, where your weakness lies. You are, at heart, a man of the bureau, the staff and the court; I am, at heart, an infantry officer, and such I will ever remain. The front line is my natural home, where I belong, amidst the smell of powder smoke and the thrill of command. You are at a loss. For all your wit and your clever games, when it comes down to it, you have no real stomach for battle.

Keane spurred through the thick of the fight towards Macnab. The marine's sword felt light in his hand – too light – and he looked around desperately for something better.

Garland called to him, 'Sir, take this,' and held out his own sword, a heavy British dragoon, issue 1796 pattern sabre – a 'meat cleaver'. Dropping the lighter infantry sword, Keane took it with thanks and saw, to his relief, that Garland was already armed with another weapon, taken, he presumed, from one of the students.

He turned back to Macnab, but the man had vanished – and Archer with him. Keane swore and scanned the mass of milling horsemen for the black bicorne, but none came into view. To his left, one of the students crashed from his horse, cut through the head, and he realized that perhaps he had underestimated the fighting ability of Lievremont's marines. Heredia's men were in among them now, having disposed of the skirmishing line, and Keane could see that they, too, had a fight on their hands. As he looked to his right, past Heredia and the lieutenant, he noticed another touch of brown among the sea of blue coats: Macnab again, no mistaking him. This time, the man, as frantic as ever, had moved to the French left. Of Archer, there was no sign. But Keane counted this as a good thing. If the two had been separated, it followed that Macnab could not escape from the fight with his prisoner. Keane saw Macnab's sword flash in his hand as he dispatched one of the student horsemen with enviable ease. He might not be much of a field officer, thought Keane, but there was no denying the man's skill as a swordsman.

He turned his horse, determined now to reach the spy, and began to push through the melee. There was a marine on his left flank, an old sergeant with a black moustache, his shako tilted to an unlikely angle, four long-service chevrons on his arm. He came at Keane, his sword at the present, and reined in his horse for the fight. Keane, desperate not to lose his path to Macnab for a second time, cut at the man on the horizontal with the heavy dragoon sabre and felt the jar through his arm as the marine parried it with his thinner blade, the man's strength compensating for the lack of weight in his sword. The marine riposted with a thrust to Keane's side, which made contact, but not hard enough to penetrate his cloak. The man was slow to recover and, seeing his advantage, Keane made a cut with the cavalry sabre that took the sergeant across the chest, splitting open the gaudy yellow brocade of his uniform and slashing deep through the fabric. The man gasped and, open eyed, stared at his seeping chest before falling to the right to be trampled in the mud beneath the horses' hooves.

Keane turned to find Macnab again and, this time, was relieved to see him where he had been before. Now, he thought, you won't escape me, and, pushing hard against the flanks of his mount, spurred her on into the fighting, cutting as he went at any Frenchman who stood in his way. He was almost on Macnab now and the spy turned to see him, a smug smile spreading across his face as he did. One more push, thought Keane, and, as he dug in his spurs and prepared to fight, a horse came careering into the left flank of his own, almost pushing him from the saddle.

Keane turned towards the rider and found the weather-beaten face of Lieutenant Lievremont.

The Frenchman looked Keane in the eyes and shook his head before aiming a cut towards his head. Keane took it with his own blade and parried to the right, returning with the point towards Lievremont's heart. But the marine was quick and dodged the point before riposting with a thrust to Keane's abdomen, which cut the cloak. Keane pushed his horse against Lievremont's and tried to shout across the melee, 'Give up! You can't win. Surrender!'

But whether he heard or not Keane never knew. For Lievremont made another cut at Keane's head and, instinctively parrying, Keane automatically carried on with a thrust that caught the marine beneath his exposed right shoulder and drove on into the armpit. Lievremont grimaced and his sword fell from his hand, which dropped limp to his side as the blood began to flow from beneath the shoulder. Keane almost regretted his action, but knew there had been no alternative. As he watched, Lievremont tried to clutch the damaged right arm with his left, but the blood and the pain were too much and, as his legs became unable to grip, he started to slide from the saddle. Keane stretched out a hand to support him, but it was too late and the lieutenant dropped to his left and fell from his horse.

A voice came from Keane's right, shouting through the rain and battle noise: 'Sir, we've got Archer, sir. Archer – he's safe.'

It was Ross and, turning, Keane could see that behind him stood Silver, supporting Archer, who was still tied to the pommel of his saddle.

Keane shouted through the rain, which had become heavier, 'Get him away from here, Silver – to the rear. And untie him first.'

Silver untied Archer's hands, but kept him steady as he got his balance. They began to ride away and Keane turned back to assess the situation. To his front, the student militia were fighting well, although they had taken serious losses. But Keane sensed that the marines were now giving way.

Heredia was still in the saddle and, as far as Keane could see, so were all the others from his own company. The marines were in a tight knot of horsemen and were about to find themselves surrounded – and to discover, too, that they were leaderless, for, quite apart from Lievremont, he realized that Macnab was not among them. With a new sense of urgency, he looked again for the spy and then, turning to make sure Silver had managed to trot with Archer to a safe distance, he was surprised to see a third horseman gallop towards them through the rain. He called to Ross to come with him and dug his spurs into his horse's flanks. Ahead of him, the third horseman was gaining on Archer and Silver, who had sensed his approach and turned to face him. There was no doubt in Keane's mind. It was Macnab.

Ross was alongside him now, riding hard, as they saw Macnab reach the others. The sergeant pushed a gun towards Keane. 'Here, sir, take this; she's still loaded.'

Keane, allowing the sabre to fall from his hand, grabbed the carbine and, pulling up hard on the reins, dug the stock into his shoulder, took aim on the black bicorne and squeezed the trigger. Through the smoke, he saw the man shudder in the saddle and then fall, before his horse took off into the rain. Keane handed the gun to Ross and rode up to Archer and Silver. 'Macnab?'

'Yes, sir; well done. We didn't see him till he was on us.'

'You're hit?'

Archer held up a bleeding hand. 'Flesh wound. You stopped him, sir.'

Keane jumped down from the saddle and went across to Macnab, who was lying face down. He kicked hard at the man's back and Macnab flinched and groaned.

Keane spoke: 'Get up. Get up, you bastard. I missed.'

Slowly, Macnab raised himself in the mud and got first to his knees, then to his feet. His hand went to his shoulder where his coat was torn and bloody. 'No, Keane, you hit right enough. But just not well enough.'

'Oh, I hit you exactly the way I wanted to. Just enough to knock you down, so that I could finish the job properly.'

With a swift action, Keane kicked his booted foot hard into Macnab's groin, sending him flying to the ground. Macnab screamed and grabbed at his crotch as Keane advanced on him. 'That was for Gilpin, and this is for me.' He kicked again, with the same force, but this time hard into Macnab's right side, just about level with his kidneys. Again, Macnab screamed.

Keane knelt down beside him as Silver and Ross stood above, covering both men with their carbines. With the rain lashing down, Keane ripped open Macnab's tunic – French, this time – and, thrusting his hand inside, searched around for the book. Finding it, he pulled it out. 'Mine, I believe.' He tucked it into his own coat. 'And now I've a clean target.'

Macnab lay on the ground, squirming in pain, as Keane

prepared the coup de grâce. He called to Ross, 'Sarn't, your weapon, if you would.' Ross handed him the carbine and he cocked the hammer and stood over Macnab. The spy had stopped squirming now and lay dead still, his arms by his sides, staring directly into the barrel of the gun.

'This wasn't the way I had dreamt of it, Macnab. You've had it easy – don't you think? – after everything you've done. And I'm sure there's much, much more than I know about.'

Macnab said nothing. He stared at Keane with black, emotionless eyes, ready for his fate. Keane stared back and felt the trigger yielding to his finger. The rage was boiling inside him. He thought of Morris and Gilpin. This was the revenge he had vowed to take for them. He swallowed hard and steadied the gun and, for a moment, his finger pushed on the trigger. But, as it pushed, he began to think with a clearer head. The red mist lifted from his eyes and he relaxed his finger, feeling the trigger settle again. Macnab was still staring at the gun, but with something resembling fear in his eyes. Keane smiled at him, seeing the change and knowing now that he would not kill him.

He began to squeeze the trigger and watched as Macnab stiffened, waiting for the fatal shot. But at the last moment, Keane tipped the gun to the left. He squeezed and the gun fired, the shot missing Macnab by inches. The spy was breathing heavily now, the sweat beading on his forehead, his eyes wide and staring.

Keane lowered the gun, knowing, though, that Silver had his carbine trained firmly on Macnab.

'I'm not going to shoot you now. I shan't give you that satisfaction. We're going to take you back to Wellington and you will be tried for treason in the lines. And then you will be hanged. That's the proper way to do things. And you will also have the pleasure of knowing you're certain to die, and time to consider the prospect.'

He turned to Ross. 'We'll keep him with us. He'll need a proper escort. Just make sure he's securely tied. Use as much rope as you like and fasten him to the saddle of the slowest horse we have. Then tie it to your own.'

Ross smiled at him. 'Yes, sir. Better than killing him here. Well done, sir.'

There was no firing from the bridge now and, looking in that direction, Keane saw that the fighting had stopped. What was left of Lievremont's force could now be seen standing in small groups, their hands raised, as the students of the Coimbra militia herded them together and searched the ground for any of their comrades who might still be alive.

Keane, having retrieved his sword from the mud, watched as Ross, who carried a length of rope beneath his saddle, tied Macnab's hands and then bound him again with a noose around his neck so that any attempt to free his hands would only result in its tightening.

Archer was back on his feet now and, with Ross leading Macnab, still on foot, the five men walked back down the road towards the bridge, where Francesco's students had made the French their prisoners.

Keane, watching Macnab shuffling through the mud, his steps limited by his bonds, felt a glorious sense of elation, as if he had laid to rest some monster. He touched the book, secure in his pocket. They would take Macnab back to the duke and watch him hang. First, though, they had one more task. And, for that, Keane knew he would need all of his skill.

15

It didn't take long to reassemble the troop. Or what was left of it. Captain Francesco had, thankfully, survived and, with a bandaged arm where a marine's sabre-briquet had cut him near the wrist, was ordering his men into formation when Keane appeared. As he came into view, a cheer sped through the ranks, starting from nowhere but quickly taken up and, with three loud huzzahs, rang in his ears. The fight had been hard – harder than he had expected – and the student cavalrymen who formed up before him now showed it in their faces. Gone suddenly were the young men whom he had led down the road barely two hours earlier. These men were soldiers now.

Keane smiled and saluted them. Steadying his mount and bringing her to a halt, he addressed them. 'Well done, all of you. You and your commander, Captain Francesco, deserve more than you may know. You have all done a great duty to your country and also to the civilized world. When I meet with Lord Wellington, I shall commend you all to him and I intend, in particular, to recommend Captain Francesco for promotion.'

There was a brief silence as they translated, then another

cheer. Hats were flung into the air. Keane, for all his years of soldiering, was unused to quite such adulation.

Francesco approached him. 'Sir, we could not have managed it without you – you and your men. You have given us inspiration.'

Keane smiled. He was not an easily embarrassed man, but this had caught him by surprise.

'I am proud to have served with you, all of you. But we still have more work to do. Captain, I need your men formed up and ready to move within half an hour.'

Francesco saluted and went about making ready. Keane turned away and Ross approached him, accompanied by Archer.

Archer's face was drawn and gaunt, but he wore a smile and did not seem to have been harmed. Keane clasped his shoulder with his good hand. 'Archer. Thank God. We thought, for a moment, we'd lost you.'

'Sorry, sir. I don't think I'm quite ready for the delights of Paris, yet.'

'Or Paris for you. I dare say all you want right now is a comfortable bed and a bottle of Oporto.'

'That's about it, sir. Can't say I can think of anything I'd rather have, save a mutton pudding.'

'I hate to disappoint you, but I'm afraid that's not going to happen. Not yet, at least. We have other business. I can't risk losing you again, even if we have Macnab captive. You're a valuable man, you know.'

'Yes, sir; so it would seem.'

'Lievremont's dead.'

'Good, that's no less than he deserves.'

'What did they do to you?'

'Nothing, sir. Least, not in any way other than when they took me. I put up a good fight.'

'I'm sure you did, Archer, but even you can't beat off twenty men.'

'No, sir. They wanted to put some ground between us and you. I didn't even have time to take a look at the book.'

'Well, that can wait. Thank God we found you in time.'

'Yes, they told me that they had plans for me. Macnab assured me that he would get information from me and that I would end up telling them anything they wanted to know. Anything.'

'Well, we have him and we've got you back and that's the main thing. And the book, of course.'

Ross spoke: 'Sir, might I ask what work it is we're to be about?'

'You may, Sarn't Ross. In point of fact, we don't have a minute to waste.'

'What, sir? Are we to go back to Coimbra now or to rejoin the army at Torres Vedras?'

Keane shook his head. 'Neither. Why go back there when we still have a chance of getting a share of the gold?'

'But I thought, sir, that you said you had unfinished business in Coimbra.'

Keane smiled. 'Yes, you're right, I did. But she will have to wait.'

Silver had joined them. 'Then should we not be taking Macnab and the book to Wellington, sir?'

'No. And it's too late for that right now – too many French in our way at present. We need to rid the country of a few more, first. No, lads, we're for Pombal. And when we get there – which, I trust, will be as fast as you can manage – we're going to help Don Julian Sanchez and his bunch of peasants relieve Marshal Massena of his gold.'

*

The rain had abated by the time they reached the pass of Seguedo.

Although they had kept Macnab with them, trussed like a roasting fowl, Keane had sent the fifteen other prisoners back to Coimbra, under guard of six of the students, led by a Portuguese sergeant. The rest of them had ridden hard for the last four hours and, by nightfall, had reached Miranda do Corvo, covering a distance of about fifteen miles.

It was a full fifty miles from Ponte de Murcella to Pombal, the route that Don Sanchez's men had taken, and, by Keane's reckoning, the guerrillas, with their slower rate of march, held back by the foot, would have reached the assigned ambush position by midnight and be in place to attack on the following day, the 16th of November.

Fifty miles would take them two days at the average rate of march for cavalry. But Keane needed to cover the same distance in less than half that time. He knew that it could be done. At least, he had heard of horsemen managing twenty-five miles in under six hours. The question was, could he and his men manage it? Thus far, they had done well, but there was still over thirty miles to go.

A little to Keane's surprise, given his recent apparent animosity, it was Heredia, the seasoned trooper, who had come up with the means. They would ride, he proposed, for an hour, after which they would halt for ten or fifteen minutes to adjust their tack. From there on, they would stop every hour, for five minutes. At the second halt, though, there was to be no actual rest. Rather, they would go on with the troopers dismounted, leading the horses. This would last twenty minutes, after which they would all remount and go on at a trot, no more, for another twenty minutes. The last twenty minutes of the second hour were to be completed at a walk. The routine of lead, trot and walk would be repeated with slight variations for another three hours. After five hours, they would rest the horses for a full fifteen minutes and then begin again.

Keane had been a little sceptical, but Heredia had explained it so clearly and with such conviction that he had thought it might work and, thus far, the horses seemed to be well enough.

Ross trotted up alongside. 'How much further, sir, would you say?'

'Another thirty miles, sarn't, is my guess. How are the men?'

'The men are fine, sir. Damned tired, but they'll get a second wind. They're keen to be at the French. They'll do it. When do you reckon we might get there, sir?'

'If we carry on at our present rate, we should make Pombal a few hours before sunrise – perhaps a little after four o'clock tomorrow morning, maybe five.'

'Will that be enough, sir? Soon enough to join the fight?'

'I hope so, sarn't; really, I do. Don Julian needs us. I dare say he will have noticed our absence by now. I wonder what he will have made of it.'

For another three hours, they carried on through the hills into the night, skirting Coimbra by the south, through Miranda, before emerging out into the open plains around Soure. The going was easier here, but with the horses tiring, despite Heredia's scheme, their pace inevitably began to slow. Keane turned and rode back down the line. He looked carefully at his own men, seeing the fatigue in their faces, before riding on to see Captain Francesco.

'How are your men? It's not far now.'

'We will do it, captain. But I wonder how ready for a fight they will be at the end.'

'I'm sure they will fight well, if we can judge from what they did back at the bridge.'

Keane thought for a few moments as they rode on. They scanned the tree-lined hills, left and right, as best they could in the darkness, but there was no sign of any presence, friendly or hostile. Moving down from the stone-scoured fields of the *serra*, the horses picked their way across rocky streams and past the huge granite boulders which characterized this part of the country. The road was flanked by fields now, but where the crops had lately been, notwithstanding the season, the fields stood barren.

At last they rode into view of Pombal. The little town twinkled with the lights of lamps and fires in the windows of its whitewashed houses. They came in from the north-east, constantly on the lookout for friend and foe. Beyond the first of the outlying farms and houses, they could just make out, in the distance, the old Templar castle, which dominated the town, towering high above it. Keane imagined that the commander of the French column would have made his base up there, within the protective enclosure of the castle, on the high ground, before setting off again in the morning. It was likely that the French were still there. Never, in all his years of fighting them, had he known the French to be fond of making an early start.

The assigned rendezvous, at which Keane and Sanchez had agreed to make the ambush, was close now. To the left lay olive groves and, to the right, a dried-up riverbed. Within a few hundred yards, though, the ground began to rise on both sides. This was just as Keane had remembered it and the perfect country in which to take the column. The plan had been to position the infantry on the steep slopes, to fire down into the French column, while keeping one half of the cavalry on the road at the north and the others mobile to the south, ready to move to the road and so block the enemy route of escape.

Of course, without Keane's horsemen, such a plan would not work and he wondered what Sanchez had devised in its place.

At any moment, in fact, Keane expected to be challenged by one of Sanchez's sentries. But when none emerged after another mile along the road, by which time they had almost reached the end of the designated spot, he became concerned.

Silver was riding close to him when he spoke his mind. 'This doesn't feel right, Silver. We should have seen Sanchez's men by now. Something's not good here.'

He took from his pocket the gold hunter chronometer, which he had been given many years ago by his mother – a gift, to her, from his father – and flicked open the lid. The hands stood at twenty minutes past six. Sanchez would have arrived here shortly after midnight – perhaps as late as two in the morning. They had agreed to wait here to attack the French who, according to Dussitot's intelligence, were due to leave Pombal early that morning. But where, he wondered, was Sanchez now? On discovering Keane's absence and the lack of men, what might Sanchez have done? Keane tried to put himself in the man's place. What would he have done?

He turned to Ross. 'Sarn't Ross, what would you do? If you realized that half your force was missing, that the plan you had made might not work for lack of horse, how would you adapt it to suit the situation?'

'Well, sir, for one thing, with half my cavalry gone, I don't think I'd take on a mixed column in open country.'

'Yes, I agree, you're right. If Captain Dussitot is to be believed, then Ney's column will have dragoons and chasseurs. Sanchez boasts of his lancers, but I wonder how they would do against regular cavalry, operating en masse.'

'Not good, I'd say.'

'Then what would he do?'

'I think, if I was him, I'd have two choices. If I believed at all that you'd still come, I'd go to ground and wait.'

'And if you thought that we weren't coming?'

'I'd push on, sir. His infantry are nippy. They work like our light bobs. Specially good in built-up areas. I'd take them in the buildings where the Frenchies couldn't use their horse. Then I'd bring up the student infantry behind the guerrillas, in close support.'

'Yes. That's my thinking exactly. Advance to the town. Take the outlying buildings as a platform from which to launch an attack on the column when it eventually emerged.'

'Yes, sir. I'd get into the first houses. Get a foothold and work in from there. That's what I'd be doing. That part of the place must be empty. If you managed to get into this end of the town and take some of the houses, then, when the column started to move out, you could open fire on them. Keep the lancers back in reserve.'

Keane nodded. 'Of course there is a third alternative. He could always split his own horse and carry out the attack just the same. Then he would have all the gold for himself and we would have done him a real service.'

Keane strained to see, but could discern no signs of movement in the part of the town that lay directly below the walls of the castle. He wondered if Sanchez had done as he supposed.

He turned his head to Ross. 'I don't think they've followed our solution, sarn't, to attack in the built-up area. They'd be in these houses here, now – wouldn't they? – waiting for the

French. Who, I'm willing to bet, used the castle up there as their headquarters billet last night.'

'Yes, sir, you're right. Funny, if it had been me in Colonel Sanchez's position, I'd have had men in every one of these houses. I wonder what he's up to?'

As they watched, noise of movement came in the valley, some distance off towards the town, beyond the forest of coni-fers, cypresses and olive trees that lined the hillside – the sound of creaking wagons and marching feet. The French were on the move.

Keane muttered, to no one in particular but overheard by all, 'Where in Christ's name is Sanchez?'

They sat silent, save for the occasional whinny of a horse, listening and, for a few minutes, all they could hear was the French column. Keane pictured it in his mind, the infantry in the centre with the wagons, the horse to the front and rear. He listened out for the jangle of the harnesses and thought that he had caught it when, over on their left, there came a thunder of hooves that shook the hillside. His first thought was that, despite his care, the French must have somehow seen their approach and sent their cavalry around their flank. Keane yelled to his men: 'Cavalry! Look to your left!'

Suddenly brought to action, they turned their horses and drew their sabres, waiting for whatever might appear at the crest of the hill – dragoons or chasseurs, thought Keane. Perhaps both. They would know soon enough.

Silver, off to his right, whispered, just loud enough for him to hear, 'Come on, you green-coated buggers. We're ready for you.'

But Keane knew it was a hollow boast – brave words from a man who knew what was to come.

But it was neither dragoons nor chasseurs nor any men in green who appeared over the brow of the hill, but lancers, dressed in blue, with red and yellow pennons hanging below their glinting spear points: Don Sanchez's lancers.

At their head rode Sanchez himself. Seeing Keane, he spurred ahead and pulled up sharply beside him.

'You are late, Captain Keane. Please be so good as to explain yourself.'

Sanchez's furious expression spoke volumes. So much so that Keane decided to pre-empt any further comment that might be about to come.

'Colonel, first, allow me to apologize for not informing you of my change of plan. It was unavoidable and a direct order from the commander in chief. I hope that it did not inconvenience you.'

Sanchez stared at him. 'Inconvenience me? How dare you? How dare you leave a column on the march? Do you realize that we only discovered your move at daylight? By then, it was too late to turn back. And, besides, the gold would not wait. It was a most unsoldierly act. You have imperilled the mission.'

'I'm sorry, colonel, but, as I told you, I had other orders. We thought that you might have gone in to attack the town.'

'I thought about it, captain, but I could not decide, not having all of my force to hand.'

So, thought Keane, you did know that I would come. For all your bluster, you trusted me. He knew that Sanchez could have attacked – that he could have split his own cavalry in two – but still he had waited for them. And, with that realization, he began to warm to the colonel once again. He was different to Trant – and, as he had thought before, to most of the other guerrilla leaders. There was an intrinsic honour about Colonel

Sanchez, even though his greatest incentive would always be his desire for gold.

'Colonel, I can only apologize again.' He pointed to the rear, where Macnab sat, trussed and tied, on his feeble horse. 'We took the traitor, Macnab.'

'Congratulations, captain. I'm sure that he is a great prize and that Lord Wellington will be very pleased. But my own prize, as you know, lies over those hills – at Pombal.'

'And very soon it will be ours.' Keane emphasized the last word. 'Do you intend to attack today?'

'I was waiting for them to ride out. We could still catch them *en ambuscade*, don't you think, captain? Now that you are here . . . at last.'

Keane did not need a second hint. He nodded at Sanchez. 'Yes, colonel. I agree.' And, with no more ado, he yelled a command and set the men to taking posts. It was a little late and the French might appear, he knew, at any moment from the town gate, but, nevertheless, they would take their original, planned positions. The infantry and those who were the better marksmen of the horse would lie down and crouch on the steep slopes, just below the tree line, to fire down into the French column.

Within minutes, as they had planned, a force of cavalry would be ready on the road at the north and the others, the greater portion, would be to the south, ready to stop the French from running.

As the Portuguese officers began to give orders to the militia and Sanchez's guerrillas moved off on foot, Keane turned to the colonel.

'We will still manage this. You know we will.'

Sanchez looked at him. 'Yes, I know that. But I cannot deny

that I am surprised at you, captain. I had not thought you would abandon your comrades.'

Keane turned on him. 'Never accuse me of that, colonel. I will never abandon one of my men. You may rely on that. I swore that I would save Archer and I swore that I would avenge Gilpin. And that is what I have done. I am a man of my word, Colonel Sanchez. Let there be no doubt in your mind of that.'

'You gave me your word, captain, that you would meet me here.'

'And so I have, colonel. And together, God willing, we will take that gold.'

The sound of the column was louder now – much closer. He saw Sanchez's men riding down to the south and rallied his own to ride to the north of the road.

'Lieutenant Francesco, quick as you like, take posts to the north. Follow me.'

With Keane in the lead, his men and the students cantered together down the hillside and turned short of the road, shadowing it as they road north, towards the tail of the French column. Around twenty of the students had been killed or wounded at the bridge and, with a half dozen of the better marksmen, Martin included, now dismounted and ready to fire at the French officers, his troop now numbered a total of seventy-five men.

It was not many with which to face five thousand, but Keane told himself that their role was merely to block the road. The infantry on the slopes would do the real work, turning the road into a panicked mass of dead and dying, as Sanchez's lancers pushed the French into a better target for the muskets. They were near the rear of the column now – near enough to hear the sergeants shouting commands and the wheels of the wagons creaking through the wet mud of the road. Keane raised his hand and, from within the cover of the trees, the horsemen came to a halt and watched the road down below.

The column moved slowly, just as he had envisaged, with horse to the front and rear and mounted officers with their white plumes among the infantry. It was hard to know for sure how many of them there were. A single battalion strung out in order of march would occupy some two hundred and fifty yards of road alone.

He began to do a quick count of their numbers, working his way through the ranks, down to the wagons. Beyond these, he could see more infantry and he doubled his figures. There must have been around six hundred foot, in all, that he was now able to see. And then, to his surprise, in the far distance, he discerned more cavalry. Either the French commander had split his force on the march and scattered squadrons of horse throughout, or this was not quite the force he had been expecting. Where were the rest? The promised five thousand? The brigade-strength escort?

Keane had a sudden thought. Of course – what if it was a ruse?

Ross saw his expression. 'What's wrong, sir?'

'Don't you see? It's a decoy – a dummy. Their commander's done this just to test the water. Ney must have guessed that they would be attacked. Of course he would. He would expect it. The bulk of the force is still there in Pombal – thousands of them – and they have no intention of coming out.'

There, Keane realized, they would stay, along with their gold – unassailable by anything other than a properly equipped enemy, with siege guns and storming ladders and the rest.

'What do we do, sir?'

'What do we do? What can we do? It will be too late for Colonel Sanchez. He will have gone into the attack. Listen, that's musketry.'

He was right enough. All across the hillside, the infantry, militia and guerrillas had opened up and were firing down into the French column.

'All we can do is kill as many of them as possible. It's not the way I would have wanted it, sarn't. It's butchery. They don't have a hope and there'll be no surrender.'

He could already hear the French ahead of them crying, 'Retreat!' He watched as they scrambled through the undergrowth before running down to the river and crossing by the single bridge that led to the town and a ford some yards upstream. But, once in the town, the castle lay uphill and, for most of them, by then it was too late. A single officer might have turned them at the bridge and made them stand, but their officers were mostly dead, toppled from their horses by Martin and the sharpshooters, and their sergeants were all for sauve qui peut.

So the lancers did their devilish work too well, riding hard after them and sticking them in the back with the small steel tip of the long shaft. The lance was not a clean death. Keane had seen it many times. A man might be speared up to a dozen times before he expired and, often, those who collapsed on the field would die a horrid, lingering death, crying out for water and aid until their throats became too parched to speak.

Keane called out to the troopers, 'Here they come. Stand your ground. Take as many as you can.'

The French began to run towards his line and, as they did so, Keane gave the command to trot. They took the first of the infantry at an easy pace, cutting down into their shakos and across their bodies. As Keane had foreseen, it was no melee, but a massacre in which retreating men ran into a wall of steel and horses.

Within minutes, his little force had dispatched perhaps twice or three times their number. Three minutes more and he had had enough. 'Retire. Pull back to the trees.'

Keane's troopers, and the students with them under the captain, disengaged from the desperate French and rode quickly off the road and back up into the trees. Then, turning, they watched the end.

Sanchez's men did not give up the pursuit, and ran the enemy across the bridge, into the town and up to the castle before retiring under fire. But the gates of the castle were shut fast and the retreating French, unable to gain entry, screamed up at the walls to their comrades to open. But the commander of the convoy had a hard heart and an iron will, forged in the battlefields of central Europe. He had watched the Austrians and Russians drown at Austerlitz and seen the Prussians blown to pieces at Jena. And, once again, he had done as his marshal had requested.

He had sent out a party to test the enemy – a party of the most expendable men he had: an under-strength, underfed line battalion with walking wounded and a squadron of mutinous chasseurs on sickly nags to guard six empty wagons. Most of them had perished in the ambush, or would do soon in the pursuit. But the plan had worked. He had found his enemy and he could gauge their strength. And so now he would stay in his castle. He knew that, if he opened the gates, no matter what fire his men might pour down, there was a chance that the enemy would get in. And when that happened, all would be lost. So he kept the doors of the castle shut and the Frenchmen hammered on them and were shot and skewered, like rats in a tub.

Keane watched them die and knew what their commander had in mind. He could also guess how Sanchez would react. He would attempt a frontal assault on the place – and lose half his men in the process, with no result.

Keane, though, had another idea in mind. For that, he would have to find Sanchez and he knew that, first, they would have to get into the lower town and do what Ross and he had proposed earlier – occupy the houses and engage the enemy.

16

As the last remnants of the massacred French column made it across the bridge, retreated through the town and threw themselves against the castle walls, Keane gave the order to dismount. They tethered their horses in the wood above the road and, taking their carbines and ammunition bags, and Keane, unusually, his valise, advanced slowly along the road, across the bridge, littered with bodies, and into the town. Keane had insisted, too, on taking Macnab with them, and Silver and Garland tied him between two of the students, rendering escape impossible.

They moved in cautiously, in single file, along the first few streets of what he guessed must have been a prosperous suburb of the town, lined with two-storey terraces of white painted houses with neat grey lining and shutters, each with its own wrought iron balcony.

From up ahead came the sound of gunfire. Keane turned to Ross and the others. 'Come on.'

The streets were deserted, as he had suspected they would be, and, as they grew closer to the castle, the gunfire grew louder and more frequent.

Silver nodded in recognition. 'They're on the hill, sir, like you said – the Frenchies – in the castle.'

He was right. As they neared the action and began to encounter Sanchez's men and the students, Keane could see that they were assaulting the castle, which was heavily defended by the French. Of the lancers there was no sign and Keane supposed that they might be tucked away in safety, as a reserve.

As they drew closer, the sheer height of the castle became clear. Around them, crouched behind the cover of village walls, lay the infantry element of the student militia. The boys that Keane had spent time training now waited for an opportunity to fight. But he and his men had trained them in volley fire by company, not in the house-to-house light infantry tactics which this sort of a battle demanded.

Martin, who had returned to them from his role as a marksman, noticed it. 'Bloody shame, sir, ain't it? Fine job we did on them and they can't make use of it. Should have taken a lesson from Black Bob's boys instead.'

'Yes, Will, I dare say you're right. Light infantry's what's needed here.'

Occasionally, a French musket ball would fly towards them, zinging off the buildings about them. But it was extreme long range from the castle and there was no real danger back here. All the same, as they moved forward, Keane began to walk at a hunch and the others followed suit, trailing their weapons.

At length, they arrived at the foot of the hill on which the castle stood. Here the enemy fire was more intense and, as they watched, three of Sanchez's men fell. Others took cover behind the stone walls of the old castle buildings they had taken in the initial rush.

Two small ruined houses and what had once been a chapel

lay below the outer fortifications. At intervals, the guerrillas, and some of the students who had come forward to be with them, would pop up from behind the walls and fire at the castle's high crenellations, hoping to find a mark. But it was desperate stuff. Without artillery, such an attack was doomed to failure. Behind the houses, Keane noticed, at last, a group of lancers, standing as if on guard, and he knew that he had found the guerrilla commander.

He signalled with two fingers to Ross and Silver and, beckoning them with him, ran across the street between the houses towards Sanchez's headquarters. A single shot in the dust at his feet was enough to let Keane know that they had been spotted from the walls. At the back of the houses, Sanchez stood among an order group of his junior officers. Two wore makeshift bandages around wounds to their arms.

Keane approached the colonel. 'You do know, colonel, that you'll never take this place by a frontal assault. You're outnumbered and outgunned and you have no heavy artillery.'

Sanchez nodded, grimly. 'Is that so, captain? Can you offer me a better suggestion? And I sincerely hope you can, as it was your action that made me take this course.'

'That's untrue. I did not ask you to make a frontal assault on a fortified position.'

'But you cannot deny that you left the column. You deserted.'

'I asked you once, colonel, not to call me a deserter, and I would repeat my request. I acted on my initiative to save one of my men and the object of my original mission. This mission, to take the gold, was never in those orders. Besides, even if we had been here at the appointed hour, what difference would it have made? This is the French commander's doing. It's his plan.'

Sanchez said nothing. Then he looked at Keane and shrugged. 'So what do we do now? We cannot take the castle. We cannot get the gold. We might even lose our own lives. I have lost too many already. This is a disaster.'

Keane shook his head. 'No, colonel, it's far from that. I think we do have a chance. It just so happens that I know this place. We came through here last year, before the French invasion, and, when we did, I took a walk around that castle. I'm in the habit of making notes on topography and the like. Making sketches. It's an order from headquarters. From Wellington.'

He reached into his valise and drew out a sheaf of papers. Then, brushing aside two earthenware plates and some half-fin-ished food, he placed them on an old wooden table that stood up against the rear wall of one of the houses. There were a number of drawings and sketches of buildings and landscapes.

Keane began to pore through them. 'I'm sure it must be here.' He paused and then pulled one sheet away from the others. 'Yes, here we are.'

He laid the sheet away from the others and looked down at it with Sanchez. In the top right-hand corner, written in Keane's hand, were the words, *Castelo de Pombal.*

Sanchez looked at it, almost in disbelief. It bore a drawing in a competent hand of the castle that now towered above them and, beside it, a small sketch map.

The castle, it appeared, was centred around a tall keep with curtain walls punctuated by eight smaller towers. Beyond the main walls lay secondary walls, much lower, and, outside these, further buildings. By any standards, it was an impressive forti-fication – even in the semi-ruinous state in which it now stood.

Keane pointed to the plan. 'You see the main entrance is here, just to our left – to the south-east. But it's pointless to think we'd ever get in that way. It will be barred and heavily defended.' He took a step back. 'This is how we'll take the place.' Moving over the drawing again, he pointed with his finger to a small line on the map with a shaded gap in its centre. 'There.'

Sanchez looked at it. 'What is that?'

Keane smiled. 'A secret entrance, colonel. Or, in actual fact, a secret exit. It was built by the Templars to effect an escape if they were ever besieged and things looked desperate.'

'There is a secret way in?'

'Yes, as I say. I'll need some of your best men – just a half company. I'll take them and my own men and a few of the students. And we'll go just as soon as they're ready.'

It didn't take long to assemble the storming party. With their carbines and muskets slung over their backs and their swords drawn, Keane led them around the castle perimeter to the south-east, staying close in to the walls. Forty of Sanchez's men followed him, along with six of his own less Archer and a platoon of the students, whom Martin had previously pointed out to him as good shots. It was not a large party, sixty-four strong, but Keane thought it would be large enough to get inside the castle and, once there, to open the main gate. After that, the main force of the guerrillas and the remaining students would take over. What he was relying on was that the French, with their innate fear of being captured by guerrillas, would think they were being attacked by a larger combined force and flee or surrender. To that end, he had instructed Sanchez to double his fire at the ramparts, use his lancers to demonstrate outside the castle and then have them take cover behind the ruined chapel. A report from one of the guerrillas told him that the cavalry consisted of two squadrons of dragoons and a single squadron of Polish lancers. In the castle, these would have no room for manoeuvre, while Sanchez's lancers would act as his shock troops, storming through the gates as soon as he opened them and riding down any French unfortunate enough to be in their way.

Making as little noise as possible, the party continued its advance along the outer walls until it was some two hundred yards from where the concealed entrance was marked on Keane's map.

Keane stopped and signalled to the others. 'Sarn't Ross, we'll go in twos – up the lane and into the cover of the inner curtain wall. They can't see us there; the angle from the high tower is too steep. It's dead ground. You first, with Silver. Now, go.'

Ross and Silver ran from the wall to the foot of the castle, keeping low all the time. It took a few seconds, and a bird call from Silver let Keane know they had arrived. He waved forward the next pair and, on the next signal, did the same again.

He had just sent the sixteenth pair across when there was a shout of alarm and a shot, followed by another shot and a cry – the sound of a man being hit.

Keane swore. 'Christ, they've seen us.'

Martin, detailed as his cover man, asked, 'What now, sir?'

'We'll have to think again. There must be an open area before the lane. No cover. They've seen us now. We'll have to go in some other way. We've got to get to that door.'

Sanchez was with them now. 'What's happened? Are they discovered?'

Keane nodded. 'Yes. They'll have to stay there until we can reach them. There must be another way to get to the door.'

He drew the map from his valise and, unfolding it, looked at the position of the door. Perhaps, he thought, if they were to drop down the hill from their present position, they would be able to crawl round the walls in the cover of a high bank beneath the perimeter road. Then they would reach the ruins of the old kitchens and could make their way up a return and reach the door. It was the only way.

He explained his plan to the remaining men and together they set off, pushing through the hard grass, trying to lie as low as possible. After an uncomfortable half hour of crawling, they found themselves among broken stones and ruins. Keane held up his hand to halt and hurried forward, crouching, into a ruined building. He turned and waved them in.

He had counted on Ross and Silver to wait for him and, sure enough, they were still there.

Ross was clearly relieved. 'We were about to try, on our own, sir. Didn't know if you'd come another way.'

Silver spoke: 'I was sure you'd come, sir. I knew you would.'

Ross nodded. 'Of course we knew you'd come, sir. I said to Silver, "The captain won't let us down." We lost three men, sir – all militia. The French have got guns up on that wall.' He pointed. 'Only place they can see down. We're safe here.'

'Well done, sarn't – and you, Silver. Right, let's find that bloody door.'

Pressing himself close to the wall, Keane edged around the stones and, after a few minutes, found what he had been looking for. Cut into the bank, below the wall, was the top of what looked like a door. Pushing down on a tangle of moss and brambles, he was able to uncover more of it until the shape of the entrance became more evident.

Keane smiled. 'There.' He turned to Ross. 'You, Martin and Silver, come with me.' He signed to the guerrillas with his fingers. 'Five of you – *cinco* – with me. The rest of you – Archer,

Garland, Heredia, Leech – when we get inside, I want you to go right and secure the gate to the inner courtyard. Hold that shut at all costs. We're going left to open the main gates. Right, let's go.'

He pushed at the door, but it would not budge. Keane tried again, with no result. He turned to Garland and motioned for him to come up. Standing amid the brambles, Garland put his shoulder to the door and pushed. With a ripping noise, the door began to move. Keane pushed again and it opened.

They entered close to the keep, but, not wanting to become involved directly in a battle for its possession, skirted it, silently knifing the few sentries at its base. As Keane had predicted from his plan, the bulk of the French infantry – perhaps two full battalions, a total of two thousand men – were formed up in the main courtyard of the castle, which was separated from the area around the keep by a high curtain wall and accessible through the door which he had ordered his men to keep shut 'at all costs'. It was a classic example of medieval castle construction and, thought Keane, it would work just as well for him now.

There was, in fact, another means of moving between the keep yard and the main courtyard. There was a small door in the curtain wall, barely four feet high, and, to judge from the ivy growing around it, as yet unopened by the French.

Keane went through it, followed by the others. The door led to a flight of steps and this took them to a gallery, halfway up the curtain wall. Keane had taken a gamble that the French would not have discovered this covered walkway beneath the battlements, and it appeared that he had been right.

They moved along it at a crouch, keeping out of sight of the men on the battlements, until they came to the south-east of the castle and the main entrance. Here, a similar tower led away from the gallery and took them down to ground level.

They emerged some ten yards from the main gates – two sturdy oak doors within a point-arched gateway. Keane was out first and saw, to his relief, that, as he had thought, the area behind the gates was also separated from the main body of troops by the same curtain wall which kept them from the keep. With Silver and Ross behind him, and the five guerrillas, he ran fast across the yard, managing to reach the gates before he was spotted. There was cry of alarm from above and the sentry by the gate spun round to see him, only to be met by a rasp of steel as Keane slid the big cavalry sword between his ribs.

Martin took aim with his carbine and brought down the guard who had raised the alarm, but the game was up and, as they stood by the gates, shots began to hit the cobblestones beside their feet, sending up shards of stone. One of the guerrillas was hit and fell, but another managed to shoot one of the guards. Keane, the shots striking the gates in front of him, splintering the wood, raised the iron crossbar which had secured them shut and called to his men, 'Now, pull, for God's sake! Pull them open.'

Together they heaved on the great gates. Another patter of shots hit the ground and some of the balls slammed into the wood. One of them hit Ross in the hand and he sprang back, cursing. But the gates were moving now and, as they creaked open, Sanchez, seeing them from his position before the walls, shouted to his trumpeter, who gave three loud blasts. Instantly, Sanchez's lancers turned from where they had been concealed in the cover of the group of houses below the ruined chapel and galloped towards the entrance, up the grassy slope and the cobbled track, before crashing through the doors and into the courtyard.

The yard was filled with Frenchmen now and Keane and his party had lined up with their backs to the internal wall. But the blue ranks wavered at the sight of the lancers.

Within seconds, the French were falling to the deadly spear points. Some of the French infantry manning the parapets turned and began to fire down on the horsemen, but Keane's men had them targeted now and more fell than hit their targets, plunging the fifty feet from the battlements.

From beyond the curtain wall, they could now hear the growing panic and confusion of the French infantry within. But clearly Archer and his men were managing to keep the gate closed on their side, and Keane had used the iron bar from the main gates to immobilize the other set of double gates from the yard into the entrance. The French, all two thousand of them, were caught in his trap.

Around him, the lancers were going about their work and now the guerrillas were pouring in through the open gates, followed closely by the student militia, all of them yelling death to the French.

Keane turned to Ross. 'The gold.'

Together, followed by what remained of the assault party, they ran to the rear of the courtyard, where a gap in the wall led to the inner yard and the castle's high stone keep. Keane recalled that, when he had last visited the place, there had been a number of wooden sheds and stables here – recent constructions, used by the local peasantry for storage – and, sure enough, there they were, beneath the shadow of the tower.

Whatever guards had been posted there had gone now, fleeing from the lance points. Keane and Ross were first inside and they were not disappointed. Four wooden wagons were parked in the first barn and Keane could see others beyond.

There was an axe strapped to the side of the nearest of the wagons. Keane undid the buckle to free it and handed it to Garland, indicating that he should use it.

Garland swung the blade above his head and brought it down on the top of the wagon, splitting the wood with a crack that also severed the padlock. Keane opened the lid to reveal dozens of canvas sacks. Taking his sword, he slit one open and lifted it up. The bag split, showering hundreds of gold coins over those below.

Keane smiled and turned to Ross. 'Sarn't Ross, I think it's time that I met the French commander, don't you? Martin, here's a chance to use your French, at last. Announce me, if you will.'

The French *général de brigade* commanding at the Castelo de Pombal had known that nothing good would come of his mission. Indeed, General André Simon had tried his best to avoid it, claiming to his superior that he had dysentery. But his divisional commander would have none of it, and so here he was. And he had been quite right. His men were now penned up in a filthy old castle; dozens, perhaps hundreds, had been killed by guerrillas; he had never received most of the promised cavalry and, to cap it all, now he really did have a bout of dysentery. He stood, sweating, in the morning sunshine in the keep courtyard, facing a young, tall, unkempt English officer in a brown coat that he did not recognize and his only desire was to get out alive.

Keane smiled at him. 'General, I come under a flag of truce. I have a combined force of Spanish *guerilleros*, Portuguese militia and British soldiers. Six thousand men, all told – infantry and cavalry. You are surrounded. I ask you to surrender now and leave with honour. Otherwise, I have no alternative but to order my force to take every foot of the castle, room by room, man by man. You will all die or be taken by the guerrillas. Surrender and I personally guarantee your safe passage back to Marshal Massena's army.'

The general's English was not so good, but Martin was able to translate and he smiled at Keane. Then, with a single, elegant movement, he drew his sword and handed it to Keane.

An hour later, Keane stood with his handful of men at the top of the keep of the Castelo de Pombal and watched the blue line of French infantry as it snaked away towards the south, returning to Marshal Ney with the news that his gold had been taken and Pombal was in enemy hands. But at least their lives had been spared.

As they watched from their vantage point high above the valley, Silver asked the question in all their minds: 'Where do we go now, sir? Are we to go back to Coimbra, with Colonel Sanchez?'

'No, I don't think so. Aren't you forgetting that we still have to complete our mission? The book, Silver. We have to get the book to Wellington.'

'And Archer with it, sir, and the gold.'

'Yes, Garland, and Archer with it. And now, too, the duke's share of the gold.'

Silver spoke again: 'I know it's important, sir – the codes and all that – but was it really worth it, sir? What with Gilpin dead, and Archer nearly, too. All those others, dead and wounded. All of them, for that one book.'

Keane had been about to make the usual response he had

given previously to the question – that, of course, it had been worth it; that the book was vital to the war effort; that, with it in French hands, the British intelligence network would collapse – but, before he said it, he thought hard.

He was about to speak when Ross cut in, turning on Silver. 'Course it was worth it. We did it, didn't we? We got Archer back, and we got the book and the gold, and we captured the traitor. What more do you want, Silver? The keys to bloody Paris?'

Silver shrugged and Keane laughed. 'You're right, sarn't, we did it. You managed it – all of you. Now let's find a bed and whatever we can in the way of food. I think we may be in luck. Massena's men may be starving at the lines, but I'll bet that Marshal Ney won't have sent his column off without provisions. And don't go at it too hard; I'll be with you and we've a hard ride in the morning, trophies to lay at Wellington's feet. Just drink a toast to those who fell and be thankful you're still alive. Sarn't Ross, no more than two pints of wine a man. Silver, you can keep a watch on my share. I won't be long.'

As they went to find a billet and relieve the French of their supplies, Keane hung back for a moment. Standing high on the ramparts, he looked out from the castle across the town of Pombal and watched the sun set as the guerrillas went about the field of battle, slitting the throats of the wounded and raiding the pockets of the dead. Such, he thought, was the 'field of glory'. There was no more than a passing glory in war and precious little honour. But he was determined to seek out as much as he could of both.

They had taken Macnab and soon Keane would avenge the deaths of both a friend and a comrade. Touching the signet ring in his pocket, he wondered about Macnab's true identity. He wondered, too, about Trant's promise, whether he could trust the colonel not to renege on the promise to give him more information on his father's identity.

He would return to Coimbra – just as soon as they had seen Wellington.

Trant would wait. And Henriette, too, now that Lievremont was gone.

And so, Keane asked himself again, in response to Silver's question, was it really worth it?

The point was, it had to be. Otherwise, what were any of them about? They had to believe, as he did, that such lives as Gilpin's were not wasted.

Keane's faith in Wellington, he had to admit, had been a little shaken over the past weeks. He did not envy the commander. It was clear to him there was more going on at headquarters and at court than might be apparent, and the general was playing a game of cat and mouse with factions on his own side. He wondered how it would play out and what part he would take.

Theirs was the loneliest branch of the army and their tasks were hard, often against impossible odds and always little praised. Keane knew that he was unlikely to ever be lauded at court for leading a great charge that won a battle, that he and his men were destined to be unsung heroes. At the end of the day, he might be, as some people would insist on calling him, a 'spy', he might be shunned in the mess by his fellow officers as somehow beneath their dignity, 'not quite the gentleman', but when all was said and done, when all the polished, powdered and frock-coated gentlemen had earned their battle honours and won the grateful thanks of King and nation, Keane knew that he would be able to rest easy in his bed at night, safe in the knowledge that, through whatever means he had used – brute force, clever ruse or downright dirty trick – he had always done his duty as a soldier.

HISTORICAL NOTE

The carefully ordered retreat of the Anglo-Portuguese army to the safety of the Lines of Torres Vedras in the autumn of 1810 was Wellington's brilliant masterstroke which was to give him the upper hand and pave the way for victory in the Peninsula.

Massena was utterly taken in and had no idea of the existence of the lines until confronted by them. By then it was too late and after a terrible winter, his army was forced to retire through the barren lands of Portugal. Unfortunately, as a consequence of his retiring to the Lines, Wellington was forced to abandon much of Portugal, including the historic university city of Coimbra.

Most of the civilian population accepted Wellington's policy and, with their farms and mills in ruins and their livestock slaughtered, left with the Anglo-Portuguese army. But several thousand of the citizens of Coimbra remained and when the French took the city on 1 October 1810 a number of these met a dreadful end.

The city was sacked and much of its riches looted by Massena's army. It provided a useful diversion for Wellington who made good ground towards the Lines. Massena then moved on in pursuit of Wellington, leaving only the wounded from Bussaco in Coimbra with a guard of Imperial Guard Marines and when on 7 October a force of some 4,000 Portuguese militia, including the Coimbra Academic Corps, led by Colonel Nicholas Trant, attacked the city it did so with total surprise and without much trouble, taking 5,000 French prisoners.

The Academic Corps had been founded in the 1640s and its greatest moment was in the campaigns of 1809 and 1810. In March 1811, Trant's militia successfully held the city against the retreating French.

According to Napier, a number of French writers circulated rumours that the Portuguese militia had massacred the French wounded in Coimbra, but the fact that this was mostly propagandist exaggeration is testified to by a letter of thanks to Trant himself, signed by a number of French officers and published in appendix 3 of volume III of Napier's history of the Peninsular War, which as usual has been my constant companion in researching this latest volume of Keane's exploits.

Nicholas Trant is one of the most colourful and least well known figures of the Peninsular war and his background and character seem to have been similar to those portrayed in the book.

Dr Sobral is also based on a real character who was imprisoned by the French for supplying home-made gunpowder to the Portuguese during the French assault on the city.

The Chemical Laboratory of the University of Coimbra of which Sobral was director was housed in fact in the original refectory of the complex of sixteenth- century Jesuit colleges which had been shut down by the Inquisition.

The tunnels beneath Coimbra still exist, being part of a

system put in place beneath the colleges when the city was still a seat of Jesuit learning.

The division within Wellington's high command at the period is well recorded and we know that he was hard pressed to ensure that his policy prevailed.

At the same time as the retreat to the Lines, the Portuguese Regency, despite having initially agreed to Wellington's evacuation of the Portuguese population and scorched earth policies, had been upset by the devastation being wrought and the sacrifice expected of the Portuguese. It was suggested that the allied troops should cease their retreat and fight a pitched battle against the French, but Wellington would have none of it.

Rumours had even begun to circulate of British plans to abandon Portugal entirely to the French. Wellington was desperate for some high profile success to show the Portuguese Regent. Fortunately for him the success of the Lines and the retreat of the French army was in itself sufficient.

The *Très Sainte Trinosophie* actually existed in the exact form that I have described, although to my knowledge it was never used as the basis for a military code book. Nevertheless it was of genuine interest to Napoleon. One of only two copies of the book known to have existed was taken by Marshal Massena himself from the Vatican library and presented to Napoleon who did indeed have an interest in the occult and in the workings of secret societies.

The fight with Ney's forces at Pombal is also based upon fact although the time sequence has been changed to suit the purposes of the book.

It took Massena the entire winter to realize that he could not break the Lines of Torres Vedras. When he did decide to retreat from Portugal, he gave Ney command of the rear-guard. Ney managed his command well and the Anglo-allied army caught up with him on 11th March 1811 at Pombal. A British advance-guard attacked the town and forced the French out.

Ney himself led a counter attack and recaptured Pombal. Despite this success, Ney set fire to the town and continued his retreat on the right bank of the river Arunca. His final rear-guard action took place on 3rd April 1811 at Sabugal. By April Massena was encamped around Salamanca and the following month would meet Wellington again at the battle of Fuentes de Onoro. Five days later a despatch would arrive from Paris relieving Massena of command and spelling the end of his military career.